The leisure riots

Also by Eric Koch

A Novel:

The French Kiss 1969

Films:

The Culture Explosion
Freud

Television Plays:

Durham's Canada (written in association with Vincent Tovell)
  published in 1961 as *Success of a Mission.*
The Fourteenth Colony
The War of 1812
Reluctant Nation
Nineteen Ninety-Nine (a political fantasy, written in association
  with Vincent Tovell)
The Ninety-Ninth Day (on Kaiser Wilhelm, written in association
  with the late Melwyn Breen)

Eric Koch

The leisure riots

A comic novel

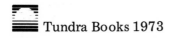 Tundra Books 1973

Published simultaneously in Canada by
Tundra Books of Montreal, Montreal 107, Quebec
and in the United States of America by
Tundra Books of Northern New York, Plattsburgh, N.Y. 12901

Library of Congress Card No. 73-76301
ISBN 0-912766-06-9

Legal Deposit, Third Quarter
Quebec National Library
ISBN 88776-0-20-1

Printed in the United States

PUBLISHER'S NOTE

This is the original manuscript written by Friedrich Bierbaum, identical with the copy given to the Russian Ambassador in Washington, Mr. Boris Lermontov, on July 6th, 1980.

Preface to the original manuscript

Since this book cannot be published until after my death, I am addressing myself to posterity. I would, of course, infinitely prefer to write for immediate publication, but this is impossible. If the manuscript were seen by an agent of Peking I would be done away with immediately, in spite of all the security measures being taken presently by the Canadian authorities to protect me and my wife, Paula, here in Montreal.

But I had to write it anyway, I had to tell how it came about that the think tank, entrusted with one of the most difficult problems America has ever had to face, fell into the hands of a Maoist.

The only person who will receive a copy of the manuscript is the delightful Russian ambassador in Washington, Mr. Boris Lermontov. It is ironical that I, who have detested Communists all my life, have authorized him, of all people, to make use of it any way he sees fit. My reasons will become clear to the reader in due course.

To present a complete picture of the events that have led to the disaster which forced me to leave the United States, I have had to dwell on many indelicate aspects of my personal life and that of others, for personalities dominate think tanks as they do all else. If this shocks my readers, I apologize in advance. However, I fervently hope that everyone will be as magnanimous as my wife who has totally forgiven me.

I confess that — who does not like to be vindicated? — I cannot conceal a certain element of *Schadenfreude*, i.e. a delicious feeling of joy in the embarrassment of others, when I think of the response this book is bound to elicit. I had better make the best of it now since, alas, I shall not be on this earth when that time comes.

Moriturus te saluto!

Friedrich Bierbaum
Montreal, Canada
July 5th, 1980

Chapter 1

Many eyebrows have been raised because America's most important and influential think tank, CRUPP (Center for Research on
Urban Policy and Planning), was built up and managed by a
former administrative assistant to the late Hermann Göring, the
second man in Hitler's Germany.

What has made this worse is that this man — myself — looks a
little like Göring. Of course, I am now much older than he was
when he swallowed that little vial of poison in his Nürnberg
cell two hours before he was to be hanged. (When I worked for
him — from 1942 to 1945 — I was in my early twenties.) But
there are many resemblances. Like him, I am fat and built like
an ox, and have quick blue eyes and a double chin. I am also
very fond of the pleasures of the flesh, and I laugh a lot. But
there are many differences between us. I like power, but of course
I do not abuse it cynically the way he did, and I am *not* corrupt.

I am resigned to ending my days here in Montreal, though I find it
extremely hard to take any interest in the life around me. My mind
and heart are still in that beautiful cement and steel structure which
houses CRUPP, and which I built within five minutes' walk of the
Pentagon. Writing this is to return there and relive our great days.

Canada is pleasant enough. We live in *Habitat*, that futuristic bee-
hive of building blocks along the St. Lawrence River, built as
model housing for Expo 67. The guards here are so busy protecting
the building against tourists that I am, in a way, automatically
protected. *Habitat* looks as though it might have been designed
by Albert Speer, Hitler's architect, whom I used to know slightly
— a comparison that would probably appal its real architect who,

9

I am told, is Israeli-born. Though Paula constantly complains about the position of some of the windows, which makes it almost impossible for her to wash them on Saturday mornings (the windows of our home in Berlin, like those of her parents' house in Potsdam, were washed regularly as clockwork on Saturday mornings), I find it comfortable enough. It is a suitable "habitat" for a man whose think tank used to do some of the most original future research in the United States. I would, of course, have preferred a little more flamboyant luxury. Like Hermann Göring, I adore expensive masterpieces and lots of space for lavish parties. But exiles must live austere lives. At any rate that is what my wife tells me. As for her, well, you will hear plenty about her in these pages. She is quite happy here — apart from the "window" annoyance — compulsively tidying up the place all day, though there is nothing to tidy up. She polishes and scrubs away as though she were a charwoman, and not the daughter of General von Lichten-felde-Königstein, and raised on the parade grounds of Potsdam.

It is hard to describe the woman one has lived with for two-thirds of one's life. Let me just say at this point that, though she disagrees with everything I do or say, I can't make a move without her. It would not be accurate to picture her as a typical high-class Prussian. She is entirely original and, in many ways, my exact opposite. I am fat and she is skinny. I am garrulous and voluble, and she is silent — except when she has something sardonic to say. I love Americans; she considers them children, adorable when she likes them, and aggravating when she doesn't. I worship sex; she hasn't had any for thirty years. I am an activist, a doer, an organizer, a promoter. Never did Hermann Göring endear himself to me as much as when he exclaimed, at one of his birthday parties in Karin-hall, *"Ideologie ist Scheisse! "* (Ideology is bullshit!) I, too, have no feeling for ideology, except that I am an anti-Communist. Even that is not quite ideological. I just can't abide them, that's all. Paula, on the other hand, is an idealist, introspective and morally correct as a German pastor. In a way, I think I am the only "fun" that she gets out of life. After all, what's the point of being morally correct unless one lives with the less moral? The monotony would be dreadful.

Sometimes, here in Montreal, I wake up convinced that this is my last day. Either the Chinese will get me, or, who knows, a man of my age may have to leave the scene any time through natural causes. Writing then becomes a race against time.

Yesterday morning I poked Paula in the ribs while she was still asleep, and as she opened her eyes I quoted Goethe's *Mephisto* to her: *"Ihr Mann ist tot und lässt Sie grüssen."* (Your husband is dead and sends his regards.)

She rubbed her eyes, patted me on my fat cheeks, and said lovingly in the best Berlin slang, *"Mensch, bei Dir piept's ja,"* which roughly translated means that the little birdie in my head must be twittering.

Paula always has *le mot juste.*

* * *

What I liked about Göring was his *joie de vivre* and the fact that he did not lie to himself. It is true that in his final phase he behaved like a "perfumed Nero," fiddling while Germany was in flames, but by then he had effectively lost his authority. Also, *he* wrecked his body through drugs. He started taking drugs to kill the pain from the wounds he had received as a commander in Baron von Richthofen's famous Fighter Squadron during the First World War, and he continued taking them until the end. I don't take drugs, and my body still functions very well in all — or nearly all — respects.

Yes, I liked Göring, and I still do. He was the only Nazi leader who was truly popular, and when they took IQ tests in Nürnberg of all the prisoners, he was among the top scorers. Yes, I liked him.

I am not allowed to say this in my wife Paula's presence. She loathed all Nazis and would condemn them to only slightly graduated purgatorial tortures before throwing them forever into the flames. She wouldn't marry me while I worked for him, and when finally after his death and my de-Nazification she accepted me, I had to promise not ever to say a good word about him in her hearing. She still thinks that, as far as he is concerned, I suffer from moral tone-deafness, and has devoted her life to tuning me in on virtue and humanity. Her antenna for anything that remotely reminds her of Nazis, or of Nazism is, if you ask me, extravagantly sensitive, but I have learned over the years to live with this, and usually succeed quite well in concealing from her any thoughts of mine which might be open to misconstruction.

The media in America have compared me to Göring so often

(to the extent of sometimes writing my name Friedrich "Göring" Bierbaum) that it is time to be quite precise about my attitudes and background.

I am — I admit — an old-fashioned German. My father was a prominent lawyer in Hanover, and a city councillor. I am not lower middle class like those dreadful people with whom Göring had to associate, the Himmlers, the Streichers, the Franks, and all the rest. Incidentally, Göring too came from a good family: his father had been Governor of German South-West Africa at the beginning of the century. It was he who introduced Hitler to high society in the twenties, to the former Crown Prince, to Prince Philip of Hesse who had married the daughter of the King of Italy, to Fritz Thyssen and other tycoons.

Nothing was more important in my childhood than to have good manners and to be able to quote Goethe and Schiller, and to show off one's Latin. This talent, learned early, I have used through my life. Even in America, a profound knowledge of the classics distinguishes the people who count from those who don't, and no matter how much Americans say this is not so, in my years in Washington I have found them as impressed by Latin-dropping as by name-dropping, just as they are impressed by aristocratic connections in spite of democratic protestations.

Let me describe the circumstances in which I write these confessions. Today is May 27th, 1980. On March 16th, I was dismissed as President of CRUPP, a position I had held for fifteen years. On April 11th — three days after the hearings examining CRUPP's relations with the White House were over — I was advised, for the sake of my personal safety, to leave the United States. I came to Montreal on May 3rd.

Already I have gained a perspective I could not possibly have acquired in the hothouse atmosphere of Washington where everybody who is anybody knows me personally. Here nobody knows me. A few may know my name, but that's all. French Canadians, in any case, are too self-involved to pay much attention to any outsider. I am being left completely alone. The authorities in Ottawa know I am here. The Royal Canadian Mounted Police is fully informed. So is the Quebec provincial police, and the Montreal police. They know I need special protection. (I was surprised at how readily Canadians believe that anyone prominent in the US is a potential assassin's victim.) I did not try to tell them that the danger was likely to come from Peking; I just couldn't face again that funny look of private "understanding" that comes into people's eyes when they decide I'm paranoid. Better to let them protect me against *everybody*.

I don't think I'm boasting if I say that Communist China has now gained control of the only really important think tank in America. All the others deal with highly specialized technological and economic problems. I might almost say *trivial* problems: they dissect and analyze and measure the trees, leaving to CRUPP the task of looking after the forest. Only CRUPP asked — and answered — the fundamental questions touching on the very fabric of American society. No doubt this is the reason why the White House became utterly dependent on CRUPP, and would not consider making a move in any area of domestic and, to some extent, foreign policy without having in its pocket a sweeping, penetrating, succinct — and often devastatingly unorthodox — CRUPP report.

It has often been said by cynics at Washington cocktail parties that the *real* reasons for the President's addiction to CRUPP were my "impeccable" credentials as a lifelong anti-Communist. I don't think that's true at all, though I admit it's never been a disadvantage for me to have been on the right side of the Cold War long before it started. But I maintain that the real reason for my success has been the excellence of the brilliant staff I assembled for CRUPP throughout the sixties and early seventies.

Chapter 2

I started CRUPP in the late fifties, but it did not become big and important until the decline of the RAND Corporation and Herman Kahn's Hudson Institute. CRUPP evolved naturally from the work I had done for the Pentagon after my honorable de-Nazification in 1947. (I had no trouble convincing the tribunal that I had never been a member of the Nazi Party, which — believe it or not — happens to be true, that I did not like Hitler, that I was never directly involved in any of the unpleasantness with which the judges were pre-occupied at the time, and that I could be useful in the fight against the Bolsheviks.) The Pentagon was much concerned with economic and technological forecasting, an area with which, as an administra-tor, I was thoroughly familiar from my work for Göring who — among other things — was head of the *Reich* Research Council. I cannot emphasize enough that I myself am not an intellectual, but an administrator. I can't do any forecasting myself, but I know how to recruit forecasters. Thanks to me, many of my former associates in Berlin found work in the American Military Govern-ment in Bad Godesberg, and proved to be invaluable. As Bismarck used to say, politics is the art of the possible, and I did everything possible to help my old friends, and thereby — nobody can deny it — I helped America. They are men like myself, like Albert Speer whom I have just mentioned as the man who might have designed *Habitat:* we are unpolitical. A problem is a problem: it has to be solved. Never mind what the politicians do with it later.

"Politik verdirbt den Charakter," I used to learn at school. Politics ruins the character, and I have always observed this to be true. Technology is neither good nor bad until the politicians get hold of it. I am a technologist, if I am any "ist" at all, and CRUPP is a paradise for technologists of a special kind, as we shall see later.

The work we did in the sixties had mainly to do with city planning, hence our name. We devised model urban systems; we worked on housing, air pollution, traffic safety, police and fire protection, and then later, when the drug problems became severe, we drew linkages between the degree of social disintegration and the narcotics addiction rate. I will not bore you with a list of our accomplishments. There is not a major American city for which we did not do at least some minor consultative jobs. We were not famous yet, but we laid the groundwork for our later fame, assembled staff and techniques, and began to make innumerable contacts which later became invaluable. As we acquired confidence, we began to develop special interests. We stayed away from weapons research and concentrated on social and human problems, i.e., *eternal* problems, and had to wait until the early seventies to make our first spectacular breakthrough. It put us on the map as the think tank that would tackle problems the others wouldn't touch. It got us maximum publicity and attracted the attention of the White House.

No doubt you will remember the case of the Secretary of Defense, Leslie Mackenzie. You may have forgotten our involvement in the case, but I am sure you will recall that the Secretary, an overt homosexual and honorary president of the Gay Liberation Movement, had been accused of actively discriminating against heterosexuals in the Defense Department. To clear his name, he asked for an independent study: not a judicial or congressional hearing such as the one I have recently had to endure, but a detached "academic" study by an unpolitical, objective agency. I contacted him immediately and, with the consent of the President, the job was assigned to CRUPP.

The facts were easily disposed of. There was no concrete way in which we could establish whether or not direct unequivocal acts of discrimination took place. We are not the police, and not in any way an investigative agency, but we had to go through the motions of conducting interviews with all the complainants, examining witnesses, and all the rest. One of our most brilliant staff members — the Reverend Soren Anderson, whom I will properly introduce later — came up with an entirely original idea which in many ways was the germ, the point of departure, of CRUPP's subsequent fame. He sent me a private memo, based on biographies he had recently read of Julius Caesar, Prince Eugene of Savoy, and Frederick the Great of Prussia, three of the greatest military geniuses of all time, and also well-known homosexuals.

"I would not go as far as to suggest," he wrote, "that it is a handicap in military affairs to be heterosexual — after all, Rommel and Eisenhower were 'straight' — but...."

We took it from there.

With the help of a number of consultants from the Institute of Sex Research, and from the psychiatry departments of various universities, we prepared a confidential paper summarizing all the recent findings about heterosexuals, to prove to the Secretary of Defense that by the time a person is two or three years old the die is cast, that no one is born either one or the other, and that high IQ, administrative talent and, above all, military prowess, are in no way limited to homosexuals and, most important of all, that a heterosexual can serve his country as conscientiously as a homosexual.

The Secretary was deeply impressed, *and* so was the President. The paper was later published and caused a sensation. There has not been any trouble in the Defense Department since. I think that Secretary Mackenzie personally checks all applicants to make sure that heterosexuals are fairly represented in the personnel of his department according to their ratio in the general US population.

One of the immediate consequences of this event — apart from President Roberts' favorable disposition towards us — was that we became the think tank well-endowed representatives of the so-called counter-culture turn to, whenever they need help in high places. Rebellious university students, blacks, Mexicans, women, all kinds of groups call on me when they want a study done to justify or substantiate their position. (For reasons I have trouble understanding, the one group which has never contacted me is the Jews.) My attitude towards these requests has been the same all along: whenever we are equipped to do a good job we will do it. I don't care whether we serve the old culture or the new, the Establishment or the anti-Establishment. CRUPP is not to be identified with any faction. We serve the truth, that's all. *Nuda veritas*, the naked truth. There is an old German song I often sing in my bath:

Wer die Wahrheit kennet und spricht sie nicht,
Der bleibt fürwahr ein erbärmlicher Wicht.

He who knows the truth but won't tell it,
Will forever remain a miserable no-goodnik.

I think I have said enough to indicate that we are a think tank very different from the others. It is our human touch rather than any bias towards one side or another that has carved out for us a very special position in this newest branch of our democratic system, the branch which has filled the formerly gaping vacuum between academic life and the life of action, between the universities and government. (God only knows what will happen to this most precious institution and to those who make use of its services, now that it is in the hands of a person who is secretly in the pay of Red China. I am convinced we will soon find out.)

Chapter 3

Though I'm sure you would like to know who it was who subverted CRUPP and is now hoping to use it as a platform for an eventual takeover of America by Communist China, I will not reveal the name at the outset. I will spare you another dull history book. Instead, you may try to guess, as my sad story unfolds, which member of my brilliant staff might do such a thing, and why. Let me introduce them to you now.

The Reverend Soren Andersen

Since I have already mentioned Soren Andersen, I may as well start with him.

CRUPP is the only think tank in America — there are about a thousand of them — which has on its staff a world-famous theologian. A native of the Danish province of Jutland, he dazzled his professors at Copenhagen with the brilliance and subtlety of his mind. His special field — naturally, I suppose — was Kierkegaard, on whom he has written the definitive monograph. At the age of twenty-three he came to America, taught at the Union Theological Seminary in New York, and took up psychoanalysis, not as a patient or even as a doctor, but as a *scholar*.

Soren Andersen is blond and blue-eyed, and has the appearance of a typical Dane. He has a schoolgirl complexion, and looks as though he has never had to shave. This, together with a characteristic giggle, has suggested to some that he is a suppressed homosexual — a possibility that perhaps is borne out by his interest in psychoanalysis and in sexual matters generally. (And I am not entirely forgetting his ingenious solution to the charges against the Secretary of Defense.)

18

He distinguished himself at CRUPP through his work on *pacem in terris,* and his contributions to the study of the effect of pornography on children. He has developed a number of innovative theories about games and various forms of play,which are highly relevant to the subject of this book. His appearance before the Senate Committee investigating CRUPP was, in my opinion, nothing less than a *tour de force.*

Hilde Hildesheim

Hilde's background is very similar to my wife Paula's: she, too, is a scion of the Prussian aristocracy. Though ten years younger than Paula, they are old friends, and it is thanks to Paula that we managed to lure her to CRUPP. Hilde is an extraordinary character: a world-renowned expert on communications theory, she was a movie star in Germany as a young girl in the late thirties, and there is not a German of my generation, or even a generation younger than mine, who does not cherish nostalgic memories of her bittersweet beauty in her two famous films: "Stolen Flowers" and "Tigers in July."

All her life she has profited from reminding everyone of the late Marlene Dietrich. Her seductive, slightly hoarse, no-nonsense Berlin voice is very much like Marlene's. That a girl like that should become a first-class scholar is an achievement second to none. That she should continue to do original work now that she must be nearly sixty, always breaking new ground on the subjects of her choice, is beyond praise. During the war she was married to Freiherr von Schleswig-Strelitz, who was involved in the Generals' Plot against Hitler, and was butchered after the events of July 20th, 1944. She has had three husbands since, each time, strangely enough, an advertising executive on Madison Avenue. She divorced her fourth husband just before joining us three years ago.

On her good days Hilde is still stunning looking. There are not many women of her age who make a fetish of never wearing a bra and get away with it. She dresses beautifully and expensively, and spends hours in front of the mirror every morning, making up her face. (It takes her twenty-five minutes, she told me the other day, when she is in a desperate rush.) She happily regales people with funny stories about her three face-lifting operations, which she compares to the ministrations Babylonian queens used to be subjected to *after* their death.

19

Tex Winter

He came from the West, from Wyoming, and is a trained astrono-
mer, a marvelous mathematician and physicist. When he joined us,
Tex was in his forties, tall, languid, soft spoken; he had a pale,
freckled face and thinning sandy-colored hair: a cowboy with a
PhD. Of all CRUPP people, he was the most future oriented, and
I think he still is. He is thoroughly familiar with the concept that
we are now able to study the future the way we study the past,
that we can know both equally well, since both contain the same
mixture of fact and fantasy — in Goethe's words, of *Dichtung und
Wahrheit*, of Poetry and Truth.

During the five years Tex has been with us, he has specialized in a
vast variety of fields, some of them very far from his chosen disci-
plines. I refer particularly to his work on criminal justice and law
enforcement, as well as to his studies on International Development
and Foreign Aid. We have always tried to encourage our staff members to move as far away as possible from their own fields, and
thereby to broaden their horizons. Tex has also written a first-class
paper on Disaster Simulation.

Richard Toshima

This is our resident psychologist. A Japanese American from San
Francisco who spent part of his childhood years in an internment
camp, Toshima is impossible to imagine except in hippie costume,
wearing long hair, granny glasses, headband and leather jacket. This,
of course, is now hopelessly old-fashioned, but I suspect he has not
changed clothes since his university days at Caltech and Yale. He is
the kindest man in the world, and, undisguised, could be a movie
star. An expert in all aspects of the counter-culture, his life style
(except for his clothes) is by no means that of a hippie: an
excellent amateur clarinetist, he prefers the nineteenth century
to both baroque music and contemporary compositions. He hates
the guitar. His apartment in Richmond, Virginia, does not have a
single piece of furniture, or picture on the wall, made after 1890,
and he is a great expert on Proust.

A disciple of Skinner and Skinnerism, he believes that our behavior
is primarily learned and not determined by genetic components
to any important extent. For a mild-mannered man who became
famous in his middle twenties through two popular books on brain
research, he is a curious mixture of modesty and intellectual arro-

gance. Like the late Skinner, he believes that there is no such thing as freedom of will: our choices are predetermined by behavior patterns acquired early in life. "Freedom" and "Dignity" are pure rhetoric in his book, and he believes that anyone who uses such terms is a liar or a fool.

Cedric Douglas-Whyte

Since the time I joined Hermann Göring's staff in 1942, I have been familiar with the idea of Renaissance Man. The *Reichsmarschall* often said to me: *"Ich bin, was ich immer gewesen bin: der letzte Renaissance-Mensch, mit Verlaub zu sagen."* (I am what I've always been: the last Renaissance Man, if you'll allow me to say so.) Obviously I was not the only person to whom he made that observation, since it is quoted in a number of biographies. I know *exactly* what Göring meant. He thought of himself as a *condottiere,* a well-rounded (in every sense of the word), sensuous, luxury-loving, fearless, rough-and-ready soldier-adventurer who is also a patron of the arts, a man who lives in sumptuous palaces, usually stolen.

Cedric Douglas-Whyte is a Renaissance Man in a very different sense. He is a modern Leonardo da Vinci. An English scientist and artist, he knows everything. I have never met anyone who can catch him out. He has a typical Oxford stutter, a habit peculiar to educated Englishmen that I have yet to have explained to me. He is tall, wears a well-groomed Vandyke, has piercing eyes, and never stops talking. I have been told on the best authority, that even at night, with the very young girls he cherishes, he talks right through his, and her, orgasm — an accomplishment for which, I suppose, a special taste has to be developed. It has been said about him that he is likely to continue talking even an hour or two after the moment of death, just as a man's hair and fingernails, it is said, go on growing. He is utterly democratic; he does not care to whom he talks. For him life is a long monologue, and his audience has included kings and chambermaids, presidents and office boys. He specializes in esoteric information of the most far-fetched kind, and I know certain philistines who, though everyone who knows him really well shares my admiration and affection for him, want to run away after five minutes of his monologue.

Karin Hamsun

I would have fallen in love with her, even if her name had not been

Karin. With her sky-blue eyes, her tousled blond hair, her gorgeous figure, she is one of the most beautiful girls I have ever met, let alone gone to bed with. But the name Karin certainly helped. It was the name of Göring's Swedish first wife, whose maiden name — forgive me — was Baroness Fock. The dashing war hero loved her deeply, and after her death in the late twenties — she was an epileptic who had contracted TB — made a cult of her memory. To anyone who associated with him, Karin was always a name with a halo, and therefore, when I met Karin Hamsun, six months before this story begins, I was already predisposed towards her.

She is also one of the most brilliant computer scientists in the country, and in a relatively short time made herself indispensable. An account of my affair with her will occupy a number of pages in this book, and the dramatic end of it is part of the climax, so I don't want to anticipate it now. Let me just sketch her background.

Karin had emigrated, with her parents, from Sweden to Wisconsin when she was in her teens. In her first year at Madison, she dazzled her professors with her flair for higher mathematics. By the time she did her MA, she had won every prize the university had to offer. Like Newton and Einstein, she developed her mathematical genius in her early twenties: by the time she was twenty-five, she had written a textbook on the mathematical aspects of in-plant systems which is now required reading for every IBM employee

She was teaching at the University of Texas when she heard about our search for a top-rank computer scientist. She wrote me a business-like letter signed "K. Hamsun" which was singularly unimpressive; I left it lying about for three weeks before answering it. When she came for an interview, I didn't understand a word she said, but I hired her immediately, (1) because of her eye-boggling beauty, and (2) because I found out the "K" stood for Karin. As for being able to decode the peculiar computer language she uses, I have never managed it.

"Why don't you use English subtitles? " I sometimes asked her during tender moments in bed.

She would laugh her delightful laugh and say, "Get on with your nexus, or we will have a failure logging," or something like that.

Although Karin has always tried to observe the academic detachment customary at CRUPP and carefully avoided any appearance

22

of commitment to causes, I knew for a long time that she had deep sympathies with the Women's Liberation Movement, and considered herself in some ways the prototype of what Ibsen used to call the "New Woman." I often teased her about playing Nora in my Doll's House.

This, then, is the CRUPP staff. The brain power assembled under my roof was singularly well equipped to do honor to our house motto, *cogitamus ergo sumus.* One of them betrayed this motto, for nothing could be more obvious than that it is impossible to cogitate freely in a think tank run by an agent of Communist China. How this came about is the subject of this account of the fateful events which I am now ready to report in chronological order.

Chapter 4

My downfall began a little over a year ago with a phone call from the White House. The date: March 3rd, 1979. It came from my old friend, Bill Bush, one of the youngest members of President Roberts' personal staff. His official title was "Liaison Officer of the President's Science Secretariat." I never have any trouble remembering Bill's name, since it's identical with that of Germany's most famous humorist, Wilhelm Busch, the author of *Max und Moritz*. Bill, however, is a very different type: horn-rimmed and hard working, cold and businesslike, and utterly humorless. He was not on the President's staff at the time of the Secretary of Defense's problems when we endeared ourselves to the Administration, but we have talked about it often on various occasions, and he was fully aware of the President's inclination towards us.

"Are you free for lunch, Friedrich? " he asked. "There's something I would like to discuss with you."

"I'm sorry, but I'm tied up today, Bill," I said, lying, but faithful to my principle that it's always a good idea to play hard to get.

"It's important," said Bill. "*Very* important."

"All right," I yielded. "I'll make it. Where? "

"At Marbella's in Georgetown. Twelve thirty."

He was there five minutes early. We chose a table in a corner, ordered double martinis and began talking right away.

"The President thinks he has a project for you," he said. "It's something quite extraordinary. Absolutely puzzling. Something has been happening across the country that's stumped everybody, the police, the FBI, various social agencies, *everybody*. It seems quite innocuous and insignificant, and that's why the press hasn't got hold of it. Not yet anyway, as far as I know. But what with the election in November next year, it's become vital for us to get to the bottom of this thing. It may well turn out to be the number one election issue, and the President thinks it's bound to determine the nature of his campaign. You may remember that he has a very good nose: when he sniffs something in the air that's disturbing and that he doesn't understand, he won't rest until somebody has figured it out for him. That's what he wants CRUPP to do."

"What is it, Bill? " I asked softly, sipping my martini.

"It sounds kind of crazy, I know, but there's been a rash of seemingly unconnected and quite harmless little incidents all over the country. They look like routine vandalism of one kind or another. In fact, that's what it may be, nothing more than that. But, on the other hand, it may be something more serious."

"What kind of incidents? " I asked.

"Let's order first. What will you have? "

I asked for calves' liver, and he ordered a roast beef sandwich, rare, and a bottle of Beaujolais. Then he started on the list.

"Well, now, let me see. In Kansas City pages were torn out of a hundred and fifty books in the Public Library — always the same page: page fifty-seven. In Pebble Beach, the locks in the golf course's locker rooms were tampered with. In New York, somebody put airplane cement in the Steinway in Carnegie Hall, just before a piano recital by Lin Mo Tao. Here in Washington somebody wrote 'Fuck you' on the behind of one of the best dinosaurs in the Smithsonian. In Houston, Texas, a person or persons raided a handicraft store, and pinched all the instructions for making lamps out of Chianti bottles; in Poughkeepsie, New York, they scribbled profanities on thirty-three travel posters urging customers to go to the Passion Plays in Oberammergau; in St. Louis, Missouri, somebody took one piece out of each of two thousand different jigsaw puzzles,

and in Atlanta, Georgia, they smashed the windows of the
Berlitz School. Now, what do you make of that, Friedrich? "

"I haven't a clue, Bill. I only drum up business, you know: others
have to do the work."

"Will you take it on? "

"Of course," I said. "You didn't doubt it, did you? "

"As a matter of fact, I did," he confessed. "I was afraid you were
going to say you were a think tank, not a detective agency."

"For the President we'll do anything," I replied. "Or *almost* anything. We're not going to raise money for the party, that's for sure.
Remember that we are unpolitical."

"Of course," he said seriously, chewing his roast beef sandwich.
"But tell me honestly, what do you make of all these incidents?
Aren't they strange? "

"I suppose so. This sort of thing is really not my cup of tea. Let
me quote some of your great namesake, Wilhelm Busch."

"Please don't," he said. "I have no time for fun and games."

"Sorry, I simply *have* to give you my quote. It expresses exactly
what I feel.

"*Max und Moritz ihrerseits
Fanden darin keinen Reiz*

"I'm sorry I can't make up an English translation which rhymes,
and it sounds kind of silly, but it means 'As for Max and Moritz,
they saw no charm in it.' Those little incidents you rattled off,
I doubt whether they mean anything. They don't sound very
interesting to me. But don't worry, Bill. We'll come up with the
answer. What are we having for dessert? "

We ordered some *pâtisserie* and coffee.

"When do you think you'll be able to submit your report, Friedrich? " he asked me when we were finished.

"That depends entirely on the kind of cooperation we get from your people. If all doors are opened to us, I would think we'll have something ready in six weeks."

"Very good, Friedrich. I know the President will be very happy to hear it."

"We'll do what we can."

Oh, how I wish I had turned him down!

Chapter 5

"What kind of a hare-brained scheme is this? " asked Paula at
dinner that night in our house on Meadowlark Lane in Bethesda.
It's a huge house with sixteen rooms and a swimming pool. The
Italian ambassador used to live there before we moved in twelve
years ago. He had four servants. Paula won't have any servants
in the house: she insists on doing everything herself. She even
cleans out the swimming pool in the garden every fall — a garden,
incidentally, dominated by a huge sandstone Buddha imported,
I believe, by a previous occupant who, when he was Roosevelt's
special envoy to Burma (or was it Nepal or Ceylon or Thailand?)
had "acquired" it in return for a large loan at low interest. I mention this only because many people have remarked on the resemblance between the smiling Buddha, with his magnificent double
chin, and myself.

It was agreed when Paula and I got married that she would have
nothing to say about my paintings — which to buy, and where
to hang them. This is my field, and I decided to hang my Böcklin
— a beautiful picture of a Greek island that used to be my father's
pride and joy — over the mantelpiece, my Lenbach — a portrait
of a Munich dowager — in the library, and my authentic Dürer
print in one of the four guest rooms upstairs. Mementos of my
Göring period, such as a gold model of one of the fighter planes
he flew during the First World War, are stacked away in the attic.
You won't find a single swastika in the house, nor any of the
uniforms I used to wear. The main difference between my house
and the dozens of houses Göring used to own is that, in contrast
to him, I paid for mine and all its belongings, including three
abstract expressionists he would have had confiscated from any

German art dealer as "degenerate art" and sold surreptitiously
for a huge sum in Zürich.

Paula's touches are visible mainly in the kitchen, the pantry, and
the fifteen linen closets. She loves gadgets. An electric can opener,
presented to her on her birthday in a brown paper bag, would
give her infinitely more pleasure than a gift-wrapped mink coat
which, in any case, she would reject. The gods need protect any
visitor who comes to dinner armed with a bottle of French perfume
for the hostess. But anyone who has the brains to arrive equipped
with a special knife with which to peel onions without tears, will
be invited again and again, and might even get third helpings of
her famous Bulgarian meatballs.

On this occasion, when she chided me predictably about my latest
"hare-brained scheme," she was wearing one of her three black
dresses and an apron. Instead of replying to her, I asked her to pass
the butter, *bitte.*

"Why should you do the President's dirty work? " she asked.
"The place is crawling with police, and here he comes begging you to
to do his police work for him! I think the man's got a screw loose,"
she said, tapping the side of her gray head, the way we used to do
at school. "And look at yourself, Friedrich, you've got half your
breakfast on your tie! Disgusting! " She dipped her napkin in
some water, and removed a bit of dried egg. "These are just some
American hooligans at work. Typical *Kindereien.* I would have
thought the President had other things to worry about. When some
kid in Potsdam put my pigtails in an inkwell, I don't remember
Kaiser Wilhelm calling a Council of War! "

"I've said yes, and we're going to do it. That's all," I said with
authority.

"Then don't come running to me crying when this has gone sour,
the way you did when you couldn't solve the Serbo-Croat labor
problems. Remember? "

Yes, I remembered. It was Paula who eventually came up with the
answer: eleven and a half percent increase for the garbagemen in
Serajewo over three years, and vacations with pay for the concierges
in Dubrovnik hotels.

We finished the meal in silence.

* * *

The next morning at ten, we assembled as usual at the High Table on the second floor of CRUPP. This is our brainstorming room. Cedric Douglas-Whyte called it the High Table — apparently the section of the dining halls where Oxford professors sit — because a table is conspicuously absent from our room. We lounge on semi-horizontal chair-couches designed specially for me by a young Polish architect. From the High Table's windows we have an excellent view of the Pentagon.

Everyone was there. Tex Winter looked as though he needed some sleep. Cedric Douglas-Whyte was flaunting an Elizabethan lute he had borrowed from the Library of Congress, and was talking about the Haida Indians. The Rev. Soren Andersen was smiling blandly. Hilde Hildesheim was braless ("Look, Ma, I'm sixty: no bra! "), and Karin Hamsun — ah — Karin Hamsun looked like the sunrise over a cool Swedish lake. She wore a dark blue pant suit and a yellow scarf, and I could not take my eyes off her. May I mention once more that the time of this meeting was March 4th last year. My affair with Karin began two weeks later.

I summarized the new project, trying to remember all the details of Bill Bush's recital of horrors: page fifty-seven missing from the public library books in Kansas City; the tampered locks in Pebble Beach golf courses; the cement in the Steinway in Carnegie Hall; "Fuck you" written on a Smithsonian dinosaur's behind; the Houston handicraft store raided; Poughkeepsie travel posters profaned; ruined jigsaw puzzles in St. Louis; and smashed windows at the Berlitz school in Atlanta.

"G-g-g-gorgeous," said Cedric Douglas-Whyte. "Just the right case for an anthropological Sherlock Holmes like me."

"We should ask Karin to put the computers to work," suggested Soren Andersen.

"One would first have to choose reasonably well-related variables," Karin ventured. "I would want to control the dynamic allocation of all the peripheral units before going to work."

"That goes without saying," replied Richard Toshima, teasing her. "But I think we might make some progress before embarking on one of Karin's multiprogramming systems. Sight unseen, I think we could detect some common denominators right now. For example, each one of the incidents has as its most characteristic ingredient a demonstration against what one may call a 'leisure activity'."

"Well, that's p-p-p-pretty obvious," said Cedric who could not abide anybody cleverer than himself. "Even the famous Bill Bush, with his ridiculous horn-rimmed glasses, could have made *that* deduction. After all, what's more self-evident? The culprits don't like reading books, playing golf, going to piano recitals or museums; they don't like fooling around with handicrafts — for God's sake, who does? — they are bored by jigsaw puzzles, just as I am, and they hate learning French. I must say, they have my sympathy."

"I see the word *alienation* written all over this project," said Hilde Hildesheim, sounding more than ever like a lesbian sergeant major in the Berlin girl guides. "It does look like a pretty interesting catalogue though. Why didn't those kids smash computers? Or break the windows of the head office of General Motors? That's what I would do if I were alienated, wouldn't you? "

"We don't know the culprits are kids," said Tex Winter sternly. "You're jumping. Besides, I'm as alienated as anybody, and I have never smashed a computer or a head office in my life."

"Order, please," I said with mock severity. I always try to nip any incipient conflict in the bud, with humor if possible; if not, through the exercise of brute authority. "I would like to hear from Soren. What do you think, Reverend? "

"Well," Soren said, rubbing his beardless schoolgirl chin, "what I find significant is the absence of any overt sexual content in these manifestations. Unless page fifty-seven in all those books in Kansas City contain purple passages," he added with his Danish giggle. "What I am trying to say is that there's nothing sexually stimulating in a dinosaur, is there? Playing golf, or the piano, or doing jigsaw puzzles, doesn't reflect any repression or projection of the usual kind. It's not sexual games or pastimes or recreations the evil-doers are after, but — as Richard Toshima noted so well — leisure activities, pure and simple."

"Th-th-there is another thing that's interesting," said Cedric,

31

stroking his well-groomed Vandyke. "The demonstrations seem to me curiously neutral," he said with his Oxford stutter. "What I mean to say is that they don't reflect any anger on the part of the Establishment people against revolutionaries, or the counter-culture, or whatever you want to call them, nor the other way round. Who's ever heard of some long-haired Maoist going after jigsaw puzzles, for Christ's sake? Jigsaw puzzles don't symbolize anything, do they? "

"Oh yes, they do," said Toshima. "Most certainly they do. They symbolize boredom. Or rather the attempt to overcome, to defeat, boredom. To fill the empty spaces of time unused and time un-spent."

"B-b-b-bullshit! " replied Cedric vehemently. (He loved using crude American expressions. His Anthony Eden accent and stutter made them very effective.) "I've never heard anything as foolish in my life, if you allow me to say this, Dick. I see nothing more symbolic in jigsaw puzzles than in any other exercise of human ingenuity, such as running think tanks, making war, or writing ninth sympho-nies. If jigsaw puzzles are a waste of time, so is writing poetry or doing algebra."

"You can't tell me," replied Toshima, clearly stung, but not wanting to show it too much, "that all human occupations are on the same level: that there is no inherent difference — not just a difference in degree, but a *categorical* difference — between killing time by doing jigsaw puzzles and writing the ninth symphony."

"That's enough of that," I said, using my prerogative as chairman. "I don't think this is getting us anywhere. What do you say we should do now? What's the next step? Any suggestions? "

"We should ask the White House to secure for us all the files on each one of the incidents," said Hilde. "Let's study them, and then meet again."

"We should tell the President to stick them up his you-know-what," said Tex Winter.

"That's not a very helpful observation, Tex," I said.

"I think Hilde is right," Toshima said, looking at her approvingly. I have known for a long time that Toshima has tremendous appeal

32

for younger women who find him irresistible, but he regards them as silly and superficial. He likes to go to bed only with women at least fifteen years older than he is. I now noticed for the first time that he was embarking on a systematic campaign of flattery, aimed no doubt at landing Hilde in bed.

"Let's get the facts first, " he said. "I'd be happy to work with you, Hilde, on a detailed analytical breakdown of the various components."

"I'll do as 1 am told," she said, looking at me, putting down Toshima's advance.

"And what are your views, Karin? " I asked, softening my voice.

"Before I can be of any use," she said, her bright blue eyes looking directly into mine, "we would have to translate the questions we need answered into the machine code language of the computer. We would need input buffers which would require peripheral units to be operated continuously. I'm not sure we're ready for that."

"Probably not, Karin," I replied, my heart pounding with longing for her. What charm, what poise! She wore her tousled blond hair like an old-fashioned *Bubikopf* which suited her magnificently shaped round face perfectly, and gave it a natural, improvised look. Of course I had wondered, from the moment I hired her, what her attachments were, whether she was available to all of us, to any of us, or to none of us. What were *her* needs? Swedish girls are very sensible, I know, and consider sex a fundamental human activity comparable to eating or breathing. Would she do it with Cedric? With Andersen, a fellow Scandinavian? Surely not with the obstructionist, Tex? She was too young for Toshima, that I knew. How would she respond to a direct approach from me, who could almost be her grandfather? Was it conceivable that she was a lesbian? Could she and Hilde....? No, impossible!

"I-I-I think it's perfectly obvious what we must do," said Cedric. "I gather we're in a bit of a rush. Six weeks, did you say, Bierbaum? Well, that doesn't give us too much time, if we want to do a good job. Hilde is right, we must get the files. But I think there's something else we can do in the meantime. Let's try and find out, right away, who it was who wrote 'F-f-f-fuck you' on that dinosaur's behind. That was here in Washington, right under our nose. If we can get hold of the arch-criminal who did that, and do an in depth study on him, we might make a little progress. Or we might not. In any case, there's a chance that we might learn something."

"Well, we might try it," said Anderson.

"Not a bad idea," Hilde agreed.

"That's what we'll do then. I'll talk to Bill Bush, and let's see how far we can go. The meeting is adjourned."

Chapter 6

How we found the author of the seminal "Fuck you" is one of the more amusing episodes in these annals.

When we started our search I was reminded of the line from Goethe's famous poem "*Kennst Du das Land*" which reads "*Das Maultier sucht im Nebel seinen Weg,*" meaning the mule finds its way in the fog. Well, the mule did, and the fog could not have been thicker.

Even the world's greatest handwriting expert would have been of no use, because the *derrière* of the Smithsonian dinosaur had been scrubbed with Paula-esque thoroughness using a particularly efficient turpentine solution. There was only one way in which we could proceed with at least some remote chance of success, and that was to alert the museum authorities, and all the uniformed guards, and ask them to keep their eyes open for any suspect who might return to the place of his crime and do it — or something like it — again. Within a week the culprit was in our net. This time he had tried to remove the glass on one of the coffin-like boxes housing an Egyptian mummy of the twenty-first dynasty, in order to commit an unspecified act of molestation. He was caught red-handed, and in response to our request not to have him delivered to the civil authorities, he was handed over to CRUPP.

The man's name was Eddie MacIntosh — henceforth to be called simply Mac. One of the curators of the Egyptian Room brought him to CRUPP in a taxi, delivered him, and then excused himself.

I had him shepherded directly to my office.

Mac was a man in his early forties, pleasant looking, with a small brown mustache. He was well-dressed in a gray flannel suit that is the uniform of American businessmen. He was very polite. Of course, he had no idea why — of all places — he was brought to CRUPP.

"Please relax, Mr. MacIntosh," I said, offering him a cigarette. "This is not the police, and you are in no danger whatsoever."

"I know who you are, Mr. Bierbaum, and I know all about CRUPP," he said, then added with some embarrassment, "I must say I'm a little surprised to find myself here."

"I'm sure you are. *We* are also surprised," I said with a benevolent smile. "This is not our usual line of work. I'm afraid I don't quite know how to proceed. It's true, isn't it, that you have been writing rude words on an object in the museum, and that you were about to do some more damage when you were caught? "

"I guess that's true," Mac said, squirming in his chair. "I don't know *what* to say."

"You can be quite frank with me, Mr. MacIntosh," I went on in the manner of an avuncular prison chaplain. "It's obvious to me that normally you are a perfectly respectable citizen. You don't look like a psychopath, or a Communist, or something like that."

"I'm not," Mac said quietly, lowering his eyes.

"Well then, why do you do such things? "

"I don't know how to answer that, Mr. Bierbaum," he replied. "It's a way of telling how I feel."

"Well, that's a pretty good answer, I would say," I said. "And how *do* you feel? "

He laughed sheepishly.

"Bored, I guess," he said. "I don't know how else to put it."

"Well, have you ever had any trouble with the law, Mr. MacIntosh? "

"Parking tickets, that's all."

36

"Are you a family man? "

"Yes, sir. I have a wife and two children."

"Any trouble at home? "

"No more than anyone else. No, sir, I would say."

"Where do you live? "

"On Hunt Avenue in Chevy Chase. Near Wisconsin Avenue."

"And what do you do for a living? "

"Nothing."

"*Nothing?* "

"That's precisely what I mean," he said, tightening up. "Nothing at all. It drives me up the wall."

"Do you have enough to live on, I mean, without any work or employment? "

"More than enough. I'm on early retirement from Jupiter Aircraft in Baltimore. I had to leave them a year ago, with a very good pension. Add to that all the benefits I get, and the income from my investments, I have far more than I need."

"But don't you have to worry about the children's education? "

"That's all looked after."

"Then why don't you go around the world? Have yourself a ball? Take the wife along."

"Because I don't feel like it, that's why." The anger was return-ing again. "I want to stay right here. I don't want to go anywhere."

"I see." I was trying to think of some other questions. "Very interesting." I paused. "Would you say there are other people like you? "

"Thousands and thousands," he said quickly. "So far we haven't made any noise. But you wait, Mr. Bierbaum, you'll hear plenty from us! We've had enough of this! "

What did this remind me of, this talk of having had enough? Oh, yes, the Nazi speeches in the thirties. "We've had enough. *Wir haben die Nase voll!* " (We have our nose full!) Hitler used it. "Fourteen years of *Systemszeit,*" he used to rant, meaning the Weimar Republic. "We've had enough! *Es wird anders werden!* Things are going to change! " I suddenly had a terrible feeling of foreboding of what was in store for America, and it took an enormous effort to sound calm.

"I suppose you would call yourself dissatisfied with your lot. Is that a fair way of putting it, Mr. MacIntosh? "

"It certainly is. Dissatisfied is not strong enough. We're fed up! "

"And to show this to the world you write rude words on dinosaurs. Is that it? "

"We'll soon think of other ways, I can tell you that."

"I see. You realize, of course, that you can get into serious trouble for what you have done. You've committed a criminal offence. A word from me, and you'll receive a summons from the police. You would mind that, wouldn't you? "

"I wouldn't like it very much. True."

"Nor, I'm sure, would Mrs. MacIntosh."

"I guess not."

"Well, then, I'd like to suggest something. Why don't you go home? I won't say a peep to the police if you promise me that you'll return to us for further talks if we telephone you. I would like to discuss this matter with my colleagues."

"May I ask why you are so interested in me? "

"That I can't answer now. But if you cooperate with us, you will discover it very quickly. I think you will find our concern interesting and constructive."

He was suddenly the eager young executive.

"If I can be of any help — I've always been interested in science."

"Especially in dinosaurs? " I smiled, as he took his leave.

Chapter 7

The next morning — March 16 — I reported this conversation to my
assembled staff at the High Table.

"That's completely in tune with everything I've learned from the
files," said Hilde who was sporting an expensive maroon dress. She
wore dark blue eye shadow, making her look more than ever like
an immortal screen diva. "All the people responsible for these
so-called pranks are affluent members of the middle class, not
young and not old, who have no employment. They all complain
of being bored, and they all use this language of veiled threats.
It's quite extraordinary! "

"I would have liked to have helped you with this analysis," said
Richard Toshima, casting a lustful glance at Hilde's braless figure.
"Did you find it tough going? "

"Not at all," she replied sharply, giving the poor man another snub.

"A typical case of bourgeois delinquency," mumbled Tex Winter
in his cowboy voice. "Not very significant, I would say."

"But if it's true that there are thousands and thousands of them?
Could this not lead to a multi-cycle feeding? " asked Karin Hamsun,
opening her sky-blue eyes wide, like an ingénue from the backwoods.

"It could," replied the Rev. Soren Andersen. "It would certainly
be another American first: a rebellion by the rich against being rich.
The Voice of America will have a hard time explaining *that* to the
starving masses of the Third World! "

"It hasn't happened yet, *Kinder*," I said, "so let's not hatch our eggs before they are fertilized. Now I'm going to give a preliminary report to Bill Bush. Unless you have something else to say first."

"I-I-I do," said Cedric Douglas-Whyte. "I think we should take one more step. If you don't mind, Bierbaum, I'd like to visit this man MacIntosh and find out what he does with his time. It's just conceivable that this may round out the picture."

"That's a good idea," said Hilde. "It may throw some light on *his* leisure activities. After all, even in America today, the vast majority would give their eyeteeth not to have to do any work."

"That's what they *say*," said Cedric, sniffing the air like a rabbit. "May I go, Bierbaum? Do you agree? "

"Go with God," said Tex, with a loud yawn.

"All right, Cedric," I said. "If you get anywhere this afternoon, I'll call Bush at home tonight. Agreed."

Around five thirty that afternoon, Cedric Douglas-Whyte returned from his visit to Hunt Avenue, Chevy Chase. Before I present his report, I would like to say a little more about him.

He paints, he writes poetry and plays, and he sings Elizabethan madrigals, usually only the voice that does *not* contain the melody. At the same time he is a trained anthropologist, biologist, bio-chemist and linguist. Much of his work for CRUPP has dealt with race relations, and he has made a great reputation for himself — in conjunction with the Center for Applied Research on Developing Nations — as an expert on the Congo. He has also written a paper-back on the Papago Indians.

But his most important achievement no doubt is his study on deca-dence. This was one of the most extraordinary projects we ever undertook. It was done for one man: the French-American multi-millionaire, Alphonse Guelph. I had met M. Guelph at a cocktail party in Manhattan. We talked about France at the end of the last century, the *fin de siècle*.

"Isn't it strange," he said, "that no country ever considered itself as decadent as France did in 1890? Decadence was a cult: think of Baudelaire and Rimbaud and that lot; think of the Paris-oriented

Aubrey Beardsley and Oscar Wilde. They *thought* they were
finished. They *thought* they resembled nothing more than Rome
during its dying days. Yet, twenty years later, France fought to
the death for the traditional values: honor and duty and *la patrie*.
Isn't that extraordinary? "

We then talked about Germany and the Nazis, and the way *they*
thought Weimar Germany was decadent, and that it was their
sacred mission to restore Germany's health and virility.

"What about America? Is America decadent, do you think? " he
asked me.

"Let me find out! " I answered, and within two days I had in my
pocket a five hundred thousand dollar contract.

Cedric Douglas-Whyte's answers to this question were characteristic. He went, in great detail, into the factors that brought about
the decline and fall of Rome. He observed that in Rome there was
a feeling that the Empire was finished at the very time when it was
at its height: during the immediate successors of Augustus. That's
when the great Juvenal wrote his satirical poems castigating Roman
hedonism.

Cedric wrote about population figures and currency problems, the
decline in agriculture and the barbarian invasions, about slavery
and sex, and in all these respects he found very little resemblance
between Rome and America. He poured particular scorn on the idea
that the hippies were the early Christians of our day.

Alphonse Guelph was much reassured by the CRUPP report,
and joyfully paid us our fee.

This is what Cedric had to say about his visit to the MacIntosh
ménage.

"J-j-jolly nice house. Worth about $90,000, I would say. Good
department store furniture. Apart from bound volumes of the
Reader's Digest, no books visible. Expensive copies of Landseer
hunting scenes on the wall. Mac was a topnotch accountant
apparently. Very good at his job. No education in the humanities.
Not that that matters," he sniffed the air — a grimace he adopted
whenever he wanted to put something, or someone, down —
"considering the state of American education. Mrs. Mac decently

dressed, nice coiffure, tired face, but well looked after. No sign
that she knows anything about her husband's naughtiness.
Pretended I was an insurance salesman. Did a superb job,
considering that I know nothing about insurance.

"Mac — this might be a clue — is in the clutches of the pensions
department of Jupiter Aircraft who have some kind of compulsory
adult education scheme; Mrs. Mac thinks it's excellent. This is what
the poor man has to do: read *War and Peace*, learn the violin, take
paleontology, archaeology and history lectures at the Smithsonian,
and learn Spanish. What's more, he has to perform all kinds of good
works in the ghetto, activities for which he has absolutely no
talent. He was compelled to act as nursemaid, dishwasher, social
worker and plumber for a black family called Jefferson Lincoln
in the slums, not far from the station on H Street. They don't
want him but are forced to accept him as a condition of their
welfare allotments. They really dislike him, and bully and
exploit him to take revenge on the white man. No wonder the
bloke is ready to scream. Mrs. Mac is of no help. She sympathizes
with him only with regard to the black family. She feels the
authorities should find a more receptive family for him, one that
would treat him with kindness and consideration, treat him as a
person, not a machine. But as far as learning and culture are
concerned, she pushes him all day. Those g-g-g-goddam American
women: they're culture mad. It used to be religion; now it's
culture. It's all those prairie schoolmarms, the frontier tradition
and all that. Males had to build the country, women to supply
the culture. It's the ruin of America, I have no doubt. Talk about
motivation: the poor man has absolutely no motivation to learn
anything: he does it only because he's being pressured into it. If he
refuses, they stop the pension cheques. Man's inhumanity to man!

"Mac took me to his den, and we had a heart-to-heart talk. He nearly
broke down. He wants work — any work. He's tried everything; selec-
tive service, social security, private agencies; he's put ads in the paper.
No good. He would even take unskilled work, laborer's work, if the
unions would let him, but of course they won't. He's at his wits' end.
He was brought up to work, he said, not to fool around with culture.
There are more and more people like him who've had enough. He
wishes his wife were more understanding, but she means well, and
he doesn't hold it against her that she keeps pushing. Anyway, it
can't go on like this. 'Thank God I'm not a drinker,' he said,
'otherwise I'd be a raving alcoholic by now.' Unless he gets relief
somehow, something's going to snap soon. That's all."

43

A report from our research department waited for me on my desk the next morning, with some vital information about Mac. Indeed we had hit the jackpot; he was splendidly characteristic of affluent Middle America. Religion: Episcopalian. Father: lower middle class, Wisconsin, of Scottish and German origin, worked all his life in a paper mill. The youngest of a family of eight. Mother: a minister's only daughter from a small town in Minnesota, an old American family with a sprinkling of Indian blood. Mac himself had won a couple of scholarships and done very well in Business and Finance at the Ohio State University at Columbus, and then worked his way up to the top of the Accounting Department at Jupiter. Got married at the age of twenty-three, first child born a year later, second one two years after that. He seemed to come straight out of a textbook on the typical American husband, father — and executive.

After digesting this material, I phoned Bill Bush and told him the results of our findings so far.

"Good work, Friedrich," he said. "Illuminating as hell. There's been more trouble. It's all beginning to fit."

"What kind of trouble, Bill? "

"More disturbances. Sabotage. Obstructionism. Call it what you like. Vandalism. I can't find the right word. In Cleveland some people broke into the yacht club, and managed to melt down the sails on some sixteen boats. The sails are made of nylon which melts easily. What would you call that? "

"Bolshevism," I said, with a feeble laugh.

"Please take it a little more seriously, Friedrich," Bill replied. I had momentarily forgotten that Bill's main claim to fame was his complete lack of humor. "As a matter of fact, the newspapers agree with you. They also think it's a Communist plot."

"So the press got hold of it now, eh? " I asked.

"Yes, but for once we're far ahead of them. They report the incidents and write editorials about them, but they haven't as yet detected an overall pattern. In Watertown, N.Y., some people stole the mailing lists from the YMCA's adult education office,

44

and the *Watertown Examiner* thinks it's the work of Jehovah's Witnesses who apparently feel the YMCA has been out to get them. In Memphis, Tennessee, the troublemakers took some arsenic solution and poisoned about two hundred thousand worms in various establishments catering to the devotees of fishing, thereby forcing them to use other bait, or no bait at all. Normally fishing people have a lot of patience, but with that they had no patience at all."

"Did they have any theories in Memphis as to who may have perpetrated this? "

"The police think the Black Power people are to blame, but I guess that's routine. Then there's been the hassle in Portland, Oregon, which again is quite different."

"Oh? "

"It seems that in the middle of the night some people sneaked into the local concert hall, made their way to the rooms in the back where all the orchestral instruments were being kept, and cut the C-strings of all the cellos. Only the C-strings. I would have thought that cellists normally take their instruments home to practice their scales, but apparently not in Portland. Fortunately, it was discovered in time before the evening concert that day, and it wasn't very difficult to put in new C-strings. Nevertheless, the incident is significant, mainly because the local television station made it their lead item in the news bulletin that night, and appealed to the public to report the culprits to the authorities, but nothing happened. This was repeated for several days, and unleashed a violent editorial in the newspaper about the breakdown of morals in Portland and the decline of the West."

"It sounds very much like *Max und Moritz*," I said.

"Like *what?* "

"Like the two German pranksters whom your great namesake, Wilhelm Busch, immortalized."

"Oh, *please*," said Bill.

"*Dieses war der erste Streich, doch der zweite folgt sogleich.*
This was the first prank, but the second one follows immediately."

45

"You're not being very helpful, Friedrich," Bill said sternly, "remember, there's an election at stake."

"I know," I said contritely.

"Well, what do you propose to do now? "

"I think we'd better do some work on our man MacIntosh, don't you? "

"Work? What do you mean, work? "

"I propose to ask our resident psychologist, Dr. Richard Toshima, to give him therapy. If he makes progress with him, surely we may establish a pattern that can be followed to help others. What do you think?"

"But suppose something goes wrong? If there's trouble, the White House is bound to be implicated. Imagine the row! "

"What can go wrong, Bill? "

"You may kill the poor bastard."

I laughed a happy laugh.

"Yes, that's very likely," I said. "I'll make sure the President will be charged with murder. No, seriously, Bill. There's no danger. Toshima is the mildest man, and he knows his stuff inside out. Let me go ahead with it. It's the only positive thing I can think of."

"Well, if you say so. But be careful! "

"Don't worry! "

"All right then, go ahead. I'll keep the President informed."

Chapter 8

I canceled the usual High Table meeting the next morning, and instead summoned Richard Toshima and the Reverend Soren Andersen to my office and told them what I had in mind. I wanted Andersen there because of his background in psycho-analysis, and the special religious slant he gives to psychological problems.

I first heard about him at a dinner party at the house of Mr. Justice Alexander, one of our better Supreme Court judges. I sat next to a white-haired lady whose nephew had come under Soren Andersen's spell in Minneapolis, where Andersen was conducting classes for troubled executives, men who drank too much, had marital problems, were suffering from ulcers or had heart conditions. Through a combination of religious — I suppose the word is — "wisdom," and a modicum of conventional psychotherapy, Andersen apparently helped hundreds of these people. Since I was aware that the time was ripe for think tanks to branch out from narrowly governmental, industrial and economic problems, and deal in novel ways with broader human affairs, I contacted Andersen and invited him to visit us at CRUPP. We made friends immediately, and he agreed to join us.

As for Toshima, his orientation was, of course, entirely different. I knew he was a Skinner man, going in, as I understood it as a layman, for straightforward Pavlovian conditioning. He was, however, by no means orthodox.

Perhaps his most significant work for CRUPP dealt with sleep. According to him, we would be far more efficient if we slept, not through the night for six to nine hours, but throughout the twenty-four hour day in three to four hour periods. The southern custom of long siestas, which comes close to Toshima's recipe, makes much better biological and psychological sense, he feels, than our usual sleep patterns, and he has recommended his formula to a number of mental institutions and hospitals in Utah. There they call this the "CRUPP sleep pattern" and, I am told, they are very happy with it.

Toshima has also done much research on drugs and the drug culture, but he says he is now bored with it. Far more interesting as a contemporary phenomenon, he feels, are the various meditation cults that bring about deepened forms of consciousness without chemical help, and he is very well read in the literature of Buddhism and Hinduism.

I put my plan before them.

"I think I want Toshima to go to work on him," I said, "but before doing so, I'd like to have your view, Rev."

"Well, Friedrich," Soren said, rubbing his girlish chin, "what we have to do is to cure this man of his addiction to work. He now loves work, he wants it more than anything else. We must induce him to hate it, and to want the so-called Higher Things in life."

"On which you are the expert, Rev. *Crede experto*, as Silius Italicus used to say."

"Quite," he smiled. "I admire your erudition, Friedrich."

"It gets a bit on my nerves," said Toshima, smiling.

"Well," continued Soren, tossing his mane of blond hair off his forehead, "basically, of course, it boils down to a question of sex. If he had a more satisfying sexual life, he would undoubtedly be happier. He would not *want* to work. A society like ours which is based on the work ethic can function only if its members live in a constant state of sexual frustration."

I thought this over for a minute.

"If it's a matter of providing women for Mac," I said, thinking, as always, positively, "I can't imagine anything easier. CRUPP

48

has lots of money, and Washington is full of lonely, beautiful women. I think we might manage to select some very choice specimens."

"Or we might send him to Copenhagen, capital of the Kingdom of Love," the Dane said, smiling. "But no, I'm afraid it's not as simple as that. To provide erotic satisfaction for him deep enough to cure him of his work addiction, the whole of society would have to change, and this is even beyond the power of CRUPP. No, I think you're right, Richard should give him some treatments. There are also other ways of tackling the problem, but why not try the psychological approach first."

"So could you tell us what treatments you have in mind? " I turned to Toshima with polite curiosity.

"I don't see any particular difficulties," he replied, adjusting his bright yellow headband. "I'll condition the Protestant work ethic out of him, that's all. It's simply a matter of behavior modification. I'll make the patient hate work, just as I can make a smoker hate the taste of tobacco."

"But surely you'll also have to make him enjoy life without work? " I said. "Isn't that a little more difficult? "

"Perhaps," Richard answered, examining his fingernails. "I have my methods. We'll have to wait and see."

"How much time do you need? "

"One month."

"Fair enough, Richard."

"May I ask one favor, Bierbaum," he said, taking off his granny glasses, and beginning to polish them with a huge red handkerchief. "I want you to assign Hilde to work with me. I think her understanding of the cultural makeup of *homo americanis* may help me a good deal, and a spot of psychological training can't do her any harm, either."

Of course I knew exactly what he was after. He thought daily proximity could not fail to land her in his bed, or for that matter, him in her bed. But I had observed the two rebuffs she had given him and I did not wish to promise her to him without consultation.

49

"I have no objection, Richard, but I must ask her first."

"Of course," he said.

Most reluctantly, Hilde agreed.

"If you really insist," she shrugged. "But I'm not going to bed with him. There's nothing in our contract that obliges me to do *that.*"

"This is a free country," I replied.

Chapter 9

Before I report on Toshima's calamitous ministrations, there are other things — more pleasant — which I should like to describe. First of all, I had a visit in my office from Senator Hollinger, the Chairman of our Board. I mention it mainly because he plays a prominent role in the chapters to follow. He is one of the two senators from Massachusetts, a vigorous man in his early fifties, who flatters himself on his resemblance to the late Cary Grant. He enjoys an excellent relationship with the White House.

"The President tells me you've undertaken to look into those curious happenings. I want to tell you how pleased I am."

"Thank you, Senator," I said. "It's a rather mysterious phenomenon."

"So it seems. I'm pleased CRUPP is once again working on all cylinders. You realize, of course, that he considers your findings essential to his campaign. But I gather this time we'll have to do without publicity."

"At this stage, most certainly. The country is unaware of what's happening. It's not up to us to tell, is it? "

"Of course not," said the Senator, nodding seriously. What a handsome man, I thought, looking at him: tanned and healthy.

"Tell me, Bierbaum, I understand your psychologist is giving in-depth treatment to your man, I mean the man who committed that sacrilege at the Smithsonian." He smiled avuncularly. "Obviously a man with some spirit. Now, I hope your psychologist knows what he's doing. If not, this could cause us quite a bit of trouble, couldn't it? "

"There's nothing in the world to worry about, I assure you, Senator," I said. "He's one of the leading operant-conditioning men in the country. He's worked on hundreds of people without any ill effect. I assure you nothing can go wrong."

"Well, I'm pleased to hear that. That's really all I wanted to say. Your reassurance calms me considerably."

He left happy. He was, however, not so happy at the end of the month. But I must not anticipate. I now want to report a gloriously happy event in my private life: the beginning of my affair with Karin Hamsun. But first I should explain about Paula.

When I came home that evening, Paula was waxing the dining room table.

"Isn't dinner ready? " I asked irritably.

"No," she said. "This place is like a pigsty. All you look at is your goddam pictures. You don't notice the filth around here. I won't start cooking until I've made the place inhabitable. "

"Look, Paula," I said, raising my voice. "You've nothing to do all day, and you start fussing around the moment I come home. I've had enough! "

"*I've* had enough of your bellowing at me, I can tell you that. Every day you become more like that screamer Göring who thought a man wasn't a man unless he screamed at his wife and his hundred and twenty thousand subordinates at least three times a day."

May I make a short pause? The deal Paula and I made when she finally agreed to marry me in 1947 specified that I was not to mention Göring in her presence, and I faithfully stuck to these terms. But there was nothing in the contract that precluded her from mentioning him in *my* presence, and she does so with Prussian regularity whenever she gets mad at me, which is about three or four times a day. I have learned to endure this with truly Christian forbearance. I don't even smile anymore when she rails at me about my "idol, that fat, brutal buffoon who was too much of a coward to take his just punishment for the unspeakable crimes he committed."

On two or three occasions she threatened to leave me, not because of anything I said about Göring — as I have mentioned, his name never crossed my lips when we were together — but because she was jealous of some woman or other. Normally, she was very good about my engaging in occasional *Seitensprünge* — literally "side jumps," the picturesque German expression for relatively harmless little marital infidelities. She discreetly looked the other way, or tolerantly *drückte ein Auge zu,* closed one eye. But occasionally it seemed to her that things got out of hand, that a mini-affair had turned into a maxi-affair. Then she invariably raised the roof, and threatened to "pack her suitcase." In the end she'd stay and always deny having been serious about her threatened intention to leave me.

"You're helpless without me," she would say. "You're just a fat German *Faulkerl* who can't get through a single day without my wiping his nose."

I mention this because it's relevant to the evening under discussion, when I took it upon myself gently to remind her that I like dinner to be ready when I come home from work. She calmly finished polishing the dining room table, while I had three Scotches, and then went to the kitchen to make a fairly respectable *Wiener-schnitzel.* The whole procedure took about an hour. Sometimes, when I am less patient, I suggest we go out to eat.

"*Kommt nicht in Frage,*" she always says in her Berlin slang. "It's out of the question. *Bei Dir piepts mal wieder.* Your little birdie is twittering again. You can't get a decent meal anywhere in Washington. Heinz fifty-seven varieties. *Ohne mich.* Count me out."

During dinner I told her about Mac, Toshima, Hilde, and the Senator.

"It all sounds awful to me," she said. "I *like* Toshima, but sometimes he reminds me of one of those Nazi doctors who used to hang around Himmler. Of course, I'm sure you've repressed all that."

"*Du bist völlig verrückt!* " I retorted, my gall rising. This means you're completely crazy. "Toshima has *nothing* in common with those quacks. You're downright insulting. Besides, I've repressed nothing."

53

I could have killed that woman. Why does she see a Nazi under every bed?

"Don't get so excited, Friedrich. I told you I liked Toshima, even if he doesn't know the difference between an inferiority complex and my arse."

"*Verdammte Scheisse*, why don't you shut up? " I nearly choked on my *Schnitzel.*

"You're in terrible shape, Friedrich," she said, her voice suddenly sweet and loving. "A fat man your age should take it easy. He shouldn't shout so much. Or one day he'll have a heart attack. I don't know why Germans always shout. At least Americans don't shout. You should have some diversions. I wish you played golf."

"I'm in perfectly good shape," I said. "There's nothing wrong with me."

"I can always tell," she went on, a knowing smile playing on her lips, "when you're contemplating a fling. *Ich habe 'ne gute Nase.*" (I have a good nose.)

"What *zum Teufel* are you talking about? "

"You want to go to bed with that Swedish morsel. Confess it! Yes, or no? "

How the hell did she know?

"The thought has never crossed my mind," I lied.

"That girl is pure poison, Besides," she went on, "never put your pen into company ink. *Das klappt nie.* That never works."

While I was munching Paula's delicious crumb cake, I resolved that the time had come for me to launch a decisive *Blitzkrieg* on Karin's honor.

Chapter 10

As it happened, there was no need for me to devise elaborate tactics and strategies, because Karin and I synchronized our approaches. Precisely at the time I decided to invade her territory, she must have decided to invade mine. I was going to be very direct and ask her whether she would like a drink after work. Her approach was slightly more devious.

She called me on the intercom around noon.

"Richard and I were wondering whether you can spare an hour for us tonight for some further discussions about the Mac-therapy," she said, sounding very businesslike.

My heart was pounding like that of a youth in the throes of puberty.

"Of course," I said. "Where? "

"We thought my apartment was more convenient than his. You wouldn't have to drive all the way to Richmond."

"I'd love to come," I replied, my throat dry with excitement.

* * *

As soon as she opened the door, I knew paradise was awaiting me.

She was wearing a blue-green see-through gown, half pyjamas, half cocktail dress. There was soft music. My highly receptive nostrils inhaled the most aphrodisiac scent I have ever smelled.

"Why don't you come in? " she said, smiling the smile of Aphrodite.

I did, and found myself in the twenty-first century. The furniture in the living room was made of translucent plexiglass, so that at first glance all you could see were the cushions on the chairs, and a wooden bowl on the table. The door to the bedroom was open, and I could catch a glimpse of a huge round bed hanging from the ceiling.

"You must forgive me," she said, in the voice of an *ingénue* in an old Bergman film, "but Richard had to back out at the last minute. He mumbled something about having to try out some of his equipment."

"Good," I said, with feeling.

We were still in the hall. I tried to absorb all I saw. The bathroom did not seem to have a door at all, and was dominated by what I first thought was a space capsule, but then turned out to be a prefabricated shower-sink.

"A French design," she explained. "Exhibited at last year's *Triennale*. You may try it out later."

"Thank you," I said, my heart pounding. I followed her into the living room, which was dominated by a huge canvas primarily in black and white depicting about fifty different copulatory positions, with great emphasis on the tumescent male member which was painted in a triumphant red.

"Do you like it? " she asked sweetly.

"Very much," I replied, in the manner of an experienced art connoisseur.

"It helps me with my control brakes," she said. "I'm sure you'll find it useful too. What would you like to drink? Aquavit, Slivovitz, Schnapps? "

"An ordinary American Scotch, please."

My eyes were fixed on the picture as she poured me the drink. For herself she made a vodka on the rocks. She joined me on the plastic sofa, and without further preliminaries we kissed. It was heaven.

56

"You taste of Swedish sunshine in the spring, Karin," I said, at my most poetic, during a pause.

"And you, my dear, seem to be anxious to evaluate your input stimulus."

"I am, I am," I answered.

"I will do my best to reward your input with adequate reinforcing responses. What shall we talk about before we digit? "

"Before we *what?* " I said, very quietly.

"Before we interfix, stupid! You'd better get used to my language, or this won't last very long," she said, laughing a delectable silvery laugh.

We kissed again, and then I said, " Let's talk about you," tousling her *Bubikopf*, her gorgeously untidy blond hair, the way one musses up a child's.

"My, you're rough, you brute," she said. "What do you want to know about me? "

"How come you're both beautiful and brainy? "

"That's how I came out of my mother's connection box," she said, putting her hand on my thigh. "Why don't you send her a distance signal, congratulating her? "

"I might just do that, Karin. What do you think of us all at CRUPP? Do you find the work congenial? "

"I'm happy wherever I can fool around with my model building. The people are OK. *You* know, garbage in, garbage out. Tell me this, Friedrich. What's your delay time? "

She took off her top. I gulped down my Scotch and pounced on her.

"Not so hard," she said. "You're hurting my clutch points. That comes from overdoing your deprivation-satiation ratio. If you're not careful, it may easily upset your digital pattern recognition. Shall we use the bed for interacting? "

We took off our clothes.

"Do you like the rectiliniar approach or do you prefer cyclic motions? " she asked me, as we embraced on her magnificently round bed.

"Oh anything, anything," I gasped.

"Well then, let's do it the cyclic way. That's more interesting for my software. I think it's good for your toggle switch too. I suppose you're used to the elementary horizontal feed, eh? "

"By no means," I said, burying my head in her clutch points. "I often feed vertically."

"What a nice amplifier you have! " she said, seizing it eagerly.

"Thank you," I whispered.

Our interaction was perfect.

"I like your input," she said, afterwards.

"And I your feedback." I was beginning to learn her language.

"Have you a cigaret? " she asked.

"I'm afraid not."

She got up and took one out of her purse. I lit it for her and put it in her mouth. She smoked it silently. Then she said, "Come on, Friedrich. Let's digit again."

"My dear child," I said soothingly. "I don't think my amplifier will amplify for a little while."

"Of course it will," she insisted.

It did, after about twenty minutes' considerable effort by the two of us.

Chapter 11

I have always adhered to the principle that any member of my staff must be left alone to do his, or her, job without being pestered by me. Therefore, I did not bother Toshima with any questions, quite willing to wait the full month before he made his report. But in the present instance I was fortunate to be able to ask Hilde occasionally how they were getting along. About one week or ten days after the beginning of the treatment — it must have been around March 25th — she came to see me in my office towards four o'clock in the afternoon. She looked a little disheveled, considering how carefully she normally is about her appearance, and I noted unusually dark circles under her eyes.

Hilde's academic background (not to mention her past as a movie queen forty years ago) was totally different from that of Richard Toshima.

Her contributions to CRUPP have all dealt with the media. Her study of private and public television is considered superior to anything sponsored by the Ford Foundation. Her work on cassettes and cable technology has attracted the attention of both RCA and Siemens. Her preoccupation with what she calls the "phenomenology" of advertising has endeared her to many practitioners of the trade all over the country, and possibly won her those three wealthy American husbands. In a series of learned publications she developed the theory that advertising and jazz are the only original American art forms. No one, she claimed, could understand America without having a profound insight into the psychology of commercial mass persuasion. Moreover, it was advertising that gave American television its vitality and popularity. These studies brought her into contact with all kinds of market research organizations, ratings and polling systems, and she developed considerable expertise in these fields. She has also retained her interest in motion pictures, capitalizing perhaps a little on the tremendous prestige of the German cinema of the twenties with which she had nothing to do. Her talent and beauty were not discovered, I think, until 1938.

I must also mention that she is thoroughly at home in the world of mass culture generally, not just television and movies. She looks upon it all as part of our *Kulturgeschichte*, and makes marvelously ingenious connections and comparisons. I once heard her talk at a party about Ghiberti's famous doors to the Baptistery in Florence, which she called a "Renaissance comic strip." When you think of it, that is exactly what it is. But she is a serious scholar, tackling her studies with German thoroughness. She has assembled a filing system which, though not computerized, is one of the marvels of CRUPP. She asked me the other day whether it was all right for her to leave it in her will to the Library of Congress. Since it is her property, I said, "Of course."

On the day she visited me in my office to report on Toshima's progress, she was in a less serene mood.

"I can't tell you how badly this started, Friedrich," she said, plunging into one of my deep armchairs. "Such idiotic bad luck! I can't really say it was all my fault, though, in a sense, of course it was. In many ways it couldn't have been worse."

"Hilde, please speak English or German, but make yourself understood one way or another."

"Well, years ago I wrote a piece in *Harper's* about Japanese television, and I said how wonderful it was that they had a whole network devoted to nothing but education. But I went on to say that in their psychology they were light years behind us, and their 'Pearl Harbor mentality' was visible all over the place, especially in their programming for teen-agers. For some reason Toshima got hold of this article the evening before we were to get together on this project. You remember how keen he was to work with me?"

"I certainly do," recalling his two approaches at the meeting and her rather obvious rebuffs.

"He certainly changed his mind about me when he read that piece. To say that he took offense would be grossly understating the

60

case. He was mortally wounded. When I arrived in his office he asked me whether I really wanted.to work with a man who was genetically related to people with a 'Pearl Harbor mentality.' At first I didn't know what he was talking about, and then he practically rubbed my nose in that old article. Who would have thought that this sophisticated man would have such a sensitive skin? As you know, I didn't want to work with him in the first place, but when he said *that* to me, I got obstinate and told him not to be silly. He said I was free to go. But I wouldn't go, and since then he's been treating me like shit. I feel awful about this, since obviously he is very good at his job and I'm much impressed."

"Oh good," I said, sitting up in my chair. "Tell me about that."

"He says, first things first. The first thing to do is to make Mac hate Jupiter Aircraft; that's the place where he used to be a top-notch accountant. Then he has to make him hate work as such. All this is called aversion therapy, and is pretty straightforward. Then, when he's succeeded with that, he has to make him *like* the so-called Good Things in Life, and he'll start with that in a day or two, with a process of reinforcements, i.e. rewards. He seems to be completely professional at his work, and Mac is co-operating beautifully."

"And how does this aversion therapy operate? "

"It's really quite interesting. You may have noticed a funny smell in the building during the last few days. That's apomorphine, the drug he uses. He gives him intramuscular injections. It all takes place in the little room on the third floor. He put up a little projection device, and a screen. When the drug takes effect, making the man increasingly nauseated, he flashes pictures on the screen — just ordinary still photos — of the outside of the Jupiter head office in Baltimore, his office, the john, the adding machines and books, his secretary, and then, at the climax — yesterday it was a picture of the Jupiter cafeteria — the man vomits. And this is repeated again and again and again, with slight variations."

"It sounds brutal to me," I said, feeling sick to *my* stomach.

"You can't make an omelet without breaking eggs, as they used to say in good old *Deutschland*," she said, with a dry laugh.

I thought this over for a minute, frowning, not much reassured.

61

"Don't worry, Friedrich. Toshima is excellent at this game, utterly professional. I must confess I'm beginning to like him a lot."

"But you say he's treating you like shit? " I said.

Again she laughed that unamused laugh.

"Maybe that's why. I'm a masochist from way back."

"So what's the next step? "

"Mac already loathes the very thought of Jupiter. We've just started branching out to making him loathe *all* work, and we've defined this as making an effort for financial or material gain. We're not against making efforts, but we're against making efforts *for gain*, do you understand? This will take another few days, as you can imagine. Then we have to go into reverse: rewarding him for enjoying the things he *should* enjoy."

"And you think Toshima can really complete this program on time? "

"He's only promised to do his best, remember. I think we have a chance."

"Well, I'll keep my fingers crossed. And one more thing, Hilde. Go easy on him, eh? I want him to keep his mind on his work."

"I'll try," she said, with a wan smile.

"Well, *Hals und Beinbruch!* "

When Germans wish each other good luck, they say "I hope you break your neck and your leg," in that order.

I had to wait ten days for Hilde's second report, which I am afraid made me fear the worst. Again she appeared in my office in the late afternoon. She looked distinctly worse than the first time, and I noticed the little bags of skin under her ears, the scars of her face-lifting operations, had a strange bluish tinge to them.

"It's not going well, and it's not going badly," Hilde said, this time pacing the floor rather than sitting down. "The trouble is, I don't think Mac is in very good physical condition, and therefore doesn't respond quite as well as he should to Toshima's treatment. But don't worry, he responds, and we're making progress. Toshima is very optimistic."

"How far have you got, Hilde? " I asked.

"I think the first part is pretty well under control, he can't bear to hear the very word Jupiter mentioned without vomiting. As to his attitude towards work as such, I'm not quite so sure; perhaps it's too early to tell. But we're having trouble with the reverse process."

"How come? "

"Well, it's difficult to *reward* him, you know. The only thing he likes is work, and" she laughed her bitter laugh "that's the one thing we can't recognize as a legitimate reward."

"What about sexual rewards? Most men would do anything for sex."

"Not Mac. He's much too uptight for that. The trouble is he only likes making love to his wife, and doesn't need *us* to procure her for him, does he? "

"Doesn't he like little nymphets, or girls with large breasts, or any of the conventional dream figures of American men? "

"The naughtiest thing he can think of is Playboy, which he subscribed to when he was at college, and the old Playmates of the Month, but that's no good, because of all puritan magazines, the old Playboy was the most puritan."

"Why do you say that? "

"Because the whole idea is that you mustn't touch those girls. They are so clean, so remote, so unreal, that they don't do the trick at all. They look as though they had never had a period in their lives. They are not the dream figures of American men, but of American adolescents! The idea of the old Playboy Clubs, and all those bunnies with their breasts hanging out which you're not allowed to touch! Disgusting! Talk about the Protestant ethic, for Christ's sake! "

63

"Noli me tangere," I mumbled. Do not touch me.

"Absolutely. The ideal thing would be to make him read a page or two of *War and Peace* and then, when the Rosenzweig Boredom Index shows twenty or twenty-five, let him make love to a *real* woman, not a dream woman. If only he liked real women other than his wife. It would make Toshima's work much easier."

"What was that? The Rosenzweig Boredom Index? "

"Oh yes, a lovely little device. It measures your rate of attention. I don't know how it works. Registers brain waves or something. Anyway, as soon as your mind begins to wander, the thermometer goes up. When it's up to twenty, it's quite high. When Mac has to practice the violin, it goes up to thirty, and boy, does it ever show! His intonation is unbelievable! "

Hilde had wanted to become a concert violinist when she was in her teens in Berlin.

"So you see, it's hard to give him any positive incentives. Work is out, and sex is out. I tried some hard-core pornography on him. You know, the stuff you get around Times Square — gorgeously *pubic* pictures. Insatiable women enticing you passionately with hot genitalia. But it's no good. He finds them revolting. I read some highly explicit passages to him, using all the right four letter words, but he won't have any of it. He says, 'Shut up, will you? ' No, Richard thinks we have no choice but to resort to electric shock treatment."

"Electric shock? " I repeated, not liking the sound of that at all. "Why? The man is perfectly sane, isn't he? "

"Very *light* electric shocks, don't worry, Friedrich. The alternative would be to starve him, and then to reward him with food, in conjunction with cultural goodies, photographs of Mona Lisa, snatches of Shakespeare, a spot or two of Mozart. Above all, pictures of dinosaurs, to make him love *them*. But that takes too much time, if we want to meet our deadline. Electric shocks are more effective, anyway. The technique is to give him sequences of accelerating shocks, and to reward him by turning the machine off at the moment he is exposed to culture with a capital K. The relief is the reward, you understand."

"It sounds awful to me," I said.

"It isn't," she cried. "Not at all. Richard says it's worked many, many times. He himself developed the techniques at Caltech. I have nothing but respect for the quiet, efficient way he is handling this case. The man is most impressive. *Ich nehm meinen Hut ab.*" I take my hat off.

"But you say he won't forgive you for that article? " I asked quietly.

A dark shadow fell over her face.

"No, he won't," she said. "Isn't that strange? You know, reading all those purple passages to Mac, what I really had in mind was to arouse *him*, Toshima, so that he'll pay some attention to *me!* I'd go to bed with him tonight, if he so much as smiled at me. But he won't. It's pure torture."

"But you're a masochist. You enjoy torture."

"I suppose in a way I do," she replied frowning. "But I've had enough of it now. He won't look at me, and I'm going insane with desire."

"I'm sorry to hear that," I said sympathetically. "How much more time does he need? "

"The month will be up tomorrow week."

"Well, let's hope for the best," I said, my voice, I'm sure, sounding a little lukewarm.

"Don't worry, Friedrich. We may not have a complete success, but I have no doubt the results will be positive."

"*Hoffentlich,*" I concluded. "I certainly hope so."

Chapter 12

During the next week I was, in Virgil's word, *spemque metumque inter dubii*, swaying between fear and hope. I was reminded of the time, in 1943 or 1944, when, as a young assistant to Göring in his capacity as Commissioner of the Four-Year Plan, I was messenger boy between a group of engineers who, because of the shortage of steel, had been asked to design locomotives made of cement. Göring kept bellowing at me, demanding to see the drawings. The engineers weren't ready to show them.

"I make you personally responsible, Bierbaum," he yelled.

The scene took place in his Berlin *palazzo*. He was sitting behind his heavily ornate *Louis Seize* desk which I believe had belonged to one of the Rothschilds. The diamond-studded *Pour le Mérite* decoration on the front of his maroon uniform reflected the light from the huge crystal chandelier. It was about the time when the joke about Göring wearing rubber models of his decorations in his bath was doing the rounds among the higher echelons of the SS.

"Either I have those drawings in my hands by tonight, or you'll be sent to the Eastern Front," he went on.

That was the one place I didn't want to go to, naturally. My God, was I ever swaying between fear and hope that evening. In the end, the engineers came through with flying colors. They presented magnificently ingenious plans which delighted Göring, but for some reason — I don't recall precisely — the cement locomotives were never built.

Well, Toshima did *not* come through with flying colors. *Au contraire.* Four days before the month was up, Eddie MacInstosh collapsed

completely, and had to be sent by ambulance to the Walter Reed
Hospital. The combination of apomorphine and electric shocks
had utterly wrecked his constitution, both physical and mental.
Two days were enough to restore his physical well-being, more or less,
but he was then sent to the psychiatric wing, to be cured of the
effects of his breakdown, the worst symptom of which was general
amnesia.

In the meantime, Mrs. MacIntosh went to see Cedric Douglas-Whyte
whom she had met during his visit to their house. He sent her directly
to me. We had a painful scene.

"I'm sure you mean well,"·the poor woman said. She was very much
as Cedric had described her, not bad looking, with a careful hairdo,
but a face that was a little drawn and faded. She wore a well-cut
navy blue suit. "But whom can I blame but you? Eddie was in perfectly good condition until your treatment started. In fact, I think
it's an outrage what you people have been doing to him," she
continued, gaining momentum as she went on. "I can't help feeling
society should be protected from you."

"Oh," I said, soothingly,"I don't think that's the way to put it at all."

"It certainly is. I just thought I should let you know that I have
called up the *Washington Post*, and they're sending a reporter to my
house tonight. I will tell him all. I'm sure he will want to interview
you and Dr. Toshima as well."

Mein Herz ist in die Hosen gefallen — my heart fell into my pants.

"I wouldn't do that, Mrs. MacIntosh," I said, desperately trying not to
sound too frightened. But how could I deal with her? What weapons
did I have in my hand? After all, in her place, I would have screamed
my head off.

Suddenly I had a brainwave, an absolutely brilliant brainwave. I remembered that she knew nothing about her husband's misdemeanor in the
Smithsonian. I *did* have a weapon, after all.

"Well, you see, Mrs. MacIntosh, I don't think you know the full story.
If the press gets hold of what your husband has done, and he goes to
prison...." I let my voice trail off, as if I could not bear to face the end
of the sentence.

67

"What are you talking about? " she said, shrinking back from me.

"You don't know about it? " I asked, wide-eyed. "He didn't tell you? That's strange. Your marriage is all right, isn't it? "

"What are you talking about? " She now raised her voice. "What business is it of yours whether my marriage is all right? And what is this about prison? Are you trying to blackmail me, or something? I will immediately go and see my lawyer."

"You can do that, of course," I said, smiling confidently. "In fact, I think that's a very good idea. It may be better if I tell him about your husband's criminal tendencies. I don't think I have the right to tell you anyway."

Suddenly the woman burst into tears. "I don't have a lawyer," she sobbed. "Why don't you tell me what all this is about? "

"Now, that's better." I adopted my most elaborate Göring charm. "Would you like a cognac, Mrs. MacIntosh? "

"Yes, that would be very nice."

"You see, Mrs. MacIntosh," I said, as I walked over to my bar to pour her (and me) some cognac, "it's quite true that I'm not sure I should tell you. If your husband didn't, I don't think I should."

"Please do," she said, sipping her drink. "I'm sure he'll understand. What is all this about? "

So I told her the full story, leaving out nothing. I told her about her husband's defacement of the dinosaur (can one deface a *derrière?*), the President's concern, our desperate efforts to save him, the attempted therapy.

"It may still have highly beneficial effects on him, you know," I said, cheerfully, "once he has achieved full recovery. It is only a question of days. These little breakdowns are very common. Every time somebody says he's had a nervous breakdown, *that's* what he means. It happens to everybody, some time in his life."

"But when I went to see him this morning at the hospital, he didn't recognize me."

68

"Routine," I said, magnificently. "Routine. You wait. In a week he'll be as good as new."

"Well, I hope so," she said, swallowing her sobs, and sipping her cognac.

Appeasing Bill Bush and Senator Hollinger was not so easy. Bill just gasped when I told him that sickness had prevented a happy conclusion of the therapy.

"Sickness, Friedrich? What are you covering up? " he asked on the White House telephone.

"Nothing serious, I assure you."

"Oh, come off it. I can hear it in your voice. There's been some kind of trouble."

"The man just fell sick, that's all," I said. "It can happen to you or to me or to anybody. No need to make a federal case out of it."

"God Almighty! " He uttered a deep sigh. "Just as news of further disturbances is coming in from all over the country. The President will be livid."

"Disturbances? "

"Care for an example? In Charleston, West Virginia, somebody fooled around with the clock during a chess tournament."

"That would cause a revolution," I said seriously.

"Well, it practically did. Chess players have no sense of humor about that sort of thing at all."

"Whom did they blame, Bill? "

"The authorities blamed the Communists, and the Communists blamed the authorities," he replied with a dry laugh. "And have you heard about the goings on in Little Rock, Arkansas? "

"I'm afraid I haven't."

"There the saboteurs have been fooling around with adult games.

69

It seems that 'Squaring the Circle' is all the rage in Little Rock. It's some kind of mathematical game. Well, the culprits have been messing around with the paper circles, and you can't buy a set without there being highly obscene drawings all over them. Naturally, it's the Gay Lib people who are being blamed."

"And so far nobody has put two and two together? " I asked, incredulously. "I mean, it seems to me overwhelmingly clear that the country is full of Eddie MacIntoshes, all out to make trouble. Bored, unemployed executives."

"There isn't a doubt at all in President Roberts' mind. He has no difficulty with the diagnosis. It's the search for the right therapy that's troubling him. I can't emphasize enough how much he's counting on you people to come up with the answers."

"Tell him he has nothing to worry about, Bill. We're on our way. The whole of CRUPP has been mobilized," I replied, soothingly.

"There's nobody else in the country who can do this. The President knows this."

"Good. He's absolutely right."

"He's convinced a major work-leisure crisis is shaping up all over the country. Imagine what the Opposition can make of this in the forthcoming campaign! The very system is at stake! Here we are, the wealthiest nation in the world with hundreds of thousands of people in it who are so bored by their wealth that they've decided to throw spanners in the works — not by traditional means such as smashing computers or burning down the White House, but by attacking all the activities that are designed to make life enjoyable and meaningful. Unless you people come up with the answer, we're headed for disaster."

"I repeat. The President has nothing to worry about."

"How can you say this, Bierbaum? " Bill Bush's voice nearly cracked with emotion. "You've just told me your psychologist has made your man Mac *sick*. Suppose the press gets hold of this story? "

"My dear Bill, I have seen to it that they won't."

"You'd better make damned sure, that's all I can say. And please don't give me any of your Wilhelm Busch quotes. I'm not in the mood." And he hung up.

Senator Hollinger was even more difficult. In that infuriatingly urbane way of his, he said — again on the telephone — that I really had no choice but to dismiss Toshima.

"Out of the question, Senator," I said, my temper rising. "There's no evidence anywhere that Dr. Toshima's treatment hasn't been professional in all respects. In fact, he worked on this case jointly with another very eminent member of our staff, who repeatedly told me how exemplary his work was, how scrupulous and careful and considerate. These things happen, that's all. Nobody is to blame."

"That's not the way I regard it, Bierbaum," he said. "I have to look after CRUPP's reputation. I'm Chairman of the Board."

"We've suffered a temporary setback, that's all," I said, calmness itself.

"I wish you'd follow my advice, Bierbaum. The President depends on CRUPP. It's vital we show him we're serious. But I'm not going to force you. Do what you think right, and call me if you need me. Good-bye."

Toshima himself was crushed by his debacle. He was hardly coherent when he called me. I told him not to worry, and to take a few days' holiday. While he was away, an extraordinary thing happened.

Chapter 13

Paula and I were having our after-dinner coffee in my library in Bethesda under my recently acquired Holbein print, when there was an excited telephone call from Mrs. Mac. Could she come and see me right away? There had been a most puzzling development, she said; she couldn't understand it at all.

"What kind of a development, Mrs. MacIntosh? " I asked.

"I'd rather tell you in person. May I come? "

I gave her my address, and fifteen minutes later she rang my bell. I introduced her to Paula who — I could see this right away — took to her immediately.

The story that emerged was indeed fantastic. Mac apparently was still suffering from amnesia, though he was slowly beginning to remember events that had happened as recently as two months ago. However, one of the first things he did after becoming coherent again was to ask Mrs. Mac to buy the complete works of Tolstoy. *War and Peace* wasn't good enough anymore; he had to read *all* of Tolstoy. Furthermore, Mac insisted on taking five hours of Spanish grammar every day, and Mrs. Mac was instructed to hire a private Spanish tutor within twenty-four hours, which wasn't as easy as one might have thought. He also wanted to practice the Tschaikovsky violin concerto, though he still had trouble with the A-major scale. But the most interesting thing of all was that he had already registered himself in an enriched course in paleontology at the Smithsonian, in order to learn all there is to know about dinosaurs.

"Well, well, well," said Paula, with her characteristic frown-smile.
"So Toshima has triumphed after all. I take back all the nasty things
I said about him."

"But don't you see," Mrs. Mac said, her voice trembling slightly,
"your psychologist has done his work *too* well! How can Mac do
all these things simultaneously? And he is so insistent! I've never
seen him like that. I know I should be pleased that he wants to do
all the things I've been preaching to him all these years, but now he's
become positively *obsessive* about them. He told me this morning
life would not be worth living if he didn't master the Tschaikovsky
concerto in two weeks."

"He'll simmer down," said Paula reassuringly. "Men always talk
big. You should be used to this by now, Mrs. MacIntosh."

"I'm not so sure he will," she went on. "He used to be such a quiet,
moderate man, until you people began to fool around with his
psyche. He always said that the most important thing for a man
was to know his own limitations. And now — *this!* "

"I think my wife is right," I said. "He's bound to find his own level
again. Never mind that the pendulum is swinging a little too far.
You must admit it's swinging in the right direction."

"Yes, I do," she said, a little calmer now. "And I forgot to mention
that he's already telephoned the Jefferson Lincoln family — you
know, that black family in the slums — to tell them he will report
for work tomorrow morning at seven o'clock. He asked me to buy
some new type of diapers he saw advertised on television. The
last time I heard him talk about their baby he wanted to strangle
it. What am I going to do? "

"If you like, I'll come home with you, Mrs. MacIntosh," Paula
said. "Perhaps I can talk some sense into him."

"That's very nice of you, Mrs. Bierbaum. Perhaps later this week.
I know all this is for the good of science, and I'm not blaming
you any more, especially after what you told me about what my
husband did to that dinosaur. But you still haven't told me how
this treatment of Dr. Toshima's could be made to apply to the
thousands and thousands of people who feel the way he does."

So I explained to her how the therapy could easily be repeated on a mass scale. The treatment was much simpler, and less time consuming than encounter groups, and how many millions of Americans were participating in those? Eight? Ten? The drugs required, and the equipment for applying mild electric shocks, were within the means of the smallest and poorest communities, and no advanced training was required to administer the therapy. Toshima had explained all this to me, I told her, in detail. It could be done in any men's locker room, after a massage or a sauna, between the ninth and tenth holes on a golf course, at drive-in clinics which could advertise "Stop for a treatment instead of a treat," or something like that. Or special facilities could be built at the local bank or trust company.

Mrs. Mac listened to my explanation with rapt attention, but I caught an expression on Paula's face which barely managed to conceal her profound distaste.

"Of course, once it became known how beneficial the treatment was," I said quickly, to prevent my wife from making a foolish remark, "one could reasonably expect a mass demand. Unless the person truly wanted it, it wouldn't work, naturally. So there's no question of interfering with people's freedom of choice. It would be simply a matter of making it known that such facilities exist."

"I suppose I should be pleased that my husband was chosen," Mrs. Mac said, swallowing hard.

"He'll become famous, like those early astronauts," Paula said. I was delighted that in spite of her distaste she stood by me, as always in critical situations.

"And I guess I'll have to learn how to behave like those astronauts' wives? " Mrs. Mac asked with a frown. "Fearless and brave, and always smiling like those women in that TV program called 'Cinema Art'."

"Just be yourself, Mrs. MacIntosh," I said gallantly," and nothing can go wrong."

She did not seem altogether convinced.

"I'll certainly do what I can," she said.

"I'll tell Dr. Toshima as soon as he comes back from his holidays. I know he'll want to see your husband right away."

"Well, thank you for listening to me," Mrs. Mac said, rising. "I feel a little better now."

As soon as she had gone, the telephone rang. It was Hilde, asking whether she could drop in, she had something urgent to say. I told her I was tired, I had just had a visit from Mrs. Mac, couldn't it wait until morning?

"Mrs. Mac? " Hilde asked, all excited. "Why did *she* come and see you? "

"Look, Hilde. I'm *tod-müde.* I'll tell you in the morning."

"Oh, *please* tell me," she insisted. "Are things worse? "

"On the contrary," I replied.

"What do you mean? "

I told her about the pendulum swinging too far in the direction of the Higher Things in Life.

Nothing could have pleased her more.

"Richard will be *im siebten Himmel,* " she exclaimed. "He's in a terrible state, you know."

"*Mein Kind,* his problems are not over yet."

"*I* know, I know," she said irritably. "All right, Friedrich. I'll leave you alone now, since you're tired. I'll just tell you what I have to say on the telephone. Are you strong enough to listen? "

"Shoot."

"I've made up my mind," she said, sounding like her ancestors the generals when fighting the Poles or the French or the Austrians. "I'm going to develop a plan of my own. It'll complement Richard's therapy. Didn't the President ask for a number of suggestions? Well, let him pick and choose. I'm sure Richard's on the right path, but there *are* other avenues, you know."

75

"A plan? " I asked, picking up my ears. "What kind of a plan? "

"I want to deal with this as a problem in communications. That's my subject. I'm a world authority, if you remember."

"Yes, I remember," I smiled.

"Give me a week to think things out."

"Have I any choice? "

"You don't," she laughed. "Sleep well, Friedrich! "

Chapter 14

I remember Göring once telling me about Goebbels' marital troubles. Of course, he couldn't abide Goebbels. Before I arrived on the scene — in 1939, just before the war — Frau Goebbels had a love affair with a man called Hanke. He was about ten years her junior, young and awkward, whereas she prided herself on being worldly and experienced. It was a great passion, and Hanke petitioned Hitler for permission to marry her. (It wasn't the husband or wife who asked Pope Adolf for a divorce; it was the lover.) Hitler refused for *raisons d'état*. It was in the Fatherland's interest, he said, that the Goebbels couple stay together, no matter who slept with whom. The thing died down very quickly after that; Goebbels husband and wife celebrated their reconciliation by going to Bayreuth to hear *Tristan*. A suitable choice, I would think. I mention this only to say that I am grateful, whatever Paula's weaknesses may be, that I have been spared any such embarrassment.

Paula's reaction to our little ordeal was a good example of the way she always comes through when the going gets rough.

"Du bist wieder mal mit 'nem blauen Auge davongekommen," Paula said the next morning, referring to Mac's pendulum. It meant I got away, once more, with only a black eye. In German, a black eye is a blue eye. I replied, perhaps a little smugly, with the words of Schiller, *"Dem Mutigen hilft Gott"* — God helps the one who is courageous.

"A man as morally tone deaf as you certainly doesn't deserve to be so lucky all the time."

"What *are* you talking about? " I asked, irritably.

"Don't you realize Toshima is behaving like one of those Nazi doctors? Nearly giving a man permanent brain damage to prove some hare-brained theory or other? "

"Don't talk about things you know nothing about," I shouted. "When I want your opinion, I'll ask for it. *Verstanden?* "

During the next week, while I waited for Hilde's plans, I heard on the radio that in Santa Fe, New Mexico, a person or persons unknown had interfered with a tennis match on the university campus by providing the linesman with the wrong kind of glasses, so that every time the ball was in, it was really out, and vice versa. Except for the general context, perhaps a rather innocuous incident. But the explanation the local radio station gave struck me as unusually ingenious. "There is some evidence," the commentator said, "that this is the work of the local Mafia. Whether this is confirmed or not, it's obvious that Congress should appropriate larger funds to combat organized crime."

Toshima was incommunicado in his holiday retreat, probably reading his beloved Proust and playing the clarinet, so it was impossible for Hilde or me to convey the good news to him. When he returned — I think it was on a Monday — and heard about it, he had to go to the Jefferson Lincoln house on H Street near the station to see Mac, who was heavily engaged cleaning the toilet in the damp basement. But, according to the report I received immediately afterwards from Mrs. Mac, they couldn't talk about anything except *Anna Karenina* which, alas, Toshima had never read.

It was during that week that Karin and I made love three times. Karin praised me to the skies.

"Your linear optimization is magnificent," she often said, "even if your toggle-switch is a little out of practice."

I couldn't very well tell her that I found it very hard going, and that I should have responded to her praise, of which I was unworthy, with one of my favorite Ovid quotes, *"Ut desint vires, tamen est laudanda voluntas,"* meaning that even if there is a lack of potency, the will is laudable. The truth is that Karin — how can I put it decently? — made considerable demands on me. She went to work on me systematically, in the X, Y and Z positions.

"We'll run through the whole alphabet backwards before we're through," she threatened me at one point. "Your cyclic shift is improving all the time, but I'm afraid you have a tendency to deblock."

Observations like that made me work twice as hard and, on the whole, my efforts paid off. I remember one occasion particularly, when she rewarded me, smoking her post-coital cigaret, by calling me "the greatest liveware in Christendom." No words of love and tenderness had ever given me more intense satisfaction.

* * *

Precisely one week after our last conversation, Hilde called and asked me to visit her in her apartment on Brandywine Street, not far from Massachusetts Avenue, to tell me about her "plan." I had been there often, of course, and was always amused by the way she had decorated it. It looked like a movie set for that old film "Cabaret," which some of you may remember: Berlin 1932. (I must mention once more that Hilde was always cashing in on the great reputation of Berlin in its brilliant, though morally dubious heyday, though she was only a child at the time Marlene Dietrich made her historic splash, in the late twenties.)

The apartment was modern in a very different sense from Karin's. What was modern for Hilde was the *Bauhaus* and, of course, even today that furniture looks modern, though it is more than half a century old. Karin's style is futuristic; Hilde's nostalgic. On her living room wall were large posters of the movie stars of her day, Hans Albers, Renate Müller, Theo Lingen, even Adele Sandrock, that marvelous old actress who was the Margaret Rutherford of her time. There was even a picture of Otto Gebühr, playing Frederick the Great.

Hilde was thirteen when Hitler came to power. She spent her adolescence in the B. d. M., the *Bund deutscher Mädchen*, the female version of the Hitler Youth. If I now stated that she saw through the whole Nazi thing from the very beginning, I would be just as wrong as if I said this about myself. (I have heard millions of my contemporaries tell atrocious lies about this.) Neither of us understood what was going on until things began to go wrong, towards the end of the war. The only excuse we can offer is that we were very young and had a marvelous time, while it lasted. She became a famous beauty and I — how shall I put this modestly? — an agreeable young officer, and we simply could not resist the pleasure and excitement of success in our respective spheres.

At this point I might just as well confess that when I first met her — at a reception in the Adlon Hotel in Berlin during the winter 1942-43 — I tried very hard to go to bed with her, but — how terrible this sounds as I now write it down — I was rebuffed. I am not quite sure what the occasion for the reception was; it may have been the capture of Novorossisk, a few days before the Russians counterattacked northeast of Stalingrad. We must have fêted some general or other. At any rate, she was at the height of her fame at the time, and there were few SS barracks without pinups of her over every bed. She had not yet married Freiherr von Schleswig-Strelitz and was, as far as I could tell, available, and so was I who got engaged to Paula only a year later. An affair with her then when we were both in high fashion in our different ways might have been gorgeous. But she turned me down. She allowed me to kiss her passionately — I think it was in the corridor of the eighth floor, near the window facing the Brandenburger Tor — but smilingly shook her head when I wanted to proceed from mezzo-forte to fortissimo. Neither of us has ever alluded since to this near-miss on my part, and it is barely conceivable (since almost every man she met in wartime Berlin must have made a pass at her some time or other) that she has forgotten it.

Braless as ever, Hilde looked dazzling as she received me. She was wearing a beige and green pant suit which suited her perfectly. She looked ten years younger than the last time I had seen her, only a week or so earlier: all the wrinkles had gone from her face, her make-up was perfect. I was sure that her passion for Richard Toshima had been quenched during the last few days. But I was wrong, she hadn't seen him at all. What had rejuvenated her was the challenge and excitement of her new project.

As I sat down in her living room, on a functional streamlined rocking chair made in Dessau in 1925, I innocently hummed one of the hit tunes of the early forties, Zarah Leander's *Ich bin ein Star.*

"Friedrich, stop it! " she shouted, with unexpected fury.

80

I looked at her in wide-eyed astonishment.

"You know perfectly well. Zarah Leander."

"Oh, of course," I confessed, suddenly understanding. "I guess my sub-conscious was walking down memory lane."

"Don't let me catch you doing that again," she replied. "Those days were pure *Scheisse*, and you know it."

I promised to control myself in future. "Now tell me about your plan, Hilde."

"*Amerika gähnt*," she said. "The country is bored stiff, one great big yawn. Of course, it's going to get much worse: this is only the beginning. Look at poor old Mac. The man is lost without work. He's completely *ungebildet;* he's had lots of training but no education to speak of. It's tragic."

"True," I said. "Have you anything to drink, Hilde? "

"Oh, I'm sorry." She went to a red lacquered side table on which there were about half a dozen bottles. She knew I liked my Scotch with lots of water.

"So you've designed a great big advertising campaign, eh? " I asked her, as she handed me the glass.

"Wrong, Friedrich. Dead wrong. Of course nothing would have been easier. It would have been a *Kinderspiel* to sell the joys of not having to work, of arts and crafts, and all that crap, of games and recreation, of travel and adventure, of *Kultur*. I mean, anybody could do *that*."

"You mean," I said, not too maliciously, "you could have com-missioned any one of your three ex-husbands on Madison Avenue? "

She roared with laughter.

"Absolutely! Even *they* could have done it. You are wicked, you know, Friedrich! "

She wiped her eyes, and then inspected her handkerchief to make sure that not too much mascara had come off.

"I could have done better myself, of course," she continued. "After all, who better to design such a campaign than a member of the Prussian aristocracy whose ancestors never did a day's work for generations? "

"We could have drafted Paula, too," I threw in.

"Exactly! Although her ancestors were not nearly as magnificent as mine. To tell you the truth, I never had any use for the Lichtenfelde-Königsteins. Don't tell her I said this. Please. They were too stingy even to fix the leaking roof on their place near Magdeburg. Stinginess runs right through the family, way back to the *Grosse Kurfürst*. But mine — the Unterlinden-Hohenfrieds — they had style, they threw their money around, they spoke French, and every little servant girl from the Mark Brandenburg was deflowered ceremoniously within an hour after she was hired. Paula's people weren't like that at all."

"I despise people who brag about their ancestors," I said haughtily. "I think it's the height of vulgarity."

"You old prude," she said.

"So you've decided against advertising the virtues of the Prussian aristocracy? " I asked, leaning back on my rocking chair.

"I have. With regrets. Though nothing would have been easier, I repeat, than to demonstrate that any little American Joe Doe can today, with a bit of luck, live like any count, prince, marquis, duke, baron or lord in the eighteenth or nineteenth century."

She went to her *Soenecken* bookcase, picked a big folder from the bottom shelf, and fished out a few large sheets of paper showing charcoal sketches done with great *panache*.

"This," she explained, "is some American Joe Doe gambling in the casino in Baden-Baden. Note his Brooks Brothers suit."

"Very nice," I said.

"And this is the same guy walking up and down the promenade at Biarritz." She turned the page. "I like this one better, Joe

Doe having tea with the Queen at Buckingham Palace."

"*Lèse-majesté!* " I cried.

"Nonsense! " She quickly showed me the rest, Joe Doe hunting
and fishing in Scotland, going to the races in Bad Homburg,
dancing the waltz at the *Faschingsball* in Vienna."

"Not bad, eh? " she asked.

"But you say you're not going ahead with it? "

"No, I've decided against it. Too superficial, and at the same time
too complicated. How could one ever get all the points across?
I know advertising lends itself very well as an appeal to snobbery.
It's even more effective than sex. But it wouldn't be easy to switch
the direction of snobbery, from making people feel superior to the
hoi polloi generally, to merely feeling superior to the contemptible
fools who still have to work for a living. No, we've got to dig
deeper."

Hilde made a *Kunstpause*, a theatrical pause for effect. Then she
threw herself on her chromium-plated chaise longue, covered with
a leopard skin which, she claimed, was the result of a safari undertaken by her third husband on his honeymoon with his second wife.

"I propose," she said, closing her eyes, "that you go to your
friend, Bill Bush, and ask him to let me mastermind a season of
television programs on the White House network. Everybody
knows television can do miracles selling goods, but do you
remember how beautifully it also sold the ecological crisis? "

"I suppose it did," I said. "I never thought about it that way."

"Well, you *should*," she said, her eyes still closed. "You live in
your ivory tower, fooling around with your computers, and
you don't know what's going on in the world. Without television
it would take ten times as long to get that message across. And
boy, did it ever work! You can't sneeze anymore anywhere in
America without somebody arresting you for polluting the air. All
this thanks to television. Well, I'm going to go after the American
guilt complex in the same way."

"*Bitte schön?* "

"You heard what I said, Friedrich. Don't pretend to be more stupid than you are. Americans can't have any pleasure unless they've worked for it. At least, that's what they think. They feel guilty about having fun unless they have first made a colossal investment in blood, sweat and tears. That's at the root of the incipient leisure crisis in this country."

"And you think you can combat this on television? " I asked, trying hard not to sound too skeptical.

"But of course! Take for instance the idea that every gratification has to be postponed to be legitimately enjoyed. That's absurd, but it's American. If you can stop people from littering the beaches, you can teach them the much more agreeable lesson that such waiting periods are bad for their system."

"I suppose so," I said, without much enthusiasm.

"I didn't expect you to jump at this," Hilde said, opening her eyes and looking me straight in the face. "But if you let it sink in, you'll see how right I am. All we have to do is convince people that efforts are worth making for their own sake, if they're worth making at all, rather than for the sake of material or psychological gain. Every one of my programs will teach a very simple lesson, namely that work is to living what prostitution is to sex. Why do we despise prostitution? Because it turns something that ought to be voluntary and enjoyable into *work*."

"Yes, that makes sense. I follow you."

Hilde got up, and started pacing the room.

"Both self-fulfillment and the good of society are served best if people spend their time doing things for the love of them. They should stop worrying so much about the future, too. You don't realize that futurists like Tex Winter are the worst puritans of the lot. I've told him that many times, but he just smiles that clean-cut cowboy smile of his, and tells me to run away and play."

"That's very rude of him," I said sternly. "I will have to reprimand him."

Hilde was by now examining her face in the mirror above the bar.

"As you may have observed once or twice in your long life, Friedrich," she said, opening her purse to take out her lipstick, "the good things in life fortunately don't only come to people who make an effort towards them, or who plan them far ahead of time. They often come to people who haven't done any work at all to earn them, if they have the right attitude."

"And how do you define good things? "

"Very simple," she said, looking in the mirror and putting on some lipstick. "Anything that stretches the human mind or body to capacity, or that is pleasant to our senses. Any questions? "

"Yes. As a matter of fact, I have. Do you really expect them to hand over to *you* a whole season of television broadcasting? "

"They don't have to," she said lightly. "No one forces them to. It's up to them."

"True."

"But this is a rare opportunity for the Administration to show some intellectual leadership. For once they're ahead of public opinion. If they know what's good for them, they'll accept the deal."

"But they may say they'll buy the plan from CRUPP, and put it into effect themselves."

"They can do that. Sure. I won't sulk. But they'd be much better advised to let me handle it. All I'm asking you to do, Friedrich, is to present this as a package, with me as a key ingredient. I *want* to do this. But they can have the package without me."

"I think you're being very generous," I said. "I'm not being sarcastic. I really mean it."

"*Quatsch*," she replied. "Cut it out, Friedrich. I want to see this thing done. It's entirely feasible. All it requires is a little imagination. Oh, there's another thing I nearly forgot. We must use Mac. After all, he's a case in point. The very incarnation of the Protestant work ethic. A good man ruined by it."

"How would you use him? " I asked Hilde. "Better be careful. Paula

85

already thinks I'm an arch-criminal, and a typical Nazi to boot, for having permitted Toshima's experiments."

"Don't worry. I'll deal with her. After all, I'm willing to give him what he wants most in life, namely work. Besides, I'll make him a celebrity. He'll be cured in no time."

"Let's hope so." I got up from my rocking chair. "Let me try this out on Bill. Everything will depend on the President. In the meantime, all I can say is *dum spiramus, speramus.* While we breathe, we hope."

She came over to kiss me. "You'll let me know? "

"Of course."

Like an old-fashioned hostess, she led me to the door. Her parting words were *"Hoff, o Du arme Seele! "* — Hope, oh you poor soul! a very apt quotation from the *Evangelische Kirchengesangbuch.*

Chapter 15

Before calling Bill Bush, I spoke to Paula who was dusting the upstairs library.

"I wouldn't put it past them," she said. "Those Americans may just buy this. It's childish enough for them."

If Paula says a thing like that, it's as good as sold.

" *'Arbeit macht das Leben süss,'* we used to sing at school," she continued. "But apparently no longer." This is a famous German song that says work makes life sweet.

"Do you know the second line we used to make up to go with it? " I asked.

"Something obscene, no doubt."

"Not at all," I answered. " *'Und Faulheit stärkt die Glieder!* ' " (And laziness makes you strong.)

"I'm not impressed," she said, continuing her dusting.

"No one is going to interfere with *your* work ethic," I promised her.

To be completely up-to-date on the state of Mac's mental health before speaking to Bill, I first called the MacIntosh residence on Hunt Avenue. Mac himself answered the phone, having just been released from the Walter Reed Hospital. It was the first time I had spoken to him since his collapse.

"Hello, Mac! " I shouted, delighted to be able to speak to him directly.

"*Buenas días, señor Bierbaum,*" he replied in an even voice. "*¿Como esta usted?* "

I must confess I was a little dumbfounded, but decided to play it straight. "I'm sorry my Spanish is a little rusty, but I'm very well, thank you."

"*¿Y como esta la señora?* "

"Paula is fine," I replied. "But how are you? *You're* much more interesting, you know, Mac."

"*Estoy mucho mejor, gracias, pero mi cabeza me hace un poco dueño.*"

"And what does that mean, Mac? "

"I'm much better, thanks, but I have a bit of a headache."

"I'm sure that'll clear up in no time." I was glad he was still able to speak English. "And how's the old fiddle? "

"How nice of you to ask, Mr. Bierbaum," he said. "I'm afraid it's a terrible torture to my poor family, but I'm progressing. That stuff Dr. Toshima gave me seems to have relaxed my fingers a lot. I used to be terribly tense, and that's why I always played out of tune."

"That's very good news, Mac."

"I'll never play as well as Heifetz did in his heyday. But you should hear me play the slow movement of the Tschaikovsky! "

"You must play for me sometime, Mac," I said, perhaps sounding not quite enthusiastic enough. "Perhaps we can arrange a little concert at CRUPP."

"I would enjoy that," he said. "Dr. Toshima seems to be satisfied with my progress generally. Did you know he played the clarinet? "

"Yes, I did, Mac."

"He told me he wanted to play duets with me," he went on.

"That's splendid, Mac. When are you going to come and visit me? "

"I might be able to squeeze you in next week between my course at the Smithsonian and the Jefferson Lincolns."

"Please try. I'd love to see you. Cheers."

I called Bill Bush immediately afterwards. I told him it would only take two or three weeks more therapy before Toshima would be ready to begin work on his scientific report. This would then form the basis of discussion for the mass application of the Toshima technique. I then informed him of Hilde's plans. He whistled through his teeth.

"Boy, oh boy," he said. "This sounds like great stuff."

"I know it's asking for a lot," I said modestly, and went on, repeating Hilde's phrase, "but the problem is going to get worse before it gets better."

"You can say that again, Friedrich," he answered with a sigh. "Have you heard the news? "

"No. What news? "

"In Black Hills, South Dakota, some jokers let loose a herd of moles on the local golf course. Within two days they had drilled two hundred and seventy-two holes indistinguishable from the real ones, thereby ruining the course."

Knowing Bill's somber disposition, I did not dare to make a funny remark, or to fake some kind of unctuous commiseration.

"I'm sorry to hear that," I said, my voice suitably neutral.

He went on.

"Apparently last Sunday morning the minister in the Pentecostal church preached a fiery sermon to the effect that this was undoubtedly a divine punishment for all the extra-marital sex that was raging in Black Hills, especially among the members of the

89

golf club. It seems that in the locker rooms immoral deals were made between husbands and wives to swap their respective spouses."

"I find it remarkable," I said, again refraining from comment on the situation in Black Hills, "that nobody seems to have caught on yet."

"It certainly is, Friedrich. Any day now, some smart sociologist is bound to come up with a theory very close to the truth. And then every editorial writer in the country, and every politician, is going to boast that they've known it all along. You wait."

"That's why I think this is the right psychological moment to prepare Dr. Hildesheim's television approach."

"I agree with you, Friedrich, but at the moment it'll take a lot of selling. We must give ourselves a little time. You'll need a few months to prepare and pre-tape the programs anyway. They couldn't be ready before September, the beginning of the fall schedule. By then there are likely to be much more serious leisure riots all over the country. The Opposition will scream bloody murder, holding the President personally responsible. They'll consider it a perfect issue for the campaign."

"I have explained all this to Dr. Hildesheim," I said.

"Before speaking to the President about it, I think I'd like to have a word with the director of the network, Friedrich. Just to sound him out."

"Are you sure that's a good idea, Bill? He's *bound* to oppose it."

"Not necessarily. Depends on how it's put. It's better to have him on our side beforehand. No good forcing things down his throat."

"Well," I said skeptically, "I'll have to leave that to you. When will I hear from you, Bill? "

"Give me twenty-four hours. Good work, Friedrich. Keep it up! "

The next afternoon he called me in ecstasy to give me the news that the proposal had been enthusiastically accepted, lock, stock and Hilde Hildesheim. We were invited to a conference at the White House Thursday next.

The only thing the meeting in the President's Oval Room on
April l9th and my previous summit meeting — a situation conference in the Führer's headquarters in East Prussia in the summer
of 1942 — had in common was that in both cases I had a splitting
headache. But whereas in the German case my headache was due
to a common or garden hangover — too much schnapps the
night before with one of Göring's young adjutants who (that's the
only thing I can remember about him) had a terrible stutter — this
time my headache was due to an excessively exhausting use of my
toggle-switch the night before with Karin, who simply would not
let go.

"Come on," she kept saying. "You can do it. No point sparing
your digitizer. You've direct access to my socket. For Christ's
sake, make use of it! "

As I said, the headache was the only thing the two meetings had
in common. At the Führer's headquarters there were about thirty
people — staff officers of the OKW and the Army General Staff,
liaison officers with the Air Force, the Navy, the Waffen-SS and
Himmler, Göring, Generals Keitler, Jodl and Zeitzler, and God
knows who else. Only two men were seated: Hitler and Göring,
the latter only as a concession to his status of Reich Marshal and
his almost grotesque corpulence. (When Göring was not present,
only Hitler was seated.) The center of the room was the map
table. The meeting had lasted at least three hours.

In the President's office, everyone sat down. Only five people
attended: the President, Bill Bush, the Director of the White
House network, Hilde and I. The meeting lasted ten minutes.
Whereas the atmosphere at Hitler's situation conference was so
unbelievably tense that one had the feeling the whole thing
would explode if anyone lit a match (two years later, on July
20th, 1944, a conference of this type *did* explode), in the present
case the spirit was friendly, relaxed and optimistic. Another
point of difference is that in East Prussia I had nothing to do
but carry two of Göring's briefcases; now, in the White House,
I was a V.I.P. and treated as such.

As everybody knows, President Roberts is an extraordinary man.
He is only thirty-eight, the youngest president in American
history. Apart from his youth, the most remarkable thing about
his appearance is his ears. Rarely have I seen a man with larger
ears, sticking out from each side of his head like radar screens.

On innumerable occasions campaign managers and PR men have
suggested to him that simple surgery could improve his image
a hundredfold. But he refused.

"Why should I make life difficult for the cartoonists? " was his
usual reply.

The other striking characteristic is the rapidity of his speech. He
talks like a machine gun. Again, his advisers have asked him to
slow down, for example, at press conferences, and whenever he
appears on television. He *does* try for a minute or two, and then
he speeds up again. I am not sure whether this reflects an unusually
high IQ. No doubt he *is* unusually intelligent, but I think his speech
pattern only reflects the rapidity of his mind, not its quality.

We have never had a president like him before. He has all the usual
characteristics of an American politician: a flair for making deals, an
amazing virtuosity with facts and figures, and an almost sensuous enjoyment of power and a willingness to use it forcefully. As a young
professor of political science at Berkeley in the middle sixties, he was
very sympathetic to the moderate radicals, and was one of their ablest
lobbyists — mostly behind the scenes — at the Board of Regents.

This experience, combined with a natural empathy for the affluent
bored who were on the verge of a massive attack on America's
lifestyle, enabled him to recognize, long before anybody else,
that the various isolated, and seemingly innocuous, anti-leisure
incidents across the country fell into a general pattern of
profound significance.

One of the reasons why he understood so well the mental mechanism
of the rebellious rich who lacked the inner spiritual resources to cope
with their enforced idleness, may well have been his interest in oriental
religions, and his daily practice of ten to fifteen minutes of silent
meditation. The busiest man in America deliberately took time off
to communicate with the cosmos. The rational life of action did
not satisfy him. He had in common with other members of his
generation a need for spiritual exercises which the traditional
churches could not provide, and he was often quoted as saying
privately that without these ten, fifteen minutes a day he could
not do his job. This was the same generation, I was sure, as the
millions of potential leisure rioters who lacked the inner resources
to do what the President did, namely — I suppose this is the old-
fashioned word — "*pray*." Of course he could only talk about this

off the record, for fear of offending the upholders of organized religion who remained very influential at election time. Similarly, it had to be kept secret that he had frequently participated (though not while in office) in nude encounter groups, though it *was* public knowledge that he was an ardent supporter of the Human Potential Movement.

Roberts has been twice divorced, and is now separated from his third wife. Naturally the press is always full of speculation about his love life, but nothing is known about this. If he has any surreptitious affairs, he has managed to keep them beautifully concealed. His advocacy of homosexual marriages has often sparked rumors that he himself has tendencies in that direction, but there is no evidence to that effect.

As for the Director of the White House television network, he is a man of a very different stripe. Professionally charming, he is a career civil servant, a mandarin. Small and elegant, with his quick dark eyes and black moustache, he looks like a courtier in a Velasquez picture. His name is Roger Delancey, and before getting his present job he was head of the US Information Agency. The White House Television Network is an outgrowth of the old National Educational Network for which it had become increasingly difficult, in view of the public source of its financing, to exercise any kind of political independence. It seemed easier and cleaner simply to turn it into a branch of the government. This transition was thoroughly applauded by the three commercial networks which hated the blurring of the line between public and private television under the old system.

Hilde Hildesheim had given a great deal of thought to what she would wear on her *début* in the White House. To dress like an aging movie diva would be in dubious taste, she decided, and anything unduly *décolleté* open to misconstruction. Therefore, she decided to put on one of her most expensive costumes — an antique Saint-Laurent, I think — which made her look like a convent girl: black dress, lace collar, long sleeves. She still hoped that the President would notice her bralessness underneath, but this was not a matter of top priority to her.

When she, Bill Bush and I were shown into the President's office, Roger Delancey was with him. Roberts rose from behind his desk, overshadowed by the American Eagle behind it, and the Star-Spangled Banner on the side. We shook hands, and he gestured us to sit down around a little glass table in the corner, on which there was a delectable little Giacometti bronze nude, surrounded by ashtrays, pitchers of water with ice cubes swimming in them, and glasses.

"It was good of you to come so promptly," the President opened the meeting at lightning speed. "Roger and Bill have discussed your project with me. I'm all for it, though I don't want this to be interpreted as lack of support for Dr. Toshima's epoch-making experiment with Mr. MacIntosh. I fully realize that the clinical picture is not yet entirely clear, and that it's still a touch-and-go proposition, but the possibilities of conditioning the work ethic out of hundreds of thousands of severely afflicted Americans strike me as vitally important. I'm particularly pleased that so far the press hasn't got hold of it, but I don't suppose they would understand anyway what it's all about. I take it then that we in this room — and your colleagues at CRUPP — are the only people in the whole wide world who know what's going on? "

"I suppose that's correct, sir," I said, bowing slightly in my chair.

"I need not tell you, Mr. Bierbaum, that I have put practically all my eggs into your basket. I have no doubt that the leisure issue will determine the outcome of the next election. I will be the first president in American history to attack the value — moral and political — of hard work. But I hope you don't misunderstand me. This is far more important than my re-election. I don't want to bore you with patriotic rhetoric, and I say this only to make it clear that I don't want you people at CRUPP to think that I'm involving you in party politics. This issue transcends politics. In many ways, it's true to say — however awful it sounds — that the future of the country is in your hands."

Roberts smiled as he said it, as though he had put quotation marks around the sentence.

"We will do our utmost to come through," I said, annoyed with the prosaic inadequacy of my response. But I could not think of anything better, without sounding like a speech maker on Hitler's birthday.

"I have no doubt. You've carved out for yourselves a unique

position in our intellectual life. The civil service and almost all our universities are either suffering from acute constipation of the imagination, or are so specialized that they can only deal with trivia. You're the only institution in America that's taking a sweeping look at the total scene, and are equipped to come up with some strikingly positive answers. You've proved it in the past, and I know you will prove it again. In any case, we're depending on you."

"You will not regret it, Mr. President," I said.

"I know," he rattled on. "Now to come back to your television scheme. You may have expected more resistance than you've encountered. The reason there was none was that Roger and I think you've hit the bull's eye. No arm twisting was required. Right, Roger? "

Delancey smiled.

"The important thing I want to convey to you is that this concept will work only if it's approached with the utmost secrecy. I want your relationship to our television people to be informal and confidential. Roger will see to it that you will be given the authority required: it's his authority, however, and not yours. Is that understood? "

"I prefer it that way," said Hilde.

"Good. It's more sensible. I want this thing to creep up on the public, subtly, hardly noticeably at first, slowly. I want it to *build*. If it gets out that a policy directive has been given to the White House Television Network to go after the Protestant work ethic...well, you understand? "

"Absolutely, Mr. President," I said.

Was I being too much of a sycophant? I remembered how revolted I used to be by Göring simply crawling in front of Hitler, no dignity left, disgusting. Was I doing the same thing?

"You probably know our main problem is our relation to the commercial networks. Our system is called a propaganda agency, and I suppose that's what it is. Americans think the media can only be free if they're private enterprise. It's a peculiar quirk

in our thinking which astounds Europeans — and Canadians, for
that matter. But there it is. Roger will tell you what the implica-
tions of this are."

He cued Roger to go on.

"Well, the way I see it," he said, playing with his black mustache,
"is that we're all right if we keep our place. By that I mean, in a nut-
shell, if we don't cut into their ratings to any considerable extent.
If we become too popular, they'll scream bloody murder that we've
left propaganda and gone into commercial entertainment. Our job
is to be unpopular," he added with a self-effacing chuckle.

"But not too unpopular," interjected Bill Bush, "otherwise
Congress will never give us the money we need."

"Quite," said Delancey.

I shot a quick glance at Hilde, sitting there like a convent girl. What
was she thinking, I wondered. If there was danger that her programs
would be too popular, would she then deliberately step on the brake,
and make them unpopular? How could she control that sort of thing?
No doubt she was asking herself the same question. Her face, however,
betrayed nothing. She wore a polite smile, and kept her thoughts to
herself.

"We have to dance on that tightrope all the time," Roger Delancey
continued. "We're the most investigated agency in the government.
At the moment three congressional committees are looking into us,
all at the same time. We're so busy answering their questions that
we have hardly any time to go on the air! "

We all laughed.

"The important thing, let me say it once more," the President
resumed, "is to keep this thing secret. Can I count on your people
at CRUPP to be discreet? I don't want to have to ask them to
take an oath, or anything like that. Can I count on you, Bierbaum? "

"Absolutely, Mr. President."

There I was again, bowing and scraping. Awful!

"I suppose that's it, then," the President concluded. "Let me say once more how delighted we are. You've come up with the right idea at the right time. Well, Dr. Hildesheim and gentlemen, thank you for taking the trouble to come. I shall watch your progress with the utmost interest. Good luck! "

Chapter 16

The meeting with the President took place on April 19th. Two
months later, it was still too early to say whether Mac had fully
recovered, and whether Toshima's pilot project was a success or
a failure. Mac had suffered a slight setback when he finally realized
that the Tschaikovsky concerto was after all slightly beyond his
means, and that he dozed off far too frequently while wading
through Tolstoy's *Memoirs of a Madman* and *The Living Corpse*.
Also he had been thrown out of the Jefferson Lincoln residence
on H Street, after having stuck, once too often, a safety pin into
the baby while putting on the diapers. The Lincolns actually said
they would do without welfare rather than suffer Mac's inefficiency
for one more day, that the comfort and safety of their baby was
more important to them than food or shelter!

These defeats caused Mac two or three crying spells, and a return
of the general amnesia, but the psychiatrists at Walter Reed,
with whom Toshima was in close touch, were not seriously worried.

"He'll be all right," one of them said. "All he needs is work. Regular,
steady work."

While it was too early to proclaim in a scientific paper that the
Protestant work ethic was accessible to treatment by psychological conditioning, Hilde's attack on it through the media turned out
to be an unmitigated disaster because it worked *too* well.

But I must not anticipate. It will take a little time to disentangle
the mixture of false calculations on everybody's part, sheer bad
luck and high treason. So please bear with me. For the moment all
I want to say is that I received occasional reports from Hilde that

good progress was being made, that she liked the people she worked with and received all the support she needed from Roger Delancey. They would be ready in time for the Grand Opening on September 16th. But before I come to that, I must report the *crescendo* of leisure troubles, right across the country, throughout the summer, just as had been foreseen. The prediction, however, that some bright sociologist would come up with a correct diagnosis was not fulfilled.

On May 10th, the Community College in Seattle, which had been running all kinds of extension courses, was ransacked. One would have thought that it should not have been too difficult for observers of the local scene to conclude that there was a connection between this incident and the presence of hundreds of unemployed executives in Seattle, especially since there was clear evidence that some of the consumers of the courses presented by the College were among the ringleaders of the riot. However, they did not. It was widely interpreted as a mixture of traditional hooliganism, kids on bad trips, and the protest of extramural students against amateurish professors.

On May 15th, a very similar incident was reported from Dallas, Texas, where Sunday morning services were interrupted by people who demanded that the church should get out of the education game. Though this struck me as inexplicable except in the context of the leisure crisis, i.e. people demanding work instead of education, this was not the explanation the local authorities arrived at. They thought it was an increasingly vociferous band of Texan atheists that was responsible.

More serious was a report from Denver, Colorado, on May 19th. There the singularly beautiful young lady who owned a lecture agency known for organizing courses for underemployed executives was abducted, and it was feared that the "kidnappers" would demand an immense ransom from her rich father. However, she returned home, completely intact, in fact happily tipsy, after having spent twenty-four hours with three of her students who had recently been laid off the executive ranks of a local cement factory. They wanted to shake the city up a little, while having an innocently gay time with her. The events which took place in San Diego two days later, on May 21st, were equally innocuous, but they, too, made a big splash. "Some kids" managed to free a couple of pandas from the zoo — pandas which had been presented to the American people by the Peking Government. The "liberation" of these pandas was no mean feat, since the zoo —

one of the most progressively ecological in the world — is very closely guarded. After two days they were returned to the zoo, but no one was able to find out who "the kids" were who did this thing. One theory was that they were members of the recently revived Birch Society, which has never forgiven the US Government for recognizing China. On June 3rd, two dozen white mice ran across the stage during the balcony scene of Romeo and Juliet in the Tyrone Guthrie Theater in Minneapolis, with the expected result that Juliet uttered a piercing scream. This incident was attributed to a rejected lover of the actress, a man who was known for being inventively vindictive, having, on a previous occasion, when the actress played Ophelia, jumped on the stage and unzipped her bodice.

In Oklahoma City, somebody broke into the offices of "Hobbies Inc." and spread model glue over an entire stock of painting-by-numbers boxes. On June 10th, a group of people invaded a factory making playing cards in Hastings, Nebraska, and removed the ace of spades from about ten thousand packs of cards. A local newspaper called this a "practical joke of truly lugubrious dimensions," but didn't come up with any explanation. In fact, nobody attempted any overall theory, although all these incidents were widely reported. The *St. Louis Courier* wrote that "we seem to be approaching a time of spectacular silliness when a rash of ingenious pranks make front page news. Why the press devotes any space at all to these imbecilities seems to us to be beyond human comprehension."

Hilde's television series, therefore, began without the public being aware of the nature of the incipient crisis. I thought this was probably a handicap, since those able to detect its ideological objective were not in a position to note that its conception was amply justified by events. As things turned out, however, I was totally wrong about this.

Before I begin to describe the programs, I must mention an incident which was very painful to me at the time, and which, in view of a far graver event of a similar nature later, was of some significance. The secret of Hilde's association with the White House Television Network had been impeccably well kept. This is surprising since on *their* side there were many people involved who knew all about it: producers, writers, artists, administrators, and so on. Considering that in Washington there are practically no secrets, and that the press corps watches every move with eagle eyes, this is a remarkable achievement. It was, therefore, a source of particularly acute embarrassment for me that the one leak that did occur came from the CRUPP side, and that the culprit was none other than Karin Hamsun. True, it was fairly innocuous, and, as far as I know, it was never brought to the President's attention, but Bill Bush was furious. All Karin did was to tell a reporter from the *Washington Post* that the eminent CRUPP scholar, Dr. Hilde Hildesheim, had been seconded to White House Television as an expert-consultant. This, of course, was a serious breach of trust, and I should have thrown her out there and then.

Needless to say, that was Paula's advice, when the matter came up the moment I set foot in the door that evening.

"I had that girl's number," she said, waving her dustcloth in the air like an hysterical Berlin policeman, "as soon as I saw her. Pure poison. Didn't I tell you? "

"Don't get so excited, Paula. It's not very serious. I'm sure she meant well."

Paula stopped in her tracks.

"What was that you said? Not *serious? Hast Du alle Deine Tassen im Schrank?* "

This is Berlin street language, meaning do you have all your cups in your cupboard?

"Brech Dir keine Verzierung ab," I replied. Don't break off any of your ornaments. I don't know why we always lapse into the vernacular when we have a row. I suppose it's like Americans using sex vulgarities.

"Do I *have* to listen to such *Quatsch?* " she went on. "That *Stück Scheisse* has to go immediately. You've got to throw her out on her ears."

"I'm not going to do anything of the sort," I replied calmly.

She looked at me through narrowed eyes.

101

"Did I hear you right, or do I have to wash my ears? Did you say you're not going to throw her out? "

"Yes, that's what I said."

"You're mad. Absolutely mad." She hesitated for a moment. "You're not having a little thing with her, are you? "

"No," I replied. I hate it when I have to tell a lie, but *Himmel Donnerwetter noch einmal*, the woman had no business asking me such a direct question.

"Let me tell you one thing, Friedrich," she went on. "You know damned well that I don't care with whom you *vögel*." (German popular expression for digiting. Literally, to do as the birds do.) "But stay away from that Swedish *Nutte*." (Berlin slang for hustler.) "If I ever catch you even so much as making eyes at her, I'll pack my suitcase. Do you understand? "

"Is dinner ready? " I asked.

"I asked you a question, Friedrich. Do you understand? "

"Yes, I understand," I screamed at her, ran upstairs and locked myself in my room.

The next day I summoned Karin to my office.

"What the hell did you do that for, Karin? " I asked, a stern father rather than an injured lover.

She smiled at me, the smile of a Swedish nymph in a Bergman film.

"It's good publicity for CRUPP, isn't it? " she said, sweetly.

God Almighty, when women play the *ingénue* with me, I invariably fall for it.

"But don't you remember that I practically swore you all to secrecy? "

"But that was last April," she said, her sky-blue eyes sparkling. "How long is my memory cycle supposed to last? "

"Oh, Karin! " I said, burying my face in my hands. "What an idiot you are! "

This seemed to offend her pride as a neo-Ibsenite New Woman.

"Even the boss's concubine has some rights, you know," she snapped. "I'm good enough to digit with, so I'd be grateful if you didn't treat me like some subroutine or other."

The *Washington Post* fortunately didn't make much of Karin's information. On the television page they carried a little notice to the effect that "the well-known movie star, Hilde Hildesheim who, in her recent capacity as communications theorist, has been 'lent' to White House Television, is expected to give some long overdue pep to the dreary repetition, cultural uplift, and goody-goody this-is-the-best-of-all-worlds *Kitsch* that has been dished up by the Administration's propaganda outfit for so many moons. A marriage between one of America's more venturesome think tanks and the presidential information mill might produce some odd children, but there may be a better than even chance that these children, whatever their genetic origin, will not be the sordid miscarriages with which the commercial networks have been insulting the American public in the last decade."

I could have done without such compliments. The passage, however, was interesting for another reason. The man who wrote it was the only outsider at the time who knew about Hilde's role, and he thought it was a good thing, for the reasons stated. His expectations, and those of others who subsequently found out about it, were soon to be fulfilled far beyond anybody's wildest dreams.

Chapter 17

I don't know much about television, and therefore this chapter may seem unduly amateurish to those who consider themselves experts. (By the way, I am told *everybody* thinks he is a television expert. That is, everybody but me.) Fortunately I am blessed with a wife who watches it a great deal, and therefore knows a lot about it. The fact that she never likes anything does not, I suppose, detract from her expertise. There is one man on our staff, however, who is, perhaps, a fairer and certainly a more analytical viewer than Paula, and that is — surprisingly enough — the Reverend Soren Andersen. I am about to describe some — just *some*, not all — of the programs which, thanks to Hilde's inspiration, caused, I am told, the greatest sensation in the history of American television. I will attach, when suitable or helpful, both Paula's and Soren's comments. Many of these programs the three of us watched together in our downstairs library on Meadowlark Lane in Bethesda. One of them — the program about Freud — I watched in bed with Karin, in her apartment.

The first thing to mention is the *design* of the programs in question. By design I mean the way the programs were introduced, the announcements, the little flashes and emblems that are presented *between* programs and give a certain flavor and style to the over-all presentation. Amateur though I am, I could well believe that no network had ever taken the trouble to create such a delightful environment for their programs. Without being corny or senti-mental, the designs were a pure joy: faces of children, flowers, landscapes, alternated with colorful Mondrian-like abstractions and animations: the effect was charming. However, what immedi-ately caught the eyes of the critics, and was no doubt a "first," was that pictures of male and female nudes appeared in this mix at random, as though it was the most natural thing in the world.

(The correct word, I am told, to describe the type of nudity portrayed is "frontal.") This motif had considerable ideological importance, a fact quickly diagnosed by Soren Andersen.

"Ah," he said, rubbing his girlish chin, *"retour à la nature!* Our girl has been reading Rousseau! "

I guess what he meant was that the celebration of innocence in the natural state was an invention of the famous French philosopher.

This nudity theme was one of the reasons viewers switched *en masse* from their usual channels to the White House Television Network as soon as the season was on the way — a fact, alas, very much in our disfavor. It was also a theme that formed the subject of a number of programs. But I must not rush. Let me give a synopsis of the play presented on Opening Night, September 16th.

It was simply called "Twins," and the story was elementary. It was written by a young writer from Utah, and the twins were played by the same actor, John Lighthouse, whom everybody knew but me. Twin A was a hard-working shoe salesman. Twin B lived off the proceeds of a lottery windfall. It was clear that both were equally "moral": they were both upstanding respectable citizens; one worked, the other did not work, that was the only difference. A girl appeared on the scene, played by Deborah Kingsley, who Soren thought was a great "catch," since she was so well known from her Hollywood films. Both twins want the girl; the girl likes them both. Tension builds. At one moment we — the audience — want her to land in the arms of the hard-working shoe salesman. The next moment our sympathies are with the honorable loafer. With great humor and skill, the writer tosses her from one to the other. Suddenly the play stops, and we find ourselves in an ordinary television studio. John Lighthouse is there — without make-up — and he asks the people in the studio audience whose side they are on, and why. Opinion is evenly divided. There is only one way, then, in which the play can be brought to a con-clusion, and that is through a coincidence. Back we go to the play. The twins decide to toss for the girl. The loafer wins and, one hopes, lives happily ever after with her.

"I have never seen so much *Scheisse* in my life," said Paula. "I can't stand it when they cheat like that."

Soren took a different line.

"Very significant," he said, tossing his Danish blond mane off his forehead. "Once you abandon the work ethic, you can no longer automatically reward the hard-working hero with the girl. You have to go easy. It's too early in the season for Hilde to favor the loafer directly. All she's doing is softening up the audience, by reminding it that very often the undeserving win a sweepstake. You wait, in a month from now she won't beat around the bush anymore: the loafer will win every time."

"If they're still on the air. The critics will murder them," commented Paula.

"Hilde's being very careful, hedging her bets," continued Soren, ignoring Paula's interjection. "She doesn't want to give the show away the first night. Very clever."

Paula was wrong. The critics liked the play very much. They did not rave about it, as they did about later productions, and they did not go into ecstasies, as they did — within a week after the beginning of the season — about the overall approach, the *nouvelle vague* in presidential program-making, but they treated the play with affection and respect.

"The writer's comic genius," wrote Basil Levinson in the *New York Times*, "was shown to good advantage by John Lighthouse's extraordinary versatility. It will be a long time before the commercial networks attempt to deal with the most acute of our contemporary problems in as ingenious a manner as this. It is most invigorating to watch a play which raises the question so cleverly, carefully avoiding taking sides, at a time when for tens of thousands of Americans work has become more necessary than money or status."

The next evening the same question was being raised again in a different style. It was the first of a series of historical documentaries, collectively called "God and Money." And who was the narrator? None other than Mac himself. I had thought that Hilde was going to use him merely as the subject of some sort of case history, a "case in point" I think she had said. She must have changed her mind. She must have decided to make use of him in all sorts of other ways. Indeed he was excellent, just because he was so different from the usual "television host." (This again I could not judge as well as my two fellow viewers.) He fumbled and stumbled a few times, which was refreshing. He was straight-

forward and direct, and did not pretend to know anything he
didn't know: the ordinary Joe.

The program began with a humorous version of Genesis, the
expulsion from the Garden of Eden. No frontal nudity this time,
because thanks to Adam and Eve having eaten the forbidden fruit,
they had to wear fig leaves (red roses in this version). The punch
line was the injunction: "By the sweat of thy brow, etc...." This
line, said Mac, had been misunderstood for millenia. What had
been meant was that conditions on earth, henceforth, *may* be so
terrible that survival would only be by work, "by the sweat of
thy brow." What could not be predicted was that one day, in
the distant future in America, conditions would be such that
this terrible fate, namely to have to work for a living, might *not*
be everybody's lot. And he laughed happily.

"Well, well, well," said Soren. "Very nice. This is great! "

"The New Testament," Paula remarked, "says 'if you don't want
to work, you won't eat.' Why don't they quote *that*? "

"If you know everything," I said sharply, "why don't *you* go on
television? Let's watch."

After the short biblical opening, Mac told us that the subject of
the series was the connection between religion, work and success.
There was some dispute, he said, whether the original Puritans, who
were Calvinists, put much emphasis on hard work. They believed
in predestination, that some people were "predestined" to be in
a state of grace. However, if a man had gained material success,
the Puritans soon tended to regard this as evidence of divine favor,
and so, gradually, work acquired religious significance. But even
before the Puritans had arrived on the scene, there had been a
school of Christian thought which preached that *laborare est
orare*, to work is to pray. When in the seventeenth century a
commerce-minded middle class arose, a clear distinction was
made between the aristocracy which believed that the purpose
of life was well-spent leisure, and the *bourgeosie* which pursued
wealth through work. However, the work ethic as we know it,
applying as it does not only to the middle class but to the whole
population, is very much the product of the nineteenth and
twentieth centuries, and it could be endlessly debated, Mac said,
as to what extent it had a religious basis.

This, Mac said, was the theme of the series. "In the first part —
the one seen tonight — we depict the Industrial Revolution
and what it did to the people of England, of Western Europe,
and of North America. In the second part — next week — a
program about Charles Dickens' London. Two weeks from
tonight: the seamy side of Victorian England and America:
prostitution and pornography in the nineteenth century. A week
later: capitalism in Catholic countries — how did the *other*
Christian tradition deal with the problems of industrialization?
Additional programs in this series are in preparation. Look in
your local papers for detailed information."

The program on the Industrial Revolution was horrifyingly good.
Alternating pictures of child labor in the mines with work situations
involving children in feudal and Renaissance times, factory building
with cathedral building, mass production with domestic industries
like weaving, it savagely tore into the dehumanizing effects of the
Industrial Revolution, sparing us nothing. Mac's narration was sober
and simple. I am sure every unemployed executive in the country
identified with that nice, clean, sincere openness.

"What's amazing about this," said Soren when the program was
over, "is that Hilde carefully avoided the Marxist conclusion. The
same facts are usually presented to justify red-hot Communism.
I've never seen these things described before on a mass medium
as a *religious* problem, rather than as an academic treatise im-
plicitly inciting class hatred. This was done with great skill."

"My dear Reverend," I said paternally, "if Hilde were a Communist,
she wouldn't be working for CRUPP. I've fought the bastards all
my life."

"If you ask me," ventured Paula, turning to Soren, "my husband
doesn't know the difference between a Communist and a Bavarian
chimney sweep. He just likes to *think* he's been fighting the
bastards all his life. It makes him feel good."

The next evening we saw the first of Hilde's new "Westerns."

"I hope it's as good as Karl May," said Paula. He was an immensely
popular nineteenth century writer of German Westerns who had
never left his native Saxony until after the publication of his
bestsellers. Hilde's Western, however, could not have been more
different from Karl May's and, therefore, gravely displeased Paula.

The hero was modeled on the tramp who was waiting for Godot. He kept quoting from Thoreau's *Walden*. He had no visible means of support, but was clearly an admirable character. Arriving in a little settlement in California, sometime in the eighties, he discovered that a couple of conventionally masked gunmen had just held up the local bank, and raped the bank manager's teen-age daughter. Our tramp-hero then proceeded to get himself a mask and a gun, joined the gang, and even participated in another holdup, carefully, however, manipulating the situation so that the luscious teen-ager who *that* time fell into the gunmen's clutches was not raped, but surrendered her honor happily to all three, voluptuously exercising her free will. By the end of the program, the bad men and the girl were all quoting Thoreau, and were as philosophical and worldly-wise as our tramp.

This time the critics raved.

"This is a true breakthrough," wrote Bill Bethune in the *Washington Post*. (Was he the man to whom Karin had talked?) "A literate Western is nothing new on the American scene, but it is rare indeed on television. It's a *genre* that has been tried more in the movies than on TV. But what the White House has achieved is a perfect fusion of the conventional format and the requirements of a social conscience. Congratulations! "

Other writers were even more rhapsodic. I was beginning to get cold feet. Had the President not warned us that we should avoid being too popular?

"Don't worry," said the Reverend. "The critics never reflect popular taste. They're always on Cloud Nine. This looks to me like a typical *succès d'estime*. You wait: the ratings will tell another story."

How wrong he was! But before coming to that, let me describe some more programs.

On the fourth day of the first week there was a spectacular science program about 'sensory deprivation.' Again Mac was the narrator.

"Sensory deprivation," he said, "is simply the condition when, for one reason or another, we are not allowed to use all our faculties properly. This is very bad for our brains. When our brains are deprived of sensory impressions, they deteriorate. We want to demonstrate this to you by showing you carefully edited films of

109

an experiment that was conducted at McGill University in Montreal, Canada. The first time an experiment like this was done was in the fifties because psychologists wanted to find out why a number of American prisoners of war had been induced by brainwashing into making extraordinary confessions. Also the show trials in Russia had raised questions about the effect of keeping prisoners in isolation for long periods of time. Then, later, space travel gave a new impetus to this kind of experimentation."

The program started with a meeting between a psychology professor and half a dozen students. Each was given twenty dollars a day — "an associate professor's salary at the time"— in return for allowing himself to be locked up in a cell, alone, isolated.

"You'll be allowed to go to the bathroom," the professor said. "You'll be quite comfortable. You'll have enough to eat. But you'll have to lie still. You'll be entirely covered by these blankets," and he showed them, "you'll have this foam rubber pillow wrapped around your head, and you'll have to wear these translucent goggles. Do you understand? "

They said they did.

We now saw films of the students at the end of the first day, and it was clear that their capacity to maintain any connected train of thought had already been seriously impaired. We saw an electro-encephalogram, showing certain changes in their brainwave patterns. Three out of the six students dropped out at that stage. We then saw in further edited episodes how the others fared. One stuck it out as long as six days. He said that after a while he suffered from such hallucinations that, if he didn't know he had goggles on, he would have thought he was watching a movie.

"I saw a series of old men in bathtubs on wheels come across a stage, and then a row of squirrels carrying bags over their backs and wearing snowshoes."

None of the students ever wanted to submit to such an experiment again, "for all the pot on windowsills."

At the end of the program, Mac said that these experiments showed what most of us instinctively know to be true, namely that sensory deprivation leads to diminished critical capacities, a decline in

110

intelligence, and greater susceptibility to propaganda. It's therefore essential, whether we work or play, that we use our capacities to the fullest extent, in order to keep fit.

An excellent program: even Paula agreed. There were other science and medical shows, some of which dealt specifically with the wear and tear of the daily rat race in America: one program about ulcers, another about heart conditions and other "executive diseases." Then there were travel programs, beautifully produced: mouth-watering pictures of South Sea Islands and Italian baroque.

We now come to the subject of nudity. As I have indicated, this was a recurrent theme in the White House fall schedule. It was introduced on the fifth day of the season, by a half-hour visit to a nudist colony in New Hampshire. Our guide: Mac, of course. He'd never been before, he said in his introduction, and had "approached the ordeal with maximum embarrassment and minimum curiosity. I am a happily married man. I have children. I know what the human body looks like. Who needs a bunch of exhibitionist crackpots to show us what we already know? "

At the end of the program, this was his conclusion:

"I won't say I'm converted. But it's certainly been a most exhilarating experience. I'm quite amazed how exhilarating. It's true that it may get boring if you do it too often; I can't tell. I suppose everything does. But this experience was *not* boring. I can't deny it: it has to do with the pleasure of seeing a surprisingly large number of very attractive women completely in the nude, while one is in the nude oneself. I won't comment on the less attractive ones. I'm really amazed with myself, because I'm quite prudish about skinflicks and pornography. I just don't like pornography; I think it's juvenile. I may be in the minority about that. I've been trying to figure out *why* I enjoyed this experience so much, and why I intend to go again. You see, I had expected that I would find women in the nude erotically uninteresting, because I'd been led to believe that it is clothes that make a woman attractive, or rather that clothes are designed to accentuate the suggestiveness of the female body. That's true, in a way. I won't deny it. But obviously, that is not the only way in which women are stimulating. In this natural condition, in the fresh air, with the sun shining, I found this total nudity refreshingly beautiful and — somehow — innocently titillating. I repeat, this may well have to do with the fact that one is in the nude oneself. If the ladies did not find it interesting as well, they wouldn't be there. It's not just a question

111

of being totally human and free, without clothes. It's not a question of democracy through nudity. It has to do with erotic stimulation, with the pleasure of the body, and I am told this is very rarely admitted, least of all by the organized nudists themselves. I've found it a liberating experience and I'm glad I went."

The film was beautifully put together. Focusing a good deal of the time on children at play, there was a lot of laughter and gaiety. Of course, we saw a good deal of "frontal nudity," including Mac himself, but the camera did not linger indecorously on the controversial parts of the human body. I thought it would be difficult to take offence.

Soren did not agree.

"There will be hell to pay for this," he said. "This breaks every taboo in the television rule book."

Once again he was wrong. By now CRUPP had subscribed to a clipping service, and rave reviews were flowing into our headquarters from every part of America. "At last, television for adults," was one of the *leitmotifs*. The word "honest" kept recurring. There was a chorus of praise. However, there was also a smattering of criticism from the organized nudists, who, as Mac had indicated, make a point of denying the sexual component in nudism.

"They're the *real* puritans," commented Soren.

We saw an amusing letter to the editor from one of them. "The narrator strikes us as a little too young to be a dirty old man, but he followed exactly the same approach. Perverted voyeurs should stay away from our camps, or we will have to take more stringent measures to keep them out."

Now occurred — on September 23rd — the first inkling of disasters to come. One of three commercial networks — I forget which — launched an attack on the "sex-obsessed" White House television season.

"In their desperate attempts to obtain at least a minimum of viewers," the spokesman, a vice-president, said (in US companies everybody's a vice-president, so that outsiders can be flattered such a high executive is dealing with them), "so-called public television — or should we say *pubic?* — is resorting to the oldest method in the book: sex. You wait, very soon we will be able to see, on the presidential television network, live performances of the sexual act. All this in the name of freedom and honesty. What is this country coming to? "

One other consequence of the program was an invasion by a gang of executives who had received "the golden handshake" of one of the largest nudist camps in America, a camp at Lake Winnebago in Wisconsin. The invaders would not leave the camp unless each of the nudists had put his or her clothes on. In an interview with the local paper, one of their ringleaders said that they were not going to be diverted from their search for work by "the lure of idle sensuality." The paper decided it was just old-fashioned American puritanism that had prompted the invasion.

I now come to the most original and the most successful program presented by Hilde — so stupendously successful that it, more than any other, caused the abrupt and disastrous end of our experiment. (There were, as we shall see, causes other than the programming itself.) I refer to the program called "The Last of the Puritans: Walt Disney and Hugh Hefner."

Drawing parallels between these two men and their mid-western origins — both were children of farmers — the point of the program was that these two men realized in their maturity adolescent dreams of creating fantasy worlds that had nothing to do with reality. Disney created a world of toy animals that was innocent and unself-conscious. Mice, the program contended, were really rather dirty and smelly, and no one likes them very much. But Disney created the most lovable mouse in the world when he invented Mickey Mouse. Similarly, Hefner, the program went on, invented bunny girls who have as little to do with *real* girls as Mickey Mouse has with mice. Bunny girls are clean and perfect, they have no warts or wrinkles. They wear invisible "Do not touch or pinch" signs. They are the Protestant equivalent of Catholic madonna worship. They represent women so clean that their sexuality has been sanitized out of existence.

I will never understand why, but somehow this program struck a chord which vibrated across America. Hundreds of thousands of viewers recognized that it expressed an important truth. I would have thought the point Hilde was driving at was a fairly subtle one. But if one is to believe the colossal response the

113

program evoked, it could not have been too subtle. However, it is my view that many people who liked it did not really understand it. As we shall see, there is some evidence pointing in that direction. Considerable evidence.

"What Hilde is in favor of, and will soon proclaim," said Soren, "is free and open love for one and all, preferably the unsanitized variety."

"That's pretty obvious," I nodded.

"They will break her neck. You wait and see," said Paula. "I know my Americans. They only like doing it in the dark. Turn the light on and they'll kill you."

"You're talking *Blödsinn*, as usual," I said. *Blödsinn* is a decent German word for bullshit.

There are some other programs I want to mention, none, however, as successful as the Playboy one. As one could have predicted, Hilde had arranged for a series called "The Best." She got the title from the Greek word *aristos*, and it was devoted to princes and princesses, dukes and duchesses, counts and countesses. But instead of engaging in the usual American sport of muckraking, she chose examples from the last two centuries in which the subjects were shown going about their business of living well without working, with seriousness and intelligence.

This went completely against the grain of American egalitarianism, as Soren pointed out. But the message was clear, though never directly spelled out, that one could live a useful and significant life without having a job. There was a program about the Comte de Château-Fleury who divided his time between collecting Roman coins and planting cauliflowers in his park. Another described the salon of the Duchess of Savoy-Gotha, where the conversation was brilliant and the food atrocious. Then there were the various patrons of the arts who are better known: Count Rasoumoffsky, who commissioned Beethoven's opus 59 quartets, the Medicis, and the mad and homosexual Ludwig of Bavaria, to whom justice is rarely done. The English examples showed peers with a highly developed social conscience, such as Lord Shaftesbury, and many others who glittered in Parliament, in the Army, or in the Church. The German examples, I'm afraid, were the least impressive.

"I'm not surprised Hilde kept quiet about *her* ancestors," Paula said, with a malicious twinkle.

"How come? " I asked, remembering very well what Hilde thought about Paula's.

"One of them," Paula explained, "was hanged for buggery, another sold himself to the czars. Why didn't she ask me? I could have told her a few stories about mine."

"They were horse thieves," I volunteered.

"They were *not*," she said, with haughty indignation. "One of them taught Frederick the Great everything he ever learned about beating the Austrians, and another fought the goddam revolutionaries in 1848. The one thing I usually keep quiet is that my great-great-great-great-grandmother slept with Voltaire when he was in Potsdam at Sans-Souci in 1752. But Americans wouldn't care about a thing like that. It's nothing to do with football! "

"True enough," the Reverend said solemnly.

"Now what I would have done, had I been Hilde," she continued, enjoying herself, and looking maliciously at me, "is this: I would have done a program about one of the great German aristocrats of the twentieth century, Hermann Göring."

"Halt doch die Fresse," I said, a rude Berlin request to her to keep her trap shut.

"I would have begun the program by showing him in bed," she continued, "under that huge lascivious nude he stole from somewhere, having some little storm trooper manicure his left hand, while he let a handful of stolen jewels gently glide through the fingers of his right hand. I would 'zoom in' — is that the right word? — on his fat, rouged cheeks, and then let the camera slide down to the oversized ruby brooch on his brocaded green velvet dressing gown, while he himself spouts vulgarities about Bormann and Goebbels and Himmler and his other fellow aristocrats. Why didn't you suggest such a program to Hilde? It would have done wonders for this godawful series! It would have brought it down to the people! "

"Hör auf! " I shouted.

115

"Please," the infuriating woman went on evenly. "Aren't you a great patron of the arts, of *television*? Have you no influence? Why don't you assert yourself? "

"Enough! " I screamed.

Chapter 18

Disaster loomed around the corner. But before I relate what form it took, I want to mention two other programs; one, because it was singled out by a dissident reviewer as "chichi," the other because of the uplifting circumstances in which I viewed it.

The first was a kind of "do-it-yourself" show for city planners and municipal politicians. It had to do with outdoor cafés, and it advocated, as a simple and highly effective way to help people pass the time of day pleasantly if they have no work to do, the setting up of tables and chairs on sidewalks, as it is done, as a matter of course, in other parts of the world. (It carefully avoided saying "in more *civilized* parts of the world.") I could see why this would be one of the less successful productions of Hilde's since — that's rather untypical of her — she completely ignored cultural and climatic differences between the US and France.

The other program — an original musical about Freud — I want to mention because both Karin and I, who watched it together in bed, were completely entranced by it. I should interject that I had become a virtuoso in inventing subterfuges, alibis, excuses and downright lies to engineer my digiting sessions with Karin without — touch wood — so far being caught by Paula's eagle eyes. In fact, since our row in connection with Karin's indiscretion to the *Washington Post*, her name had not been mentioned in our house.

Which brings me back to the Freud program. Even I could see how daring it was.

Its main subject was that Freud was a typical puritan Victorian, that his attitude towards women was primeval, and his views about work and leisure contemptible. It was a highly amusing slash job which did not take itself too seriously. I learned a few interesting things from that program which I did not know. The image I've always had of Freud was that of a severe, paternal figure with an all-penetrating mind who was completely unemotional in his personal relationships. But from the program I learned that during a four-year-long secret engagement to his future wife, he had been the most passionate of romantic lovers and that, most probably, his subsequent lifelong marriage was exceptionally happy, in spite of his extraordinary claim that he had had no sex after the age of forty.

A bikini-clad soprano, who enacted some kind of Greek chorus, sang this memorable verse:

Listen to his true confession
Which explains his sex obsession.
He gave advice to all mankind,
But all his sex was in his mind.

"This is beautiful," said Karin, snuggling up to me. "I would have thought the old man had done plenty of digiting. Maybe there was something wrong with his flowline. Besides he was probably lying."

A moment later we discovered that perhaps Karin had been right in her assumption that things were not exactly as he wanted them to appear. A few years ago, some slightly ambiguous evidence turned up which suggested to some that Freud had followed the Victorian party line of total hypocrisy in sexual matters. This did not necessarily mean that his marriage to Mrs. Freud had *not* been happy, though his other love object was, according to this evidence, her own sister. And all this *after* he had reached forty.

We don't think it does any harm
To recall Mrs. Freud had a sister.
And that Sigmund succumbed to her charm
And — oh horrors! — may even have kissed her!

Then there was Freud's dream song:

What do the dreams mean?
The dry dreams, the wet dreams,
The reams and reams of dreams?

118

I know what the dreams mean,
The reams and reams of dreams.
Through the maze of your days
And the craze of your ways,
They reveal the repression
Of old buried passion,
That's what the dreams mean.

And his haunting Oedipus-song:

What are you doing on Sunday night, mother dear?
Please stay home!
Because on Sunday at one o'clock
I'm giving papa a fatal knock.
So please stay home on Sunday night,
Mother dear.

Karin and I thought this was wonderful stuff. I must add that for
a short spell we were having a very good time together. Was it
because of my double enjoyment as a result of Paula's declaration
of war? Or did Karin moderate her demands on my toggle-switch
slightly because she felt guilty about her indiscreet interview with
the *Washington Post?* Or did it have some other mysterious
reason? In any case, we got on splendidly. Although the affair
did not come to an end until many months later, this was the last
time we had any kind of rapport beyond the "mere" act of digiting.

"I'm enjoying this," she said, caressing the back of my neck just
the way I like it. "I like your auxiliary equipment, Friedrich,"
she added.

"I like yours, too, sweetheart," I responded, kissing her shoulder
blades which smelled of Swedish forget-me-nots in the spring, I
think. Whenever I visited Sweden, it was always, alas, winter.

In the second part of the program, the subject was Freud on work
and leisure. The main point was that he himself distrusted any
insight he had ever had which was not the result of "arduous toil."

I woke up last night and saw
That two and two make four.
Oh no, I said, this can't be true!
A scientist needs perspiration,
He must not trust to inspiration.

119

"That old prig," said Karin, seizing my primary equipment. "I've never been able to stand him. Come on, Friedrich, let's digit! "

"In a moment," I said. "The program will be over soon. Let's do it then! "

"But my digital integrator wants it now! " she pleaded, accelerating her efforts.

"It'll have to wait, that's all there is to it," I replied, extricating myself from her attentions.

The program went on ridiculing Freud for believing that there are only three categories of men who can lead good and useful lives without "arduous toil": aristocrats, artists, and — what a surprise — *priests*!

"Soren will like that," Karin said, laughing.

The grand finale was sung by a chorus of gaudily-uniformed aristocrats, long-haired bohemian artists, and black-cassocked priests, who danced a frenzied cancan, boasting that since they belonged to the Freudian elite, they didn't ever have to do a spot of work. It was beautiful.

This was the last program before the resounding crash.

Chapter 19

One of Wilhelm Busch's most famous stories is called *Hans Hucke-bein, der Unglücksrabe*, Hans Huckebein, the unfortunate crow, and Germans speak about a *Pechvogel*, meaning a bird cursed by bad luck. I hope you don't think I am indulging excessively in self-pity if I number myself among these birds. I refrained from quoting Wilhelm Busch when Bill Bush called the morning after the Freud musical. His voice was funereal.

"Friedrich, I have terrible news. The ratings are in."

"Yes? "

"The situation couldn't be graver. We have taken 36.8 percent of the commercial audience away from the networks. The three network presidents are seeing the President at 11:30 this morning."

"May I come, please? "

"Oh, no," Bill replied with a painful laugh. "There's nothing you can conceivably contribute. No, I think our goose is cooked."

"What do you mean? " I asked, my heart in my pants. (Remember the German idiom *Mein Herz ist in die Hosen gefallen*?)

"There's no question about it. I don't think the President has a choice. We'll have to revert to normal programming."

"But what about the public? Isn't this a democracy? Doesn't public taste count for anything? "

121

"Not in this case, Friedrich. Boy, oh boy, this is terrible. There's going to be one hell of a row about this."

"Just a second, Bill. I don't understand. All this is *in our favor*. The villains are those commercial guys. The public has spoken. *Vox populi, vox dei*. They prefer *us!* "

"That's not the way it's going to look before we're through. You watch. Don't forget, they're in league with the newspapers. They will charge us with all the sins in the book: that we have abused our mandate, that we have been obscene and immoral, that we have engaged in the most vulgar sensationalism, that we're out of touch with the true America, and that we're trying to manipulate the people. Boy, am I ever glad your involvement in all this has been kept more or less secret. The *Washington Post* never followed up that piece they printed about Dr. Hildesheim. Imagine, if those network boys knew about *your* role in all this! This could become a major election issue, for Christ's sake! "

"I'll remind my people once more to keep quiet," I said.

"You'd better! Oh God, if anything happened now! "

The thought of such a calamity gave him a coughing spell. When he recovered, he told me not to worry, he'd keep me informed.

"But those critics," I said, trying to understand, "they *loved* the programs. Doesn't that count for anything? "

"That's not worth a pinch of coon shit," he said, using an expression he told me once he picked up from a former president. "Nor do the ratings. Only inside people care about ratings anyway."

"And you say the networks are in league with the press? That's not the impression one gets from reading the reviews," I said, feeling a complete stranger in a world I knew nothing about.

"The people who control the press leave the critics alone. They only appear on the entertainment pages anyway. No one reads them. My, you have a lot to learn about this game, Friedrich! "

"You people are not going to give me the chance, it seems," I replied bitterly. "Keep me posted, Bill. I won't talk to anybody about it for the time being."

"But don't forget to tell your staff to keep their mouths shut! "

"I won't."

He hung up.

It was already too late. At noon the fearsome Jerry Gorham went on television, reading extracts from the next morning's syndicated column which appears in forty-seven newspapers across the United States. Gorham — famous for his eye-patch — is the man who, two years ago, exposed the scandalous goings-on in the cafeteria of the Supreme Court.

"Official Washington," said Gorham, "is in a tizzy over the latest television ratings published last night. Seems that the sexy 'New Look' of White House television has trounced the pants off CBS, NBC and ABC. There will be a weep fest at the White House this morning. Yours truly isn't the only one who can guess the outcome. Our dirty old man of a president will have to eat crow. What makes this sex story doubly spicy, however, is the news that the famous CRUPP think tank has had a hand in juicing up these programs, a hand by the teutonic name of Hilde Hildesheim, a not-so-young damsel who used to arouse goose-stepping young storm troopers in the good old days, and who is now going straight, perhaps because her feminine charms are a little worn around the edges. Why this lady has been let loose in the Administration's show-biz department remains a bit of a mystery. A CRUPP insider, however, has told your faithful columnist that he thinks this alliance raises serious questions about the propriety of the CRUPP-White House connection, especially in view of the fact that CRUPP's founder and president narrowly escaped the rope at the Nürnberg trials as a war criminal."

Once my heartbeat had slowed down to a tolerable rate, I phoned Paula at home. My voice must have sounded a bit strained, though, because all I had to say was "Paula? " and she knew I was in the deepest trouble.

"My first suggestion is calm down," she said.

"I *have* calmed down," I said irritably. I then read her the Gorham column, and told her about the ratings and Bill Bush's warning about the need for discretion.

123

"Give me a moment to think," she said. "I've been polishing the silver. Why can't they make decent cleaning stuff in this *gott-verdammte* country? "

"*Paula,*" I said, "*concentrate!* "

"I *am* concentrating. Well now, let's see. Whatever you do, don't sue."

"The thought never occurred to me," I replied.

"What else can you do about it? " she asked, dumber than usual.

"Don't you understand? The President is going to hit the roof! This may well be the end of CRUPP in Washington."

"Aw! " she said lightly, "*die Suppe wird nie so heiss gegessen wie sie gekocht wird.*" The soup is never eaten as hot as it is cooked. "You're dramatizing! "

"What would *you* do if you were president? Wouldn't you break off all contact with CRUPP immediately? "

"Why would I do a thing like that? " she asked in amazement. "After all, what Gorham said is a lie. What would I have to be afraid of? If I were president, I would summon you today and give you an Iron Cross First Class."

"*Himmel Donnerwetter*, you're impossible, Paula! What Gorham said is not *entirely* untrue. Its only *substantially* untrue. Can't you see the difference? "

"I can't, *Dummkopf.* To me, it's untrue. *Punkt.* You'll see, to the President, it's untrue too. If he got excited like you, every time some rhinoceros of a newspaperman threw *Scheisse* at him, he wouldn't be president, would he? "

"*Dein Wort in Gottes Ohr*! " I retorted. Your word in God's ear.

"But what I want to know is whether it was that Swedish bit of poison who talked to Gorham. That's what I want to know."

Of course that thought had occurred to me, but I couldn't imagine that she would commit the same crime twice. This time, however,

124

I was firmly resolved not to have a row with Paula about her, and not to be so defensive.

"That's very unlikely," I said quietly. "I'll certainly make it my business to find out."

I have the greatest difficulty remembering exactly what happened during the following twenty-four hours. I do remember that the morning after my conversation with Paula I called in every member of my staff and extracted loyalty assurances from them. Each one denied having spoken to Gorham, solemnly, utterly convincingly. To this day I have no proof that anyone did it, though I think it is safe to assume that the person — or the persons — who a few weeks later usurped my position at CRUPP, and turned it into a tool of Communist China, were also the ones who had spoken to Gorham.

But the reason I have trouble remembering the precise course of events is that I had such vivid nightmares the night after I received those loyalty oaths that I can't distinguish *Dichtung* from *Wahrheit*, poetry from truth. The central figure in these nightmares was Karin, and the visions I had of her in relation to each and every one of her colleagues were of a highly erotic nature. I suppose one might call those nightmares the dreams of a man tormented by fears of impotence, jealousy and suspicion.

Perhaps I had not realized how much my subconscious had been puzzled by Karin's willingness to digit with a fat old man like myself, when she could so easily have had the attention of younger, more conventionally acceptable lovers. Why else should I have envisioned, in my nightmare, a scene in a narrow confessional, where Soren Andersen and Karin were making love, quickly and efficiently, both standing up, in some northern church, while a tinny organ was playing a Bach chorale? And there was Jerry Gorham, with his eye patch, dressed as a priest, listening to their sounds of love, like a cleric hearing their confession in the cubicle next door. The lovers were so good at it: the whole thing took only a couple of minutes, while normally — I was very aware of that in my dream — it took me, well, let's say it took me a little longer. When Soren and Karin had finished, they opened the door of the confessional, Jerry Gorham stepped out of *his* cubicle, and all three giggled and pointed their fingers at me.

In another scene, Richard Toshima and Karin were copulating in a Japanese garden, under the cherry blossoms. He had the features

of that marvelous actor in *Hiroshima Mon Amour* — Eiji Okada.
A number of people were strolling by, only casually taking notice
of the happy couple, until one of them emerged from the rest,
bowed low, and then asked humbly for permission to take over.
Both lovers graciously granted this permission, after which the
stranger climbed with exquisite elegance on top of Karin. Only
then did I notice that he wore an eye-patch and was, in fact, Jerry
Gorham. This in itself did not upset me at all, strangely enough.
But when he and Karin were finished, I did the same thing he had
done, i.e. bowed low, and asked for permission to proceed. At
that moment, they both kicked me in the face.

I can't remember precisely in what setting Cedric Douglas-Whyte
and Karin were doing it; I seem to recall an African thatched hut
in the center of a Tudor Oxford courtyard. But I do remember
Karin asking Cedric to caress her "zone-structure" with his Vandyke, and as I, as it were, pressed my nose against the glass to
watch more closely, it was the beardless Gorham and not Cedric
who was doing it, while Cedric bent over both of them, lecturing
them about — of all things — *my* incompetence.

"Why, this Nazi is no less dangerous merely because his sexual powers
are failing: he may even be more savage in his old age. Besides, he's
illiterate. He doesn't know the difference between the Wabuwabus
and the Kwakiutles! We must dispose of him at once! "

The dream dissolved into another scene, this time set in a midwestern
football stadium, where Tex Winter, wearing nothing but a cowboy
hat, was pawing Karin, who was completely in the nude, both of them
chewing gum, while the cheering crowd concentrated on the football
game. Suddenly I noticed that their attention was not fixed on one
another, but on a huge billboard on which Tex was scribbling incomprehensible mathematical formulas, while Karin occasionally corrected
them with a piece of chalk. Suddenly everything changed, and the
crowd, led by the one-eyed Jerry Gorham in full football uniform and
egged on by Tex and Karin, pounced on me and beat me unconscious.

But perhaps the most vivid dream of all was a lesbian love scene
between Hilde and Karin, who were writhing in rapturous ecstasies
inside Lenin's tomb on the Red Square in Moscow. And who was
Lenin? Jerry Gorham, of course, very much alive, though beautifully
embalmed, watching the happy couple, miraculously without his eye-
patch, while making notes on a paper pad. Though this was by far the
least dramatic of the dreams, it was the one that frightened me most.

126

I woke up in a cold sweat, certain that I was in a Siberian prison camp.

"*Was is denn mit Dir los*? " asked Paula, bending over me, wiping my forehead with a handkerchief drenched in eau de cologne.

It took me a few seconds before I could answer.

"Nothing at all," I answered. "I'm fine."

I went back to sleep, and for the rest of the night dreamed about being first in my Latin class in the *Gymnasium* in Hanover.

* * *

Back to reality. Bill Bush was right that the President had to cancel the new programming of his network, effective immediately. But, in great contrast to Bill Bush, who thought the world had collapsed when he heard about the Gorham commentary, the President took a far more philosophical view. Once more, Paula turned out to have been correct.

"Ah well," he was quoted as saying. "Boys will be boys."

There was, however, one entirely novel — and distinctly unpleasant — consequence of Gorham's defamatory revelations. For the first time a highly perceptive observer had spotted the connection between CRUPP's involvement in the White House programming and its hitherto beautifully concealed task in advising the President on possible solutions to end the leisure riots. Within twenty-four hours after the Gorham column had appeared, I received an anonymous letter at my home to the effect that, unless CRUPP immediately ceased and desisted from its efforts to deflect the public from the real issues of the day — which was to find work for unemployed executives — immediate action would be taken against us.

What that action was to be, my correspondent kept to himself.

While I took pains not to discuss this threat with anybody but Paula and the police, several simultaneous events received screaming headlines across the country. I first heard about these events from Reverend Soren Andersen who phoned me as soon as he heard about them.

"Bierbaum, " he asked, "is that you? "

127

"Who else? "

"Your voice sounds a little strange. Is anything wrong? "

"Not really," I replied. "I'm just a little preoccupied, that's all."

"I'm sorry to hear that." The Reverend sounded professionally solicitous. "Well, I have little bits of news that might cheer you. Disneyland has just been blown up."

"Well, that's *indeed* interesting," I replied. "Our friends are becoming a little more enterprising. Which Disneyland, by the way? "

"All five of them. California, Florida, Boston, Chicago and Baton Rouge, Louisiana."

"Well, well, well," I commented. "Have they found out who did it? "

"The prevailing assumption is that it's Arab terrorists."

"Of course," I said.

"But that's not all. Certain actions have been taken against every bunny girl in every Retired Playboys' Club in the country."

"*Certain actions?* What do you mean, Reverend? I hope nothing sadistic? "

"On the contrary, Bierbaum. There's no need to worry, though I'm touched by your concern for their well-being."

"What happened then? "

"It's very interesting, because exactly the same thing happened to all of them at the same time in every major city in America. I mean at the same time, allowing for differentials in the time zones. Some people wearing masks invaded the Retired Playboys' Clubs, sprayed the girls with a mild sedative, and then, using no more than reasonable force, dressed their normally highly decorative exposed bosoms with pitch-black cardboard bras."

I allowed a few seconds to let this news sink in.

"I'm impressed, Soren. Never underestimate the power of White

128

House television. This suggests that there is some sort of national organization at work."

"It could have been the Baptist Church that organized this," Soren said.

"It could, but you know damned well it wasn't. Anyway, I hope the leisure rioters only got together for this one purpose. If they seriously gang up, I have no doubt we will be the number one target."

"Let's not become paranoid, Bierbaum," Soren said.

"I will try to be as brave as my Prussian forefathers." I said. "I have a feeling that in the days to come I shall need all the force and cunning of the *Nibelungen.*"

Chapter 20

Some of these facts, of course, you know. There isn't a newspaper that hasn't reported them and written editorials about them. But the *nuances*, the little by-plays of which there are going to be a lot in the next episode, these will all be new to you, and, I think, interest you, for none of them has ever been made public.

The date of President Roberts' conditional surrender was October 15th, almost a month to the day after Hilde's season had begun. The threatening letter, the assaults on the Disneylands and the Retired Playboys' Clubs, took place within the next two weeks.

On the morning of October 18th, before a meeting of the staff at the High Table, I had a chance encounter with Mac in the men's room on the second floor.

"What does it feel like to be a television star? " I asked him, jovially.

"It's great, Mr. Bierbaum. The best therapy in the world. Every patient at Walter Reed should get it. I feel on top of the world."

He really seemed fully restored.

"My wife is one of your most ardent fans," I said. "I think she's fallen in love with you."

He laughed.

"Please tell her it's reciprocated."

"Well, I'm sorry for your sake that it's all come to such a sudden end."

"It's nice of you to say so, Mr. Bierbaum. But please don't worry on my account. I'm looking forward to getting back to my violin and my studies. I've never felt better in my life. I don't know what got into me when I did that thing at the Smithsonian. I must have been *sick!* "

"I guess you were just bored, Mac," I said.

"*Bored?* That's hardly the word for it. I was ready to...to SCREAM! "

"I understand," I replied, like a doctor with a good bedside manner.

"That's what makes it possible for me to put myself into the skin of all those leisure rioters. I used to be one of them myself, you see. I know that there's really no difference between writing 'Fuck you' on a dinosaur in the Smithsonian, and blowing the place up. That might very well have been the next step if Dr. Toshima hadn't come along, just in the nick of time."

"I'm very glad it turned out that way," I said. "You certainly look very well, Mac."

As a matter of fact, I was struck by his excellent appearance. His face had a healthy pink look, his little brown mustache was carefully groomed, and he seemed to be wearing a new gray suit.

"I think it's terrible what those rioters are doing," he went on, "sabotaging all those good things."

"It is," I replied. "But it's all going to be over very soon. We're seeing to that. So long, Mac."

I won't bore you with a detailed account of the staff meeting. Senator Hollinger had asked to be invited, in view of the special circumstances, but fortunately he stayed only for half an hour. As usual, he was condescending, sanctimonious and long-winded. Before the meeting, he insisted on seeing me alone in my office. He looked more than ever like the late Cary Grant, but only if one can imagine Mr. Grant being pompous.

"I'm not going to tell you your business, Bierbaum," he began, after lighting a cigar. He spoke precisely like a man about to tell another his business. "You ignored my advice when I suggested you fire that psychologist of yours who botched that job with what's-

131

his-name. You had a right to ignore me: I mustn't hold it against you. But this time, please listen. You've got to find the man — or the woman — who talked to Gorham. You can't afford to have people like that on your staff."

"My dear Senator," I said, in my most lordly fashion. "I have taken every measure humanly possible to prevent a repetition. You're quite right, we can't afford people like that. I'm losing a great deal of sleep over this thing. The idea that there's a snake in our midst makes me speechless with anger."

"Yes, Bierbaum, but what are you *doing* about it? Do you have any suspicions? "

"I have no evidence against anybody; that's all I'm prepared to say to you at this stage, Senator."

"I wish you wouldn't withhold vital information from me, Bierbaum," he continued sternly. "I have much at stake here."

"So do I," I said lamely.

"Yes, yes, yes, I know that," he continued irritably, "but as Chairman of the Board I am perhaps even more vitally concerned than you that there be no further strains in our relationship with the President. I hope this morning's meeting will be constructive, so that we can develop some positive ideas as to how to retrieve the situation. I know you understand me, Bierbaum, and I don't want to ride herd on you too hard. You don't mind my talking to you like that, I hope. We must be frank with one another at all times."

"Of course, of course," I said, not too convincingly I am afraid. "I think we'd better go in now. They'll all be assembled at the High Table."

We went across the corridor. Everybody was in position, deeply plunged into our Polish-designed brainstorming chairs. The general atmosphere was tense and serious. It was the first time Hilde attended one of our meetings since her television assignment had begun. In contrast to the others, she looked glowing. She was wearing a dazzling white dress with a gold belt, and some surrealistic jewelery which was stunning. Her eyes were bright; the eye shadow was just blue enough to be effective without drawing so much attention one felt obliged to comment on it. The dress was so skilfully cut that her bralessness was well advertised without being conspicuous. Her manner was that of a general whose armies had been defeated in open battle by an enemy outnumbering him a thousand to one. That is how the Athenians must have felt after the battle of Thermopylae. Her honor was intact. Only the vulgarity of numbers had conquered superior intelligence and organization.

"Before we proceed," I opened the meeting, "let me welcome our distinguished Chairman of the Board. It is not often that we have this pleasure, Senator."

I made a formal, old-world bow to him.

"Thank you very much, Mr. Bierbaum. I'm afraid I have only a few minutes, since I have to go to another meeting. I must congratulate you, Dr. Hildesheim, for your outstanding achievement. That things took the turn they did, is a credit to your extraordinary abilities."

"Thank you very much, Senator," said Hilde, looking like a German movie queen receiving an Oscar which, in many ways, she was.

"Well, now," he resumed on a more vigorous note. "Never before in peacetime has so much depended on so few people. This is a life-and-death proposition for our whole way of life. Quite apart from that, the President's political future is in your hands. Now, of course, I don't want to pressure you into any particular direction, but the other day, when the three network chiefs met with the President, they offered him time on their networks in return for his undertaking to cancel the current White House season. They invited him to use this time for any public purpose within his discretion. I mention this for what it's worth. Whatever you do, please make sure that there will be no further...mishaps. This is of paramount importance. No president likes to withdraw under pressure." He rose. "Well, Mr. Chairman, I'm afraid I have to leave you."

I took the Senator to the door.

The school inspector left, the class relaxed, and we got down to business. It was one of the most acrimonious meetings we'd ever had. Each staff member insisted that *his* — or *her* — approach was the only possible one, and went to great lengths to put down the others. Tex Winter sneered at all those who didn't agree with him that the leisure problem was entirely political, that it was insoluble unless the basic structure of the society was put upside down. However, he was not ready to submit his views formally to the High Table as yet.

Soren Andersen, too, was procrastinating.

"I used to think," he said, a little more aggressively than usual, "there was no harm in trying a psychological approach to start off with. But surely we know by now that it has led to a dead end. Doesn't the truth stare you in the face that what we have to deal with is basically a *religious* problem? "

I had to intervene when Tex called Soren a "misplaced Sunday school teacher." Karin did not help very much either, I am afraid, when she offered her help to work out any of our plans with her computers; it wasn't her job, she said, to be an original thinker.

"My multiplex channels are at your disposal," she said sweetly. "Give me your data, and I will deliver the control totals," or something like that.

Now it was Cedric Douglas-Whyte's turn to speak. He had brought along another Elizabethan instrument he had been lent by his friends at the Library of Congress, a *"sack-butt,"* a strange wind instrument with which he had managed (I was told) to make an awful noise when he came into the room. This time, however, he only knocked it on the floor — there was no table in the High Table — to attract everyone's attention.

He *was* ready, he said, with an interdisciplinary approach which would settle matters once and for all. If there was the proper follow-through, there wouldn't be another leisure riot for a generation at least.

"No good f-f-f-fucking around with little repair jobs here and there," he said, his eyes more piercing, his stutter more Oxfordish, than usual.

When everybody tried to pin him down, he refused to say what he had in mind. He was at his most frustrating and infuriating.

"I think the High Table has a right to know," I said, trying to assert my authority.

"Nobody can force me to disclose my plans prematurely," he replied haughtily. "When you're ready to give me the green light, I will tell you what it's all about. In the meantime, let's just say I recommend supervised gym classes for one and all."

That was not much help, but there was clearly no point in pushing him further. The next one to speak was Richard Toshima who was wearing a new pair of mauve granny glasses.

"I know that Soren has a corner on the religion market," he said, with a slight edge in his voice. "He may resent a clinical psychologist like me horning in on him, but I'd like to have a crack at something."

"Halleluja," said Tex Winter.

With Hilde's enthusiastic support, Toshima reminded us that he was, among other things, an expert on Eastern religions. If bored, unemployed executives learned to do what President Roberts does every day, namely communicate with the cosmos, their lives would very quickly assume a new meaning for them, and they would cease to make trouble.

"There's much to be said for this," said the Reverend Soren Andersen. "It would certainly be a very positive stopgap measure while the rest of us put the finishing touches on our respective projects."

"A complete waste of time," volunteered Cedric.

"Hear, hear," said Tex.

"How would you go about it, Toshima? " I asked, after a pause, scratching the back of my head.

"I think we should try television once more. There's commercial time available on the networks. It's a golden opportunity. Instead of demanding simultaneous blocks of time on the three networks, let's simply ask for commercial spots between programs. We'll then design — say — two hundred twenty-second commercial messages plugging oriental mysticism. Of course, we'll want to cash in on Mac's current popularity, and make lots of use of him. Hilde and I have discussed this, and I think we agree it's worth trying. What do you think? "

135

Remembering President Roberts' penchant for meditation, the idea immediately appealed to me.

"This time," Hilde said, sitting up on her chair and bending forward, so that we could all admire her bralessness, "let's not be over-ambitious. No need to do something like my Freud show. Nor do we have to emulate CBS, which scored such a hit last season with its thirty-nine hour-long spectaculars on the private life of former President Nixon. Our commercials would also be relatively easy to research. We all know what a terrible time they had researching the Nixon series. Everybody laughed at the idea when they started, you remember, and for a while it looked as if they would have to title the series 'The Temptations of Saint Richard.' In any case, we should use at least as much frontal nudity as they did on those shows. Don't you agree? "

I nodded, deep in thought.

"I would like to make a suggestion," Tex said, a nasty smile playing on his lips. "I think the President himself should go on the air. Let him demonstrate his favorite Yoga positions, perhaps inter-twined with a couple of his mistresses. Let him show us how to achieve total serenity by attaining unity with emptiness. Let him show us how to listen to the soles of our feet and the rumblings of our digestive apparatus. Let him tell us how to channel our sexual drives transcendentally, thereby keeping the birthrate down. Richard's suggestion is brilliant."

Though I was far from amused, I did not want to have an open fight with Tex, especially since his sarcasm had fallen visibly flat. Only Karin laughed out loud when he had finished, and Cedric snickered slightly. No doubt Toshima was furious, but he was good at concealing his feelings.

"You're not very funny today, Tex," said Hilde, who had been squirming throughout the speech.

"I've made my decision," I announced at last. "I will try out Richard's scheme on Bill Bush. If he likes it, we will go ahead."

Chapter 21

In the last week of October the leisure rioters stepped up their activities. It was conceivable that they were acting spontaneously, but it seemed to me much more plausible that they were in touch with one another, that some kind of national organization, such as the one behind the assault on the bunny girls, was emerging. At the same time, the press and all the other media spent more time and space than ever before analyzing the disturbances, and, though the election was more than a year away, the leisure crisis was beginning to become a hot political issue between the President and the Opposition, just as he had predicted. The only thing that had not been foreseen was that nobody, no newspaper, no academic, no television pundit, *nobody*, except my anonymous pen pal, connected the riots with the frustrations of hundreds of thousands of angry executives around the country.

When small retail shops selling stamps and coins for collectors were raided all along the eastern seaboard, heroin addicts were blamed. When Scotch tape was stuck on every Rembrandt in every art gallery in the country rich enough to own one, security measures against art thieves were stepped up. When the police chief of Dayton, Ohio, received anonymous phone calls calling a number of suburban citizens effete homosexuals because they were pursuing their hobby of woodworking in their recreation rooms, the local Chamber of Commerce demanded a tightening up of defamation laws. When chemicals were inserted in the spark plugs of all the snowmobiles near the Canadian border in the northwest, the anti-pollution lobby was held responsible. When travel posters luring the public to Bulgaria and Tahiti were defaced with obscenities, it was the recently revived America First Party that was held accountable.

While individual blame for all these troubles was attached to these various segments of society, certain members of Congress lost no time in blaming the President for the *overall* breakdown of civil order.

"We are not going to campaign on an old-fashioned law and order platform," the silver-haired minority leader in the Senate, Philip Cosgrove, announced early in November. "We happily concede to the President and his advisers in the notorious CRUPP think tank the privilege of engaging in totalitarian rhetoric. After all, we all know which masters the famous Friedrich Bierbaum served during the Second World War. However, we cannot idly stand by while all the things that make life in America sweet are consistently, publicly, systematically, desecrated. He must do something about this, and if he does not, he must be swept onto the dustheap of history."

This was only one of the many instances in which my name was coupled with that of the President. The Governor of Minnesota, John Reddick, who hoped to run against the President in the coming election, was interviewed at length by TIME. The story appeared, boxed like a funeral announcement, in the last November issue.

Reddick: It is surely no coincidence that Roberts has chosen as one of his principal advisers the well-known think tanker, Friedrich Bierbaum. Knowing this man's record as a Communist baiter from way back, it's obvious that the President is planning to blame the Communists for all the leisure troubles we're witnessing these days. Well, we're not going to let him get away with this. It's all too evident that the people who are attacking those things that make American life as civilized as that of ancient Athens, or of Florence at the height of the Italian Renaissance, are touching the exposed nerve ends of our system. There is no evidence whatsoever that it's the work of Communists.

TIME: Who would you say then is behind these troubles? Have you drawn any conclusions yourself?

Reddick: It seems to me it's too obvious for words that it's the work of Women's Lib.

TIME: That's a very interesting theory, Governor.

Reddick: I myself find it surprising that I seem to be the only one who has spotted this. You see, the activities the rioters are attacking — going to museums, concerts, art galleries and all that — are the traditional occupations of conservative women, the kind of women Women's Lib has been fighting. American men have never felt very strongly about these activities; those who took an interest did so because their wives insisted. That's why I regard it as a civil war among women, particularly your women's liberal college women: the new radicals against the traditional conservatives, or, you might say, 'New Rads against Old Cliffs.'

When I told Paula at breakfast about Toshima's idea to sell Eastern mysticism through two hundred twenty-second commercials on the television networks, using Mac, she touched her right temple with her index finger — a common German school kids' gesture suggesting imbecility — and said, "*Ihr kotzt mich an!* " This is a vulgar phrase indicating that we make her want to throw up.

"And why, may I ask? " I poured myself a second cup of coffee.

"Because of the way you're going to exploit Mac. Just as he's about to recover from the disease you gave him in the first place, you're going to make an ass of him in front of millions. He's a much nicer man than all you people at CRUPP put together, and you're going to ruin him once more."

"*Du bist verrückt*, Paula," I replied. I nearly spilled my coffee. "He doesn't have to do it unless he wants to. Besides it's work, isn't it, and that's what he wants most in life."

"I thought you told me that Toshima had cured him of his so-called work addiction," she said, looking straight at me, "that all he wanted was to play the fiddle and read Tolstoy. I don't know what to believe anymore. You're sure making a mess of this thing, Friedrich. I have a feeling you're all floundering. It's bound to blow up in your faces. And now you're going to make Mac advertise Buddhism! I can just see the headlines. *NAZI WAR CRIMINAL ONCE MORE USES SLAVE LABOR; THIS TIME TO SELL EASTERN MYSTICISM.* I think it's downright immoral what you're up to, using a man like Mac as your stooge, to sell something of which he knows nothing and for which he has no feeling. You want him to tell two hundred lies. It's disgusting! "

"*Du kannst mich mal!* " I shouted. (A quote from Goethe's *Götz von Berlichingen*, meaning you can kiss my rear end.)

139

When I arrived at the office, Toshima was waiting for me.

"Have you heard about Mac? " he asked anxiously.

"I saw him yesterday, and he was fine."

"You remember how priggish he's always been about sex?
That he could make love only to his wife? That pornography
could not arouse him? Well, now he's become totally obsessive
about sex."

"You're not serious," I said, half-amused.

"All he wants to do is go to bed with Karin."

"With *whom?* "

"With Karin Hamsun. *You* know. *Our* Karin."

"I don't believe it," I whispered.

"It's God's truth," Toshima said, sighing.

I took a deep breath. I want it understood that till the bitter end
I was entranced with Karin. Nothing mattered more to me than
to demonstrate to her (and to myself) that I was worthy of her,
and that I could keep up with her. Should Karin respond to someone else, my male ego would suffer a severe, perhaps an irreparable,
blow.

"Does Karin know? " I asked.

"Not yet."

"How do *you* know, Toshima? "

"He told me. He says he can't sleep at night. He has the usual puritan anguish. He says he's still in love with his wife. His desire for
Karin is merely *physical,* he claims. It's just sex, that's all, he thinks.
But I have no doubt that life will be pure hell for him until he's
accomplished his purpose."

"Well, why doesn't he just *ask* her? " I tried to sound offhand.
"It's always possible that Karin might oblige."

140

"He's too shy," Toshima replied, looking at me through his granny glasses. The thought occurred to me that he knew all about me and Karin and was kind of testing me.

"Well, I don't know what *I* can do about it," I said carefully.

"Oh, nothing," he said quickly. "I just thought I should mention it, in case Bill Bush or somebody at the White House asks you why my official report isn't ready. I now have to wait until Mac is over this."

"I suppose so," I said thoughtfully. "But isn't that sort of thing quite normal? After all, that's what happens to middle-aged men. I think you should interpret it as proof of your complete success."

"No, I don't think I can do that, Bierbaum. It's *not* normal, not to that extent. He's just become compulsively obsessive about the girl. I found him yesterday in the computer lab with his arms wrapped around one of them — around a *machine*, if you please — just because he associates computers with Karin. No, it's not normal, not normal at all."

"That's terrible," I said. "If once the thing were consummated, would he be all right? "

"I would say that's a pretty safe prognosis, but one can never be sure about that sort of thing."

"I suppose not. Anyway, thanks a lot for telling me, Richard."

He left. It took me at least five minutes before I could collect myself and start the day's work.

Chapter 22

During the next week, as I followed the increasing turbulence in the country, I could not help thinking of Paula's prediction that, because of our "floundering," the leisure troubles would spell the doom of CRUPP. There were riots everywhere. Bill Bush phoned me three times a day at least, passing on the President's demand for immediate action. The leisure-work crisis seemed well on its way to becoming the number one political issue in the country — and the election was still a *year* away.

No concert hall, no theater, no art gallery, no museum, no travel bureau, no bowling alley, was immune. Though there was still no firm indication that the rioters were nationally organized, it was becoming harder and harder to believe that all the activities were spontaneous. Each morning I woke up in fear that today some malicious newspaperman would not only intuit the true significance of the riots, but also connect them *causally* with my German past and CRUPP's mission. Each morning I felt the day ahead weighing on me — the Sword of Damocles about to fall. How much time could be left to us in this race against Destiny? For every moment I was still spared I said, like Faust, *Verweile doch! Du bist so schön!* However, time could not be stopped. Now the universities were beginning to be targets. The files of the Institute for the Leisure Studies Program of the College of Social and Behavioral Studies of the University of Southern California in Tampa, Florida, were stolen (and the same thing occurred in similar institutions across America). It seemed a signal for raids on the files of extension and adult education courses right across America.

When early in November, a performance of Carmen at the

142

Metropolitan Opera had to be stopped during the first act — the scene outside the cigaret factory in Seville — because of the chorus of catcalls from the gallery, an editorial appeared in the *New York Times* under the title "The Latest Riot." I read it with my heart in my pants.

"At first glance, the scandalous disruption appeared to be the work of the anti-smoking lobby which has, during the last year, picketed every cigaret factory in America. It seemed only logical that the cigaret factory in Seville, on the stage of the Metropolitan, should be treated in the same fashion. But the evidence by the police after careful interrogation of the ringleaders, points in an entirely different direction. The rioters seem to object to opera as an art form alien to America, that a few elitist 'culture snobs' are trying to force down the reluctant throats of clean-living Americans."

I felt my heart climb slowly back up to its normal position as I read on.

"Such incidents, and the misguided reasoning that leads to them, are an irrefutable sign of the increasing philistinism of American life. Obviously, the prime culprits are our schools and universities. Unless educators radically strengthen their efforts to inculcate into young minds a better understanding of Western values, our cultural life will soon consist of nothing but the ten thousandth re-run of 'I Love Lucy'."

Reverting to its ancient Anglophobia, the *Chicago Tribune* also wrote an editorial about this and similar incidents.

"Many of us cannot conceal a high measure of sympathy for the so-called 'leisure rioters'." (I think this was the first time the term was used in print). "So much of our cultural life — and especially Broadway — has been infiltrated by the British. It is difficult for many Americans to endure this. One cannot anymore go to the theater without being offended by patronizing English accents. When it is not Englishmen who use them, it is sexually suspect Americans trying to ape them. We are fed up, too, and we may well decide to give some rioters a helping hand."

There it was again! "We are fed up" — *wir haben die Nase voll.*

My heart was moving back and forth from my pants like a zipper on a Churchill suit.

143

At one of our staff meetings Soren Andersen, who had cut himself shaving — his girlish chin, probably not much used to a razor, sported a manly gash — posed the question whether anything could be gained by asking the President to make a series of speeches in order to present a correct diagnosis to the nation. We all advised strongly against this.

"I've never heard you talk such b-b-b-bullshit, Soren," stuttered Cedric. This time he had brought an *oliphant* along which (he explained at great length) was the father of the English horn. His Vandyke, usually so well groomed, was a little scruffy today, but in every other respect he was in singularly good form. "The riots are bound to become a hundred times worse if the explanation is brought into the open. Let's count our blessings. We have a good chance of finding a solution if people think it's the Seventh Day Adventists who're behind them. Nobody takes *them* seriously. But if the President dignifies the disturbances by calling them important social phenomena with which the country has to come to grips, we've had it."

The President, however, *did* make an indirect allusion to the true explanation in a speech he delivered a few days later to the American Society of Certified Public Accountants.

"Our opponents have begun to blame the Administration for the leisure riots. The so-called breakdown of civil order is said to be our fault," he said in his rapid-fire delivery. "I must confess I have some trouble following their reasoning. That many people have more leisure than they've ever had before is surely a credit to this Administration. How can we be blamed for the fact that many people don't seem to know what to do with it? Surely, it's one of the good things of being alive in America today that the pursuit of the arts, of the beautiful things in life, of learning and wisdom has, for many millions, become a more important goal in life than the conspicuous display and consumption of wealth. We've come a long way since the measure of a man was his bank account, his town house and his country house, his servants and his wife's jewelry. We should rejoice that we've reached a stage in our civilization — especially here in California — when excessive material possessions have become burdens rather than assets. Who wants to have servants who cost the world, are intrusive and generally limit, rather than extend, our freedom to behave as we wish in our own homes? Who wants to have jewels if the first time you wear them, they mysteriously vanish? To be wise and discriminating in matters that require good taste, has become far more important than being rich. This is *the* great achievement of America, and this Administration deserves at least part of the credit. We have not yet delivered *la dolce vita* to absolutely everyone, but we're working on it! ''

I was not convinced that accountants were the ideal group to give this kind of speech to; however, I had little time to think about this — let alone consult my staff — since that same evening, Governor Barret of California, whom many suspected of wanting the presidential nomination of his party next year, took the President to task. The Governor's speech was remarkable because — without knowing it — he actually put his finger on the reason for the leisure riots.

"What is all this talk about *la dolce vita*? '' he asked, rhetorically. "Does the President not know that most people would die of boredom after the second week? Who wants to lounge around for ever in Lotusland, sipping martinis, and staring at the Sistine Chapel? Let me tell you something, President Roberts. People want work, not leisure. They want interesting, dignified, meaningful work. They don't want to sit around, twiddling their thumbs. As for the leisure riots, it certainly *is* the responsibility of the President to stop them.

"If he doesn't, he'll have plenty of time after next November to exercise his discriminating good taste while he writes his memoirs. The general collapse of traditional values, of which these riots are symptomatic, merely reflect the way his party has been running the country during the last three years. It's no good trying to serve caviar to people who want hamburgers.''

Chapter 23

I found it extremely hard to come to terms with Toshima's bombshell about Mac's lust for Karin's body. It was clearly in CRUPP's
highest interest that the union between the two should be consummated as quickly as possible, so that Mac could be cured at
last. Toshima could then triumphantly finish his report proclaiming
the success of his therapy, and plans could be implemented to
make it available to millions of work-addicted Americans who
desperately needed it. Moreover, I could not imagine how this
nice, over-excited little American boy could out-perform me in
bed. Anyway, Karin had told me often that she liked mellow,
mature men like me to digit with.

However, this was dangerous ground. The risks were tremendous.
What if Mac did rather well? No, impossible! True, Mac was *au
fond* a solid character, even if temporarily deranged, and he had
a mysterious way of coming through. But in this case? I could not
bear to think about it, and yet I could not stop.

When, on the morning of November 29th, Karin called me to
invite me to dinner at her place — our usual formula for initiating
a digiting session — I made up my mind to test her. I just *had* to
know what her reaction would be if Mac conquered his shyness
and made direct overtures to her.

I must add that there had been a noticeable change in her attitude
towards me after I had questioned her about the leak to Jerry Gorham.
I could not explain it at all; I did not really try to analyze it until
after I had those vivid nightmares about her digiting with every member of the CRUPP staff, and betraying me with Jerry Gorham. Yet,
she seemed more clinging, more demanding, more insatiable, than

before. Occasionally, there was even a note of tearfulness quite out of character with the normally business-like, almost casual, computer girl with the incomprehensible vocabulary. This was highly flattering to me, since it suggested that I had in some curious way at last aroused her passion. On the other hand, there was a slightly feverish quality to her performance, which I found fascinating but at the same time a little puzzling.

I accepted her invitation. She prepared a delicious *coq au vin,* and we drank two bottles of Mouton-Rothschild 1975. After that, we digited on her round bed. I must confess I had considerable difficulties with her, since she insisted on the hopper position in which we both had to do it sitting up. I doubt very much whether I could have done it efficiently at the age of twenty, and it struck me as inconceivable that Mac would be able to manage it, but after considerable acrobatic twists and turns, I succeeded at last. However, she did not seem to be entirely satisfied.

"Your cyclic shift requires a little attention," she said afterwards. "I think I will have to give it some intensive scanning."

"Why don't you do that," I said, sighing. Until I wiped my forehead, I did not know how exhausted I was. Then I popped my question. "Perhaps you would prefer doing it with a younger man, Karin? " I asked, my heart beating.

"But, my dear Friedrich, why should I? " she exclaimed vehemently. "You're not tired of me, are you? You don't want to close your loop and decelerate? "

"Of course not," I said, taking her hand and lifting it up to my lips. I always enjoy performing this formal, old-fashioned ritual in bed, and am usually reminded of the old story about the Viennese who when asked by a Berliner why he always kissed ladies' hands, replied, *"Man muss doch irgendwo anfangen! "* (One's got to start somewhere.) "I'm extremely fond of you," I continued. "But I can't help it, sometimes I ask myself why you put up with a fat old man like me! "

"You're impossible, Friedrich," she said, stroking the hair on my chest. "I adore digiting with you. Don't be so sensitive about my criticizing your cyclic shift. It's still better than practically anybody else's! "

147

"Do you really mean that? " I said, deeply gratified.

"I certainly do. I'm very ambitious for you, Friedrich. You're very good already, but I want you to become perfect! "

"If I get a 'satisfactory' on my report card, that's good enough for me," I said, not wanting to rebuff her, but still hoping that I might be able to lower her sights a little. "The truth is I'm a little tired."

"Oh, nonsense, Friedrich," she said. "It's all simply a question of proper resource allocation." There was a pause. "Or are you trying to tell me something? You want to digit with someone else? "

She sounded as though she was going to cry.

"*Of course not*, Karin. How could you think of such a thing? "

"I promise I will zero-eliminate any other number you want to play. I know your control field. Don't you try anything! "

"Oh, Karin," I said, smiling. "I use all my resources to please you. How could I think of anybody else? "

"There's nothing wrong with your resources, Friedrich," she said. "Don't talk yourself into some kind of fixed block field."

"My software is all right," I said. "But at times I admit I worry about my hardware."

"Nonsense, Friedrich. If you stick with me, I'll turn your software into hardware any time, day or night. All you have to do is send me an on-the-fly printout, and I'll turn on my matrix for you."

"You're too sweet," I said.

"As long as you don't go in for any multi-project scheduling," she went on. "I couldn't bear that."

"You have absolutely nothing to worry about," I assured her. "And you? Are you *really* sure you wouldn't like to be entertained by a younger man? "

"Why do you keep asking, Friedrich? I've already said no," she replied, irritably. "I might put the odd man on my one night circuit, but that means nothing."

"I **was** thinking of a man like Mac," I said, swallowing hard. "I understand he's crazy about you."

"Mac? " she said, brightening up considerably.

"A very attractive man, I would think," I continued.

"Well, maybe one digit, but no more," she said firmly. "You wouldn't be jealous, would you? "

"To tell you the truth, Karin, I would. Just a little."

"You're cute, Friedrich," she said, laughing. "All right now. Enough dead time. Let's start again. This time, let's try a vertical feed."

"Oh no, Karin! " I gasped. "I couldn't! "

"Dont be ridiculous! Come on! No excuses! "

Afterwards, it seemed to me that even the most lovingly extensive scanning practices, stretched out over a period of weeks, would not be able to reactivate my permanently enfeebled cyclic shift.

Chapter 24

With Hilde's help — and that of Hilde's many friends on Madison Avenue — Toshima assembled the cream of America's advertising industry to compose two hundred hard and soft sell commercials for use by the three networks, in accordance with the gentlemen's agreement between their presidents and the White House. The deal was negotiated by Bill Bush. It was decided to begin using them on the first of January, after all the Christmas programs were over.

Here I want to make a small digression. You remember that Paula chastised me when we "used" Mac for Toshima's conditioning experiments, and again when Hilde decided to make him the star of her television season. Well, now I had to listen to still another harangue on the subject of "indulging in the old Nazi habit of brutally using human beings for experimental purposes." In my opinion she made far too much of this. Frankly, I did not have any moral scruples about using Mac in the commercials. I told her he was delighted with the assignment, but that made no difference to her. What struck me as far more serious — morally speaking — is that *I* should be associated with the promotion of an activity — mystic communication with the cosmos — which was utterly alien to me. I have absolutely no feeling for religion of any kind, least of all for Buddhism and Hinduism. I don't understand mystic communion. I've never had any, and don't intend to start now. Fortunately, it became clear very early in the game that much of the material had very little to do with religion as such, but rather with a way of life, with a code of ethics. Much of that was perfectly acceptable to me. But I really had difficulties with the mysticism, and felt cheap and dishonest to be a party to its propagation. However, the pressure on the President, and therefore on us, was so strong that, apart from these moral scruples of mine, I had no doubt whatsoever that what we were doing was correct. Especially since none of the alternative solutions — neither Cedric's, Tex's nor Soren's — was ready.

I want to make one further admission. It was not only a matter of my not having any "feeling" for mysticism, I had a positive aversion to it, and I know exactly why. I associate it with the power exuding from Adolf Hitler, and *ein gebranntes Kind scheut das Feuer*. A burnt child shies away from the fire. Just as millions of my countrymen refused to take any interest whatsoever in politics after the war, so I stayed clear of anything I could not see, touch, weigh or calculate.

As for Hitler, I was in his presence only a few times. I never actually shook hands with him — as I told the judges at my de-Nazification tribunal — and I never looked into his eyes. But I have known lots of people who did, and though many of these individuals were perfectly sensible about the world in general, they suddenly lost all equilibrium in this case. They were "bowled over" by that "look," that something, that aura of Destiny surrounding him. Even Göring was, what Americans call, "a sucker for it," and showed his adulation in the silliest ways. When shortly after Hitler's seizure of power in 1933, Göring "requisitioned" a palace in Berlin which used to be the residence of the Prussian Minister of Commerce, he made sure that his drapes were the same color as those in the Führer's *Reichskanzlei*.

There are many theories on how Hitler acquired this power. On one thing all are agreed: he didn't get it by contemplating the void, or by communication with the Higher and Lower Realities.

Personally, I have no doubt that the origin of Hitler's "mystical" power was sexual. More specifically, it was rooted in the need to cover up his sense of sexual inadequacy. When he noticed — early in the game — that the exercise of these powers paid off miraculously well, he worked hard to refine certain techniques which, if anyone else had used them, would have been ludicrous. I myself have tried occasionally to look a person in the eye the way he did — the long, hard, unblinking stare when shaking hands — with singularly little effect. I suppose this is because I do not suffer, the way he did, from an absence of the left testicle.

Yes, when Russian doctors performed an autopsy in 1945, they reported that "the left testicle could not be found, either in the scrotum or on the spermatic cord inside the inguinal canal, or in the small pelvis." It was, I believe, Plutarch who observed that the

151

history of the world would have taken a different course if Cleopatra's nose had been a fraction of an inch shorter.

I have been carried away, I am sorry. People have asked me questions about Hitler so often that I presume an interest. But I was talking about mystical powers, and my profound reservations regarding their use in advertising to combat the leisure riots. I need not stress how desperately important it was that this third effort of CRUPP's hit its target dead center. The tension each day was becoming unbearable. I didn't have to be told by Senator Hollinger in that threateningly urbane manner of his that "next time we'd better succeed! "

The experiment with Mac, though promising, could not as yet be pronounced a clear success and, therefore, it was too soon to contemplate seriously a mass application of Toshima's conditioning therapy. Hilde's television challenge of the Protestant work ethic had, alas, succeeded far too well to be called a success. So everything depended for the moment on these two hundred commercials. Could the Eastern techniques of contemplation and meditation be made sufficiently meaningful to the underemployed affluent middle class to induce their more frustrated members to cease and desist from attacking the Higher Things in Life? Could they be persuaded, by the most effective mass medium of persuasion ever devised by man, to emulate many of their children and commune with Nirvana? Could the methods which have so amply proved their effectiveness be used to turn America into a society devoted to ascetic and spiritual ideals which are basically anti-materialist and, therefore, in a traditional sense, profoundly un-American?

The answer is YES. A thousand times, yes. But once more we proved our point so well, so *superbly* well, that the result was unmitigated disaster. The gold that should have come to us turned into dust and ashes. We seemed to have developed the opposite of the Midas touch.

But let me recount the course of events step by step. On January 1st, the OM-note, which gave our campaign its overall theme — and visual symbol — was struck for the first time on all three networks. OM stands for the Supreme Self, symbolized by the twenty-fourth letter in the Greek alphabet. During the first three days we used Mac's face and Mac's voice in connection with the sight and sound of OM — leaving it at first deliberately obscure that OM was the highest object of meditation.

152

ABC was the first network to clarify the OM mystery, before and after the Jimmy Duggan show, on Tuesday, January 4th. Two women were having coffee in a suburban kitchen. One asked the other, "Do you find yourself getting impatient and irritable with the children for no reason at all? " The other nodded. "The thing to do," the wise one said, "is to try OM as the subject of meditation. Just once a week to start off with. It does wonders for your disposition." Then Mac appeared on camera, with the OM sign. The two other networks used variants of this approach, CBS going as far as to call OM the All-Enlightened One, just after the 7:00 news. Two days later, NBC put on a commercial showing Mac in front of a stately mansion, caressing the shiny hood of a pink Rolls Royce.

"This may be very nice," he said, "but we must turn our backs on worldly things and face that life whose body is the Universe, that Absolute Reality of which no words can tell." Then the OM sign appeared, and the Oscar Levi Comedy Hour began.

By the middle of January it was clear that these commercial spots were making a deep impression. There were Letters to the Editor galore, from one end of the country to the other, praising them as "refreshing," "showing the way to new perceptions," even "revolutionary." Mac's catch-phrase "*I AM NOT, YET I AM,*" first made its appearance on CBS in the afternoon after the soap opera "Edge of Daybreak." Three gurus analyzed and dissected the phrase on a Sunday discussion program, one speaking with a distinct Brooklyn accent.

"No phrase expresses better the secret and paradox of man," he said, to which Guru Number Two replied, in that Anglo-Indian sing-song which normally characterizes the speech of gurus, "Indeed it is a good sign that Americans finally begin to understand the eternal struggle between man's higher and lower principles. At last they're waking up, and there is hope that the lower elements will be conquered after all."

It must have been around January 16th or 17th that Soren Andersen drew my attention to the absence of any news about leisure riots. I am sure I would not have noticed it myself. The newspapers were full of reports from professional "consumerists" who had for so long labored with only moderate success to expose the greed of merchants, and who were now eloquently praising Mac for extolling the virtues of the simple life. But for twenty-four hours, there had not been a single disturbance in any theater, museum or

153

hobby shop. The papers were full of the usual kinds of calamities, but no leisure riots. I marked my dated desk pad for that day with a satisfying 0. However, there were plenty of other developments to worry about.

By the third week of January, the first serious complaints started. They came from the Association of American Jewelers, whose sales had begun to show a marked drop. "What is the purpose behind this extraordinary campaign? " a press release asked. "In the name of some strangely indistinct sect, a new form of socialism is being preached, insidiously invading the living rooms of the nation. Is no one paying attention? We demand an investigation! "

One month after the beginning of the OM campaign, the second phase of the project began. The intention now was not so much to spiritualize American sex mores in one fell swoop, but rather to introduce — slowly at first — mystical concepts into the very heart of family life, i.e. the connubial bed. Always under the OM sign, we saw Mac, posing with a sizeable number of luscious models, demonstrating the cat position, the elephant position, the cobra and zebra positions, doing breathing exercises, jointly with his partners, while standing on his head, etc. The voice-over parts varied greatly, but the unifying theme was the proper use of sexual energy, of concentration and control. Some of the texts — especially the one warning against premature ejaculation — were more explicit than is customary in television commercials.

To say the commercials were "effective" is like saying a nuclear explosion is "effective." They provided a textbook example of the power of the mass media. First, it was noted by a number of observers of the social scene in offices and factories that the subjects of conversation during coffee breaks had changed from the usual sex talk and sex jokes to the themes of *Karma* and Rebirth. Everybody seemed to have been a butterfly or a hyena in a previous incarnation. Metempsychosis was debated on every Main Street of America. Drugstores were filled to the brim with paperbacks on Concentration and Meditation. Mac had done his job. While standing on his head, contemplating the "Lotus" (the symbol of purity, and, according to the dictionary, also of the female sex organ) of some Hollywood starlet, he had swayed the hearts and minds of Americans from coast to coast. After all, nobody could tell that while he did so, he panted for lust of Karin.

There were strong indications that his hard-sell spot announcements were seriously affecting the sexual appetite of Americans. Pornography shops and movie houses were beginning to complain of a dramatic drop in customers. Similarly, the Masters and Johnson sex clinics all over America were suddenly beginning to advertise their services; up to now they'd had long waiting lists of people anxious to invest hundreds of thousands of dollars in "cures" for their various sexual inadequacies, and there had never been any need to solicit patients. Finally, employment agencies all over the country noted a sudden rise of female job seekers, as streetwalkers were thrown on the job market, unable to survive in their normal walk of life, and as call girls were no longer able to following their normal calling.

The sexual drive of Americans was being transmuted into a thousand different ways of "opening the Doors of Salvation," "inverting the Mind's Eye," and seeking "New Exits of the Physical Body."

All this would perhaps have been quite tolerable, had Mac's advocacy of Renunciation and Resignation not challenged every vested interest in the economic status quo. His simple slogans about Virtue and Goodness, Seeking and Finding, his general line that worldly possessions were not needed to attain Joy and Happiness, were absolute dynamite, and there was no doubt in my mind — after all, I had been through this before — that it was only a question of time before the axe would fall.

Towards the end of February, the campaign reached its climax. By now the basic vocabulary was known to every American: people understood what was meant by "The Light," "The Way," "Bliss," by "The Wheel of Life," by "Nothing," in the new context of OM. These were concepts which large sections of the younger generation had, of course, already grasped for years. However, the time had come to zero in on CRUPP's central purpose: to persuade people that it was better to meditate than to work. This frontal attack on the Protestant work ethic was handled with great skill.

The technique used was the oldest in the business: the before-and-after. It was all done visually, with a minimum of words, and a very subtle use of Western and Oriental music.

Before: Mac sitting in an office, dictating to a secretary.

After: Mac, wearing a loin cloth, walking across a meadow.

Before: Mac, supervising a machine shop.

After: Mac, doing nothing, looking out of the window, a contented smile on his lips.

Before: Mac, walking down Wall Street at the height of the rush hour.

After: Mac alone, sitting on a Persian rug, cross-legged.

By now, it was clear that our campaign had triumphantly achieved its objective: there had not been a leisure riot in a whole month! One might have expected the President to call me in to give me my due as the savior of America. Toshima's picture should have graced the cover of TIME. OM should have been declared the official religion of the United States. But it was not to be.

High Finance and Big Business, in holy alliance with the religious establishment, hit back with such unprecedented force that it made the "law and order" binge of the early seventies look like the permissiveness of the sixties. Since all this is still in everybody's memory, I will refrain from relating the events in detail. Everybody remembers, for example, the trumped-up charges laid against two thousand elderly men and women, rounded up near Kansas City, after having been "caught" sitting cross-legged in a field far off the beaten path, meditating. The indictment read that they had "irresponsibly and maliciously contributed to juvenile delinquency." Was it President Harding or President Coolidge who used to say that "the business of America is business"? To judge from the deluge of telegrams we received protesting in the most violent terms our part in the proceedings, from the official complaints lodged by the American Manufacturing Association and Chambers of Commerce in all parts of the country, from the dozens of highly incensed heads of companies interviewed on TV, it had become abundantly clear that we had succeeded — while putting an end to the leisure riots — in throwing a transcendental spanner into the Business of America.

156

Chapter 25

I considered the next meeting of the High Table crucial. I was determined to force Tex Winter, Cedric Douglas-Whyte and Soren Andersen to put their cards on the table.

"We cannot afford shilly-shallying around any longer," I said, in my opening remarks. "If we don't come through this time, this may very well be our last meeting. But I'm not prepared to give up without a damned good fight."

I got nowhere at all with Tex Winter. He just sat there sullenly, making the occasional sarcastic remark, and refused to cooperate. Karin seemed to support him.

"I'm not going to be bullied, Bierbaum," he said in his slow Wyoming voice. "Nobody bullied me at RAND while I did my technological forecasting, and nobody's going to bully me now. I'll let you know when I'm ready. In the meantime, you'll have to include me out."

Soren Andersen was far more elegant in the way he put his position. He was wearing a new sports jacket, exactly the color of his hair, and it suddenly occurred to me that he had beige hair. However, this was not the moment for pleasant little jokes. His position may have been more elegant than Tex's, but it was just as negative.

"I'd very much prefer to wait another week or two," Soren said. "I just don't think this is the right moment, so close to the OM disaster. I *am* ready now, but I believe it would be a mistake to rush into anything at this juncture."

"Can't you tell us roughly what you have in mind, Soren? " I asked.

"Frankly, I'd rather not. I'll tell you in a couple of weeks."

"By then it may be too late, Soren," I said, frowning heavily.

"Well, we'll just have to take that risk," he shrugged.

I noticed that Hilde and Toshima were listening to these exchanges with increasing nervousness, probably because the precariousness of the CRUPP situation was in sharp contrast to the solid and happy relationship that at last had been established between them. The dark cloud threatening CRUPP was clearly a menace to their domestic bliss.

By the way, may I interject a word about the manner in which Toshima finally forgave Hilde, and satisfied her passion for him. One evening, after having worked together on a mystical commercial showing Mac and a young lady from the Bronx assuming the Pose of the Swallow, Toshima invited Hilde home to his place in Richmond, Virginia. After dinner she said she'd like to hear him play the clarinet, but he wasn't in the mood. Since she insisted on hearing some music, he put on a record of Schubert's string quartet *Death and the Maiden*, one of her favorites. During the second movement, their union was consummated.

"He was very much alive," she told me afterwards, "and I was no maiden, but it was the best sex I've had since I was deflowered by a sweet, gentle, mature storm trooper in the Harz Mountains, way back in 1936."

Now, she and Toshima are living together in Richmond.

I am sorry I seem to become more digressive as I approach the calamitous climax of my story. After Soren Andersen declined to present his solution to the leisure riots, I turned to Cedric Douglas-Whyte, my last hope. This time he had brought along a *shawm*, a medieval oboe which — he had explained this to us on the way to the High Table — had *two* reeds and was, therefore, an important step forward in the development of woodwind instruments.

"I'm ready now," he said, beaming, his Vandyke far less scruffy than the last time I had seen it. It was actually positively glistening with eager pride. "Give me the t-t-t-tools and I will deliver the goods! "

Everyone breathed a sigh of relief.

"Tell us about your plan, Cedric," I said, smiling at him bene-volently.

"I will guarantee s-s-s-success," he stammered. "The tide will turn miraculously. We've had our Dunkirk. We've been thrown out of France. Rommel has beaten us in North Africa. I am General Montgomery. Victory is assured."

Victory might be assured, but I wasn't. I was scared. Cedric's confidence reminded me, not so much of General Montgomery as of Hermann Göring, who boasted just before the outbreak of the war, while I was still at the University of Göttingen, that the *Luftwaffe's* air defenses were so complete, "the Ruhr will not be subjected to a single bomb. If an enemy bomber reaches it, my name is not Göring. You may then call me Meier."

Alas, millions did so soon enough.

However, I had no intention of deflating Cedric's ego by reminding him of the dangers of over-confidence.

"All I need," he continued, "is the Sh-sh-sh-Shoreham Hotel for one full day, in about two weeks' time. I will make such a splash that there won't be another leisure riot in the United States for a thousand years."

"How do you intend to proceed? " Karin asked, who, by the way, looked ravishing in a light blue dress.

"I will stage a hellzapoppin', the like of which has not been seen on earth before. I will invite the President, every senator, every congress-man in Washington. I will invite the Supreme Court. Let them bring their wives and children. I will invite the whole world. *Tout le monde.* For the grownups there will be lobsters and California wine. For the children, popcorn and ice-cream. Just give me the green light. The secret of Monty's success was that he always had more tanks than he actually needed. I need a million dollars, that's all."

"Of course, *money* is not the problem," I said grandly. "But what *exactly* do you have in mind? "

"Well, I would have thought it was pretty obvious by now," Cedric

159

said, pulling down the corners of his mouth and stretching out his arms, " that what the United States needs more than anything else is to have the first week of September every year declared National Stimulation Week. There's no other way to crush the all-corroding boredom that's been causing all this trouble."

I would be overstating things if I reported that this suggestion of Cedric's was greeted by an enthusiastic response from one and all. But only Tex openly taunted Cedric.

"I see," he said nastily. "You want to do as much for Stimulation as Brotherhood Week has done for Brotherhood."

Cedric smiled.

"Tell me this, Tex, did CRUPP have anything to do with the launching of Brotherhood Week? Yes? No? Let us not forget who we are! We are the only people who can pull this off. Mark my words. We'll turn America on for seven days a year, and for the remaining fifty-one weeks the country will live off the capital accumulated during that week. A carnival! That's the only way to make life interesting again. The case I will make for this brand new concept will be irresistible. You wait and see! "

"There are other approaches one might take," said Hilde, solemnly academic. "I've never been particularly partisan in matters of drugs, but I would think that in this instance a good case can be made for putting a little marijuana in the water supply. It's after all scientifically established that this is no more harmful than fluoride. Might this not be a more ...hm...economic way to obtain the results that you intend to derive from your National Stimulation Week? "

"Out of the q-q-question," shouted Cedric, more agitated than I had seen him in a long time. "Chemical aids are all very nice in small doses, for special occasions. After all, practically the whole of mankind has used them off and on since time immemorial. But what I'm suggesting is so fundamental that it's *far* beyond their reach."

"Too bad," said Tex, "that Richard Toshima didn't condition the Protestant ethic out of *you!* "

"Enough of this," I intervened, as Cedric was drawing in his breath, to hit back at Tex. "Do we, or do we not, give Cedric the green light? "

160

"We do not," said Tex.

The rest of my staff either abstained, or said why not, Cedric may be right, it may work.

"What do you think, Hilde? " I asked.

"Let's try it," she said. "The country may be ready for it."

"All right," I said. "*In Gottes Namen,* go ahead, Cedric! "

That was my ultimate invitation to Doom and Disaster.

Chapter 26

The CRUPP hellzapoppin' at the Shoreham was divided into two parts, *in partes duas:* the Crush Boredom exhibits in the Regency Ballroom, the Executive Room, Club Rooms A and B, the Tudor Room, the Cabinet Room and the Main Exhibit Hall. The case for National Stimulation Week was made in seven rooms, one devoted to each day. The proposal for Sunday was "put forward" — that was Cedric's term — in the Ambassador Room, for Monday in the Empire Room, for Tuesday in the Palladian Room, for Wednesday in the Blue Room, for Thursday in the Diplomat Room, for Friday in the Forum, and for Saturday in the Heritage Room.

The date was March 14th. I will spare you a detailed account of the hectic preparations, the publicity campaign, the sending out of personal invitations to almost three thousand people, Cedric's euphoria. He went about his business happily singing the tenor part of Orlando Gibbons' madrigal composed, as he told me again and again, in 1612, "very late in the day," with the highly inappropriate verse:

Farewell all joys,
O Death come close my eyes,
More geese than swans now live,
More fools than wise.

When I arrived at the Shoreham around eleven in the morning, the place was crawling with politicians, judges, reporters, celebrity seekers, CRUPP people, women and children, many of whom apparently had already partaken generously of the California wine and lobster, the popcorn and ice-cream, and other goodies offered by CRUPP. I was suffering from a splitting headache and a tight feeling in my stomach, and for that reason did not touch any of the gourmet food and drink liberally displayed in all the foyers and corridors. Even a huge chocolate cake, mounted in the center of the Upper Lobby, with the CRUPP motto *cogitamus ergo sumus* beautifully inscribed, did not tempt me.

The President was not expected until three-thirty in the afternoon, by which time I was determined to be home. Paula refused to come along, on the grounds that she found waxing the kitchen floor more stimulating than any of the *Bull-Scheisse* Cedric was able to dream up.

Douglas-Whyte had recruited a regiment of hostesses from the arts and science faculty of Georgetown University, or rather from among those who agreed to perform their duties topless. Fortunately more than two hundred and fifty well-endowed young ladies were happy to do this. The one who elected to be my shepherdess had pitch-black hair and light blue eyes, was called Susie, and had a father who worked for the Bureau of Standards. Her understanding of her task, which was meagre, bore no relation to her ample physical charms. Another nice thing about her was that she had no idea who I was.

"I hope you don't mind, Susie," I said to her on the way to the Regency Ballroom, "I have time only for the highlights. I have to get back to the office after lunch."

She was very good about this, and did not insist, for example, on my inspecting the Cabinet Room which was devoted to "The World's Greatest Bores." I just caught a glimpse of two large photographs, one of the late Billy Graham, the other — for a moment I thought it was a picture of me — of King Farouk, the last king of Egypt.

Nor did she insist on my visiting a little theater showing old films by the now-forgotten Andy Warhol, who used to specialize in boredom. A film (running time: six hours) about a man asleep was scheduled to start at eleven forty-five.

Susie took me past the Executive Room which looked a little more interesting. Apparently Cedric had asked the cultural attachés of various African countries to come in and explain why primitive people are never bored. We just looked in as a beautiful bearded Nigerian, in a gorgeous silvery costume, said,

163

"Survival isn't boring, is it? If that's the main challenge, who has time to be bored? Then, religious ritual takes a lot of time, and if you're a true believer, that's not boring either. No, sir. We have our problems, but boredom isn't one of them."

Then we passed another room — I think it was the Tudor Room — which had nothing in it but a huge clock, reminding us that every minute that has gone won't come back again. *Tempus fugit.*

Now came Club Room A and Club Room B. We did not go in. Club Room A was an exhibit of the psychiatric case history of a depressed person, and Club Room B of a bored person. The point of the exhibit — Susie read from her notes — was to show the difference. Depressed people usually torture themselves with feelings of guilt and sin. They are very much aware of their unhappiness and suffering. Bored people are just listless and resigned. They lack all appetite for life. At most they can experience thrill, but they are incapable of feeling joy.

Susie read these lines without any expression, as though she were reciting the measurements of an Egyptian pyramid. I was wondering whether she was merely a thrills girl, or whether she was capable of real joy. I was about to pop the question when we suddenly found ourselves in the Regency Ballroom. About a hundred cubicles had been set up, like voting booths, and there were line-ups in front of each.

"We want to help you crush boredom," Susie told me, as she handed me a ticket with the number 4562 on it. "If you stand over here," she pointed to the end of a line, "you'll be called for an interview in one of these booths. It'll just take ten minutes."

"Sorry, Susie. I don't have time for that. But what would they ask me? "

"They'll just try to measure your boredom threshold, your attention span, and all that, and ask you what turns you on. If nothing does, they'll make a few suggestions. It's a positive individual service CRUPP is happy to provide to all its friends."

"That's very nice of them," I said, "let's move on."

My headache was getting worse.

"Just as you like," she said. "Let's wander over to the Main Exhibit Hall then. It's quite a long walk, so brace yourself."

It took us almost twenty minutes to reach it, partly because we were waylaid by dozens of people who all wanted to know what I thought of it all, partly because, in spite of Susie's expert guidance, we lost our way three times. In the V.I.P. Reception Room, where I found Toshima demonstrating the Rosenzweig Boredom Index — a huge machine that looked like an oxygen tank with a tail on it — I ran into Jim Andrews, the Deputy Secretary of the Interior who had been admiring the bust of the bearded Isidor Rosenzweig, the inventor of the index that bears his name.

"This man," said Andrews, "has a Viennese accent: I can see it in his face. Well, Bierbaum, this is a proud day for CRUPP, eh? "

I mumbled something non-committal and allowed Susie to lead me on to what, in the summer, functions as the Starlit Shoreham Terrace, but which now served as a testing ground for people suffering from sensory deprivation. Since it was freezing cold, and even Congressmen's wives wrapped in mink coats were deprived of normal warmth, I doubted whether the tests had much scientific validity. Just as we groped our way out of the Terrace and entered the Bird Cage Walk, I was stopped by Ignace Wienovsky, the Polish ambassador to the US who, with the solemn stiffness typical of old-fashioned Communist officials, congratulated me on "this highly original exhibition," and asked whether CRUPP might be interested in organizing a similar "country fair" in Warsaw, devoted perhaps to another subject, such as the industrial boom in Krakow. I thanked him politely, and said we would certainly be happy to consider it.

At last we found the Main Exhibit Hall. But just as we were about to enter it, I was stopped by Steven Horak, who runs a think tank for the Pentagon in Bismarck, North Dakota.

"Very nice, Bierbaum," he said, his left eye twitching slightly. "A little unorthodox perhaps, but very nice."

"Very kind of you, Horak," I said.

"Should you ever want to sell CRUPP," he continued, "don't

hesitate to get in touch with me. I've been looking for a place in Washington."

"I'll remember, thank you. But I'm afraid I have to rush along. Be seeing you, Horak."

We had to wait in line for a minute or two before being able to enter the Main Exhibit Hall.

"Do you by any chance have anything to do with CRUPP? " Susie asked me.

"Mein Name ist Hase, und ich weiss von nichts," I answered, making it clear to her, perhaps a little obliquely, that I did not wish to discuss the matter.

The Main Exhibit Hall is huge. It has room for two hundred and fifty display booths. They had put up a number of screens, many of them divided into several sub-areas for multi-image and split-screen projections. The noise and the confusion in the room, and the thousands of people present, had a paralyzing effect on me. By now I had a *migraine.*

"I simply can't take all this in, Susie," I said. "Do you think we could just race through? Besides, I'm more interested in the proposals for National Stimulation Week. I'm sure that's more exciting than all this stuff, anyway."

"Just as you like, sir," she said, treating me now a little more like a V.I.P. "I just thought you might like to find out what CRUPP thinks about boredom."

"I do, I do," I said, with mock eagerness.

"All we want to show is that boredom can lead to a lot of trouble. Would you like to come this way? "

Susie took me to a section devoted entirely to old Italian paintings showing Adam and Eve and the expulsion from the Garden of Eden. A recorded voice told us that we would all still be in a state of blissful ignorance if only Eve had been able to stick to her gardening, or consulted Adam about other activities which might have suited her temperament better than eating forbidden fruit. We skipped about a square mile (or so it seemed to me) of exhibits from the earliest history of man right through antiquity, and got stuck in some gruesome place showing the aftereffects of Attila the Hun's visitations: decapitated corpses galore, torn legs and arms, gallons of blood. A cacophonous electronic music track underlined the horror.

"Poor Attila and his Huns were bored," a voice said. "There they were in Outer Mongolia, or wherever they came from, twiddling their thumbs. Suddenly some bright little Hun said, 'Mummy, I have nothing to *do.*' So the Mother Hun asked the Father Hun how to keep the little Hun busy, and one thing led to another, and lo, and behold, the whole lot decided to take their horses and go West."

Another exhibit was devoted to Richard the Third. There were several sub-divisions demonstrating in various ways that Shakespeare had goofed, and that Richard had been a good man, after all. Cedric's handwriting, greatly enlarged, appeared on a big streamer. "Richard would not have put those two little innocent princes in the Tower, had he been able to avail himself of sound advice on suitable alternative occupations. He did it only because he was bored."

Another noteworthy booth depicted the fateful activities of Christopher Columbus. In the center of the exhibit was a replica of his tomb in the cathedral of Cuidad Trujillo in San Domingo.

"Had Columbus obeyed his father's wishes," we learned, "and stuck to the family business of weaving, none of the horrors that followed his discovery of America until this very day would have happened. But he was bored at home in Genoa. His career provided one of the best examples of the catastrophic effects of boredom."

We rushed on, passing an area devoted to the brilliant but bored family of the Borgias who took to corruption and murder. We had a quick look at Joan of Arc.

"CRUPP," a recorded announcement said, "could have provided sounder voices than those which impelled her towards misguided political action, merely because she was bored looking after her father's sheep in Domremy."

The exhibit about Charles I and Oliver Cromwell made the point that these two men could easily have lived in peace with one another, if only they had known how to make *meaningful* use of their spare time.

The Napoleon exhibit consisted mainly of film montages and still pictures projected concurrently on large screens.

"This volcano of a man," the commentary read, "exemplifies a type whose gargantuan energies and brain power were misdirected on a monumental scale. The world would have been spared the calamitous consequences of his boredom had he been able to benefit from CRUPP's stimulation techniques while still at an impressionable stage, such as during the period he went to the cadet school in Brienne."

Cedric had taken care to single out only the more glamorous names to make his points, but even so he presented a substantial collection of villains, each one propelled into villainy by an unresolved boredom problem. He went to town on Jack the Ripper and Rasputin, on the two Serbian assassins who killed Archduke Ferdinand in 1914 in Serajewo, and devoted a whole aisle to the crimes of Stalin, who "like all homicidal psychopaths should either have been allowed by his compatriots to grapple with his internal difficulties within the confines of a prison, or have subjected himself to a systematic course on how to use his mind and senses to obtain far deeper satisfactions than those available to him through mass murder and mass destruction."

At last we got to the Nazi section. Again, Cedric had made ingenious use of film, juxtaposing, for example, Leni Riefenstahl's *Triumph of the Will* with newsreels of Belsen and Auschwitz. A loudspeaker blared forth the *Horst Wessel Lied.*

"Let's go on," I said to Susie.

"Are you sure you don't want to see this? " she asked, looking at me as though I had a disreputable reason for a quick escape.

"Susie, I *told* you I didn't have much time."

"You're German, aren't you? " she asked, suspiciously.

"What's *that* got to do with it? " I asked, loftily.

"I was just wondering, that's all," Susie said, frowning.

"All right," I exhaled a deep sigh. "Let's get it over with fast."

There were big photographs of all the Nazi leaders except Göring. In each case there were captions telling us what good things they might have achieved, if only they had been able to overcome their boredom. Hitler might have become a third-rate architect, for example, Himmler a manufacturer of health foods (he was an early health food nut), Goebbels an advertising tycoon, Streicher a pornographer, and so on.

"Where's Göring? " I asked Susie.

"Where's who? "

"Never mind. May I go now? "

"Yes, sir."

Just as I was leaving, I caught sight of a large oil painting which I had never seen before. It showed an idealized Göring on horseback, dashing and handsome, in a white and gold uniform glittering with decorations. My first thought was how much Göring would have liked it.

I looked at the portrait, transfixed. Susie stopped too, looked back and forth from the portrait to me, then asked suddenly, "Is that man your father? "

"Of course not," I said, trying not to show how flattered I was that she should ask.

"That's good, " she answered. "He sure looks ridiculous. Who is he, anyway? "

"Ridiculous? " I asked, deeply stung. "That's Hermann Göring, the man I asked you about just now."

"Never heard of him," she said, her voice indicating she didn't want to, either.

What was wrong with the girl? With breasts like that, a little Tan-Quick, and a plate of fruit, she might have been a Nubian slave. But this younger generation had no feeling for high style, for grandeur. They thought anybody who was above average was phony.

She looked at me through narrowed eyes. "That picture looks like a whiskey ad. Don't tell me you like it."

"I do," I replied, a little defensively. Was there any point in telling her that Göring's imposing face might have been painted by Velasquez, the uniform by Titian, the horse by van Dyck, and that the whole composition reminded me of — now, what was the name of the court painter of Louis Quatorze? "An excellent picture," I said. "What a brush stroke," I added, pointing at the horse's behind.

Susie shrugged, dismissing me — and Göring — as hopeless. I took another close look at the picture, and then something curious happened. For the first time in my life it struck me — like a flash — that perhaps, after all, Paula had been right all along, and that Göring was nothing but an empty-headed buffoon, but I dismissed the possibility immediately.

"Let's go on," I said impatiently.

"Just a second," Susie had a sudden thought. "What I want to know is, why did they put that picture in a special place? "

"That's a very good question, Susie," I replied. "Perhaps you should ask Mr. Douglas-Whyte." What game was Cedric playing? Didn't he know that all over Washington knives were being whetted to stab CRUPP, and above all, its founder and president, Friedrich (Göring) Bierbaum, in the back?

Probably he was just being playful, that's all.

Susie was still looking at the picture, shaking her head in disbelief, when someone tapped me gently on the shoulder. It was Mac, looking terrible.

"Have you been to the Stimulation Area? " he asked me. "It's quite something," he added, shaking his head.

"Oh, really? "

"Of course, you'll have to judge for yourself," he said quickly.

"Susie is going to take me there right now."

"How do you do, Susie," Mac said politely, apparently not

noticing that she was most deliciously topless. Was he still fixated on Karin's charms?

"How do you like it so far? " Mac asked me.

"Very interesting," I said, cautiously.

"That comes from the Latin," Susie explained, brightening. "*Inter esse.* Being between." She glanced at her notes. "We find the things interesting that come between us and the Void."

"Quite right, Susie," I said avuncularly.

"You haven't by any chance seen Karin? " Mac asked.

So he was still obsessed.

"No, I'm afraid not," I replied. "But I'm sure she must be around somewhere. You don't look very well, Mac."

"I'm sure I'll be all right," he said bravely.

"You know, Mac, you should get back to your violin and your Tolstoy. You told me the other day these were the only things that interested you now."

"I'll never touch any of that stuff again," he answered vehemently. "I'm thoroughly fed up with it. If you want the truth," he looked suddenly as if he were about to cry, "*I want my job back.* I want to get back to Jupiter Aircraft."

I groaned inwardly. So Toshima had failed utterly. The pendulum had swung full circle.

"Then there's something else," he said, lowering his voice and biting his lips. "I don't know whether anybody told you, but I'm crazy about Karin Hamsun."

I was not prepared for such an open confession, and was completely stumped. Should I make light of it? Say I was sorry? Tell him that I would put in a good word for him? Warn him that she would eat him alive?

"Yes, I've heard about that," I said after a pause. "I'm sure you'll get over it," I added stupidly. "But let me ask you about Jupiter. Won't it be a little difficult to get back? I understand they don't need you anymore."

He gave me a bitter smile.

"I'm a celebrity now. Things have changed."

"Of course! " I exclaimed. "They're bound to take you back! How could I have been so dense not to have thought of that! Well, good luck, Mac! "

"Thank you, Mr. Bierbaum."

Susie did not hear my name, or if she did, did not recognize it.

"Are we ready now for the Stimulation, sir? " she asked, a little impatiently. "You said you were in a hurry."

We made our way through the milling crowds of politicians, judges, reporters, wives and children, to the West Lobby, while Susie explained the concept to me.

"You see, CRUPP proposed that the first week of September be declared National Stimulation Week. Every year from now on. And that on each day of the week the same things happen."

"I'm sorry I don't understand you, Susie."

The noise and my throbbing headache made me hard of hearing.

"Well, you see, sir, CRUPP has worked out a pattern for the Week. Sunday is for spiritual stimulation. Monday for mental stimulation. Tuesday to train visual perception. Wednesday is reserved for the ears, Thursday for smell and taste, Friday for the sense of touch, and finally, Saturday for sex. Do you follow me? "

"That's very ingenious, isn't it? " I said, trying to absorb this information, and wondering whether Cedric had forgotten an important sense which, thanks to his possible carelessness, would be doomed to remain unstimulated — in the United States, at least — for the rest of time.

"But how does CRUPP propose to do this? I mean, this is merely a suggestion, isn't it? What is there to show? "

Susie smiled knowingly.

"You'll see, sir," she said, wagging her breasts.

We had arrived at the Ambassador Room. At the door it said in bright red letters SUNDAY.

We entered. The usual Muzak had been turned off, and we heard the pure vocal lines of a Palestrina *motet.* The people in the room observed silence, as in church. Only the topless hostesses talked.

"You see this picture? " Susie asked. Her breasts perked up.

I had not noticed that on the east wall there was an enormous reproduction of Michelangelo's *Last Judgment.*

Susie consulted her notes.

"To stimulate our tired spirits," she read, "we have to learn once again what comes naturally to children, a feeling of awe towards the Great Mystery that is Creation. This is what is meant by spiritual stimulation. We must cease to be so *blasé.* No longer must we take everything for granted. That is why the damned in this picture — if you look more closely, sir — have the features of worldly contemporary types, of which America is all too full."

I stepped closer towards the picture. Indeed, photographs of ordinary urban Americans — businessmen, accountants, druggists, salesmen — had been superimposed on the faces of the Damned.

I moved to the other side, to see what Cedric had done with the Saved. I suppose it was predictable, but the types he had selected for *them* were people close to Nature, farmers, florists, explorers, scientists, Eskimos, children, birdwatchers and cross-country skiers.

"I suppose we're lucky," Susie said conspiratorially. "*Our* pictures aren't on either side of the ledger."

I didn't feel like embarking on a theological discussion, being more interested in the activities that were scheduled for Friday and Saturday, than those intended for the solemn and chaste Sunday.

173

"Let's move on to Monday," I said.

We made our way to the Empire Room. It was livelier. Cedric's ideas of mental stimulation were — how typical! — parlor games. On one side of the room there were little cubicles in which people were deeply absorbed in playing "Twenty Questions," "Charades," and diverse variations of games from the daytime television repertoire. On the other side, there were bridge and chess tournaments. Solitary tables were reserved for crossword puzzle addicts, and people playing solitaire.

I was interested to note that he carefully avoided any suggestion of self-improvement. Mental stimulation, he implied, does not consist of learning *new things*, but of making the best of what you have.

I cut short my visit to the Palladian Room, which was devoted to Tuesday's exercises in sharpening visual perception. Obviously this was an area where Cedric was not at his best. One section of the room was an exhibit of optical instruments, another a display of French impressionists. A special corner was reserved for a marvelous painting of a field of poppies by Monet, loaned, the credit said, by the Louvre.

"I want you to pay particular attention to this picture," Susie said.

"It's very nice. I'd love to have it," I replied. "I'm getting a little tired of my abstract expressionists in the dining room. Let's move on."

"Please, sir, please." Now Susie had a pleading look on her face. Her breasts sagged badly. "Please, how would you describe the color of these poppies? "

"Red," I said.

"Aha," Susie said, cheering up considerably. "You only say this because you're not a beetle. A beetle can't see red. It can only see ultra-violet. And we can't see ultra-violet. Our sense of color is very imperfect, and we have much to learn."

"No doubt that's true," I said, studying her, wondering if she would be as tireless as Karin.

174

"And did you know," she continued, glancing quickly at the notes Cedric had provided, "that our word *idea* comes from the Greek verb *idein* — to see — which, via the Latin *videre*, is related to the German *wissen*, to know. This is because people used to believe that we can only know the things we can see."

"No, I did not know that," I said indulgently. How could Cedric hope to crush boredom when he was being so boring himself?

I found the Blue Room, devoted to Wednesday's stimulation of our sense of hearing, a little more interesting. The room was completely silent. It was subdivided into about a hundred sound-proof booths, fully equipped with computerized sound equipment. I suddenly remembered that Cedric had asked Karin for technical advice. On arrival, each visitor was asked whether he was musical or not. If he said yes, he was directed to a booth where he was asked to listen to Indian music, or Laotian music, with its quarter tones and unfamiliar rhythms. Then he had to fill out questionnaires. The unmusical customers were asked to identify exotic nature sounds. An appeal was made to them to train their hearing up to the level of bats, whose radar equipment enables them, by catching reflected sound waves, to distinguish, for example, a piece of paper from a piece of velvet, and who can accomplish with their ears what we accomplish with our eyes.

"Let's skip Thursday," I said to Susie. "I have a very good sense of smell and taste. It requires no stimulation, thank you."

"Oh, but you must have a quick look at the Diplomat Room," she insisted.

I had expected the atmosphere of a cooking school, or a perfume factory. (I had once visited one in Grasse, in the South of France.) But it wasn't that at all. Cedric's intention was to make us feel inferior to animals, most of whom have an infinitely better developed olfactory sense than we have.

"But we can do much better, if we put our shoulders to the wheel," the prepared text read. "The world is full of smells and tastes hither-to monopolized by the lower species. Snails and earthworms attract their mating partners solely by relying on their sense of smell. Will we ever be able to do the same? "

"I'm ready for Friday," I said to Susie, suddenly feeling like a schoolboy when the bell rings at the end of a class. "I think my sense of touch requires a little attention."

She took me by the arm — it was the first time she had touched me — and we made our way to the Forum. It was — at first sight — a huge gym class. The floor was covered with soft Persian carpets, and on it there were various combinations of senators, wives, congressmen and hostesses engaged in various forms of sensory awakening. There was soft music, and the voices were subdued. In one corner strange figures were moving around: walking bed-sheets, like Bedouins, only their faces were completely covered.

"What are *they* doing? " I asked Susie.

"They can do anything they like, provided each person stays under his — or her — own sheet. They may touch and explore anybody. Want to try it? "

"Not just yet," I answered.

"Would you like to get to know my face? " Susie asked.

"That would be nice."

"Then close your eyes."

She guided me slowly through the exercise, allowing my hands to examine every soft nook and cranny of her delectable face. I found it highly erotic.

"Now I shall do it to you," she said once I had finished. "I shall want to remember you in my finger tips."

While she examined me, she gave me a short lecture.

"The purpose of these experiments," she said, "is to bring us back to our senses, to relax and release tension, to become aware again of our bodies and personalities, so that we can better realize all the possibilities in each one of us."

When she had finished, my headache was gone.

"That was very nice, Susie," I said. "Thank you."

"Thank *you*," she said. "Once CRUPP's idea is accepted, the whole of America will do these things every first week in September. But of course to learn it properly requires patience and awareness. We have to learn to be comfortable with one another. Are you comfortable with me, sir? "

"Very," I replied, wondering wistfully what was in store for the two of us on Saturday night.

"Let's wander about a bit," she said. Susie took me by the hand, and guided me through the room, neatly sidestepping groups of people lying on the floor slapping one another, or pretending to be rabbits and elephants. A few elderly couples were facing each other and pressing their palms together, eyes closed. I overheard one blonde hostess saying to a heavily made-up and bejeweled society woman, "I think you will find this very useful when you do the dishes. You'll become aware of the temperature, the shapes, the textures, the bursting soap bubbles, in an entirely new way. It's better than sex, I assure you! "

"I *never* do the dishes," the lady replied indignantly.

"You should, you should," the blonde said.

"Very interesting," I said, chuckling, and thinking of Paula.

"I believe we're ready now for Saturday," Susie said. "Or do you have to rush back to the office? "

"No, Susie," I smiled. "I think I can squeeze Saturday in."

I am sure it was no coincidence that Cedric had chosen the *Heritage* Room for his sex show.

But as soon as we arrived at the door to it, I exclaimed, "Oh, my God, Cedric, what have you done! "

"I beg your pardon? " Susie asked.

"Never mind."

The room was almost completely dark. What light there was came in various colors — predominantly red and blue — from concealed sources on the floor. Hanging from the ceiling there were about

177

fifty beds, some ordinary double beds, others huge round ones —
ten times the size of Karin's. And on these beds there were hundreds
of figures making love, in all combinations, boys with girls, boys
with boys, girls with girls, groups of three, four, six, eight and more.

At first, it seemed that these were real, live people. But aware of
the puritan restrictions of the American middle class, Cedric had
procured, for the purpose of this exhibit, *wax figures* which, thanks
to a most sophisticated mechanical device, he carefully animated.
They performed the motions of love in accordance with a computer
program worked out by Professor David Davidovitch, who had made
headlines a few months previously when he was dismissed by NASA
in Houston because he designed two space ships, one in the form of
a male sex organ, the other in the form of a female one, which would
harmoniously fit together when rendezvousing in orbit.

"Do you like it? " Susie asked sweetly.

"My God, my God," I groaned. *"Pereat mundus! "*

"What was that again? " she asked, probably thinking that I had said
something obscene.

"Let the world perish! " I translated. Suddenly a terrible thought
struck me. "What's the time? When is the President due? "

Susie looked at her watch.

"It's three twenty-five," she said. "The President will be here in five
minutes."

"I must run," I exclaimed. I kissed Susie on the forehead, and made
my exit through the Calvert Street entrance, just managing to avoid
the presidential limousine which I saw driving up Connecticut Avenue.

President Roberts stayed only forty-five minutes, so that both he and
I were spared the most damaging leisure riot in the history of the
United States.

It began at 5:10 p.m. Forty-five tear gas bombs were thrown into the
Regency Ballroom, the Executive Room, Club Rooms A and B, the
Tudor Room, the Cabinet Room, the Main Exhibit Hall, and each of
the seven rooms devoted to National Stimulation Week. Thirty-five
congressmen, nine senators, five Supreme Court judges, and twelve

members of the CRUPP staff, including Cedric who was — according to eyewitness reports — chanting his favorite verse from the Orlando Gibbons madrigal "Farewell all joys, O death come close my eyes" — as well as Mac — were among the four hundred people who were taken by ambulance to the Walter Reed Hospital from which, fortunately, they were all released the next morning.

One extraordinary and entirely unexpected thing came out of this otherwise complete disaster. Mac and Karin found themselves in the same ambulance half way to the hospital. Karin recovered from the effects of the gas much more quickly than he. I shall never know whether it was because she was sorry for Mac, who was white as a sheet and trembling all over, or whether it was simply "Frailty, thy name is woman," but she decided then and there to put him — as she had told me she was prepared to do — on her "one shot circuit." Just before arriving at their destination, she pressed her body against Mac's, and invited him to a digiting session for the following night.

Mac arrived at the hospital in a catatonic state.

Chapter 27

Two days later, on March 16th, I was summoned to Senator Hollinger's office.

Just as I was about to leave the house, the telephone rang. It was Mac. His voice sounded faint.

"I'm sorry, Mac," I said. "I don't have much time now. Do you think you could phone tonight? "

This was not the time to listen to Mac rhapsodizing about his *nuit d'amour* with Karin.

"That's all right, Mr. Bierbaum," he said. "I won't keep you now. I just wanted to ask you not to believe any rumors you might hear about me and Karin."

"Oh? "

"In the end, I couldn't do it to my wife. I guess I'd just made up the whole thing in my mind. Daydreaming, you know. It's all over. I feel much better now."

"Good! " I said, trying to hide my incredulousness. These Americans! I will never understand them.

"There's another thing I wanted to say, Mr. Bierbaum," he went on, his voice firmer now. "I'll stick by you, whatever happens. You can always count on me."

"That's very nice of you, Mac," I said, touched. "I may hold you to it."

Paula is right. They are like children — adorable children.

"Good luck, Mr. Bierbaum."

Senator Hollinger's Cary Grant face was in deep mourning when he received me. He looked at me as though my mother, father, wife and seven children had perished in a hurricane, and he had to break the news.

"My dear Bierbaum, I am so very sorry about all this, and I want you to know what an agony this has been for me, as it must have been for you," he said, lighting a cigar.

"These are the times that try men's souls," I sighed.

"I'm afraid all my fears have come true," he continued behind the blue smoke rings. "The President has told me that in the circumstances it will not be possible to continue his relationship with CRUPP under its present management."

"I see." I was amazed to note how well I took this.

"Now, Bierbaum, since our work at CRUPP has been built around the White House connection in recent years, I have no doubt you will want to hand in your resignation."

I thought this over for a minute.

"Before I do so, Senator," I said, "I would like to know in what way you consider me personally responsible for our recent misfortunes. After all, I need hardly say that it wasn't me who threw the tear gas the other afternoon, that indeed certain experiments — like the series of commercials — have succeeded beyond our wildest hopes."

"My dear Bierbaum," the Senator said expansively, "no one in his right mind would think that *you* have failed. That would be quite absurd. However, from the beginning of this leisure project I have detected — how shall I put it? — a lack of sound judgment which has been responsible for what you call your recent misfortunes."

"What you, Senator, call unsound judgment, I call bad luck. At any stage of our project we might have succeeded, in which case you would have been the first to congratulate me, as you have done on so many occasions in the past."

181

"But you're like a general who has lost a battle. Since we still need the army, we have to change generals. We need CRUPP; therefore, we will have to give you up. You will have to be replaced."

Per deos immortales! Quod abominor!

"And by whom, may I ask? "

The handsome, bronzed, polished senator looked me straight in the eye and said, "By Tex Winter."

"You're not serious," I whispered, a dark blue pain seizing the pit of my stomach.

"Absolutely. A first-class man, as you yourself have told me many times. He is the right man, in my view, to restore confidence in CRUPP. In no way has he been compromised by our recent ....'misfortunes'."

"And you've talked to him? " I asked, my lips trembling.

"Dr. Winter has agreed."

"*Dieses Arschloch*," I wanted to say. It's the worst term of abuse I can think of in my native language.

"And suppose I refuse to resign? "

"Then we will have to make use of those clauses in our contract which entitle us to dismiss you."

"Well," I said quickly, without my usual calm deliberation, "dismiss me, then! "

"I think, my friend, you had better think this over. For the moment I would like to keep this question open. In any case, you will have your hands full preparing your defense before the Special Senate Committee that's been set up to investigate you."

I looked blank.

"Oh, you haven't heard? " the Senator asked in that nauseatingly cultivated voice of his. "I wouldn't worry too much about it, Bierbaum. These things are very much routine in Washington. Still, inevitably, it will take a good deal of your time. You realize, of course, that you can always count on me to help you in any way I can. I can lay my hands on a good deal of information you may find useful. The President and I are, naturally, very much interested in your presenting as good a case as possible. I have no doubt you will acquit yourself with great distinction."

"Thank you, Senator," I said, "Thank you very much."

Selig, wer sich vor der Welt
Ohne Hass verschliesst.

Happy is the man
Who withdraws from the world
Without hatred.

* * *

Paula was peeling potatoes in the kitchen when I told her.

"*Nette Leute sind das,*" she commented. Lovely people.

"Is that all you can say? " I asked.

"What else is there to say? *Mit der Dummheit kämpfen Götter selbst vergebens.*" Even the gods fight in vain against stupidity.

"And you don't mind if I have to retire and twiddle my thumbs? "

"Why should I mind? " she said calmly, continuing her peeling operation. "You can help me fix the roof. Besides, you can take up the violin, like Mac."

"*Gutes Kind,*" I said, kissing her wrinkled forehead.

"Do you know something? " she went on, ignoring my compliment. "I'm sure that Swedish morsel has something to do with all this."

"Why do you say that? " I asked.

"I don't know," she said quietly. "Intuition, I guess."

At this moment the telephone rang. It was Tex Winter. Could he come and see me?

183

The gall! The last thing I wanted was to receive that *Arschloch* in my house.

"I have to go back to the office after dinner," I said, my voice as steady as I could make it. "If you insist, I'll spend a few minutes with you there."

"That's fine," he said.

"Let's say eight-thirty. All right? "

"Perfect," he said.

"What are you going to say to him? " Paula asked, still concentrating on her potatoes.

"I'm going to award him the Iron Cross, First Class," I replied sweetly.

He arrived five minutes early. I thought his freckled face was a little paler than usual, and his sandy-colored hair more disheveled.

"You wanted to see me, Tex? " I asked directly, without a smile, without a word of greeting.

"I wanted to see you *before* your interview with the Senator, but I timed it badly. I understand you have been informed."

He spoke slowly, as usual, with that Wyoming drawl. There was nothing particularly defensive or sheepish in his tone. If anything, it was self-righteous.

"Yes, Tex, I've been informed," I said, deliberately avoiding any touch of self pity.

"I think you had it coming to you, Bierbaum," he said sharply, aggressively — quite out of character. Normally, this cowboy with a PhD is calm and restrained, occasionally sarcastic, and I had never heard him speak so rudely before.

"I did? " I asked, raising my eyebrows.

"Oh, for Christ's sake, man," he went on attacking. "You've allowed this thing to go completely *wild*! I'm not going to blast my colleagues, while they're not here to defend themselves, but all

I can say is that none of them has done a decent day's work since this leisure thing started. It's a bloody disgrace."

"And *you* have," I said, feeling my gall rising.

"I've already said more than I wanted to say about *them*. It's really immaterial." He shrugged. "What's material is that *you* have completely abandoned any kind of critical leadership. From the beginning you haven't understood what this thing is about. You've allowed your staff to play games with the Protestant ethic, with television, with Buddhism — *Buddhism, my ass!* — you've encouraged them to indulge themselves to their hearts' content, while all the time the ship has been sinking. And now that it's sunk, you don't know that it's *you* who pulled the plug, if you will allow me to mix a metaphor."

"You're out of your mind," I said, my heart pounding.

"Tell me this, Bierbaum. Do you know *why* we're having leisure riots? "

"If I did, I wouldn't have commissioned all this work. It's not my job to *know* these things. It's my job to find them out."

"Please, please, don't play the non-intellectual promoter, the administrator who doesn't have to know anything. You know plenty. But on *this* you have failed, and the Senator was quite right when he said you have to take the consequences."

"And, of course, *you* know what's been the trouble all along? "
I said, nastily.

"As a matter of fact, I do," he replied, deadly serious. "America has lost its sense of community. Everybody's out for himself. Things are not going to improve until people learn to share their good luck and their misery. We must transform all the outworn habits of thought which have turned Americans into tools of imperialism and materialism. Only then will they once more have a sense of purpose. That's what's lacking now, and that's why we're having these riots."

"Oh, I know. I know. If we only loved one another...." I sighed.

"You're old, Bierbaum. The world belongs to us young people — we who are in the bloom of life like the sun at eight or nine in the morning."

185

What the hell was he quoting, I wondered. "Like the sun at eight or nine in the morning." I searched my mental anthology of quotations, but drew a blank.

"You had your chance to make your views known at the High Table. Why didn't you? "

"I told you the other day I was working on a paper about all this. But the level of our discussions recently has been so abysmally low that I didn't see how my ideas could fit in. They did not involve renting the Mayflower Hotel and a bunch of bottomless girls."

"There are many ways," I said, still furious, "in which you could have made your views known without going to Senator Hollinger and stabbing me in the back."

"I didn't go to him. We met at a party. He asked me a few questions, and I told him what I thought. I was quite sober and so was he. I have no reason to apologize to you for anything."

I was so angry with him, so hurt and indignant, that I can't remember exactly how the conversation ended. His tone of moral superiority, his arrogant self-assurance, made me heartsick with frustration and helplessness. I think I just said to him, "Look Tex, I think you'd better leave me alone now," and he went, without another word.

The next morning Mac and his wife came to see me, both looking wonderful.

"We just thought we should tell you how terrible we feel about all this," he said.

"Mac's been so upset," Mrs. MacIntosh added, reminding me more than ever of an astronaut's wife.

"We've all been trying so hard," Mac said. "I don't know why we've had such lousy luck all along."

"I don't understand it either," I said. "You've certainly done all you could."

"We all have," he went on. "I myself have some ideas on how to handle the riots. But I don't suppose this is the time to tell you what they are? "

186

"I'd like to hear them, of course," I replied. "But you're right. At the moment I'm busy preparing myself for the Senate hearings."

"I quite understand, Mr. Bierbaum. Anyway, I thought I should tell you that I have very good news."

"You have? "

"I'm back at Jupiter Aircraft. I hoped they would take me back now that I'm famous. And they did."

"Oh, I'm glad," I said. "I really am."

And I really was.

"You can imagine how pleased I am," Mrs. MacIntosh said. "We have a lot to be grateful for. Grateful to you, I mean."

"Not at all," I said. "Mac worked hard. In fact, everything he's achieved, he's worked for." It wasn't until I said it that the irony struck me.

"He certainly has," she said, looking lovingly at her husband.

"And to think that it all started with my writing 'Fuck you' on that dinosaur's behind," he said.

Mrs. MacIntosh seemed a little embarrassed as he said that.

"I've forgiven him long ago," she remarked softly.

"It's difficult to describe what made me do that. Now I'm appalled by what all those rioters are doing. I understand them, but I'm appalled. Destroying all those lovely things! We've got to put a stop to it. We've simply got to."

"I don't see what more we can do," I said, "now that they've pulled the rug from under us."

"The Reverend Andersen has still to be heard from," Mac said. "Maybe he has a good answer."

"We'll have to wait and see," I said. "It's probably too late to save the situation."

187

"Where there's life, there's hope," volunteered Mrs. MacIntosh valiantly.

* * *

There's only one interesting thing to be said about my last meeting of the High Table, when I formally announced my resignation and handed the reins of office to my successor, Tex Winter. It was a lugubrious occasion, but everybody — including Tex — made a monumental effort to behave well and get it over with fast. The one interesting thing was Cedric Douglas-Whyte's speech. Here's an extract:

"....We certainly touched a nerve at the Sh-Sh-Sh-Shoreham. By Jove, we have. We sure made our point! Boredom is now on everybody's lips. *Of course*, they'll try to crucify us for what we've done; we're not the first ones to be crucified for pointing the finger at something no one's been willing to admit. I have a favorite Masai proverb that will take care of this situation. 'The mouth that ate fat shall eat e-e-excrement and that which ate e-e-excrement shall eat fat'...."

Chapter 28

On the morning of March 18th — I think it was a Tuesday — Bill
Bush phoned me. I had not spoken to him since before the
Shoreham disaster.

"The President feels we should spill the beans at the Senate hearing," he said cheerfully.

"I'm afraid I don't understand," I said.

"He thinks this is the perfect time for you to make the opposition
look stupid."

I hesitated for a moment, remembering the President's fervent
assurances that he would not dream of ever using CRUPP — an
independent scientific institution — for partisan political purposes.

"CRUPP's job is to discover the truth," I said loftily, "not to make
anybody look stupid. Anyhow, what does the President mean by
spilling the beans? "

"He thinks he should engage in the ancient game of one-upmanship,
and steal the thunder from the Opposition."

"Forgive me, Bill, I'm still not with you." What *was* he talking about?

"They've been saying all along that the leisure riots were caused
by drug addicts, Communists, the women's lib, religious fanatics
and whatnot. Well, we know better, don't we? "

"We certainly do," I agreed.

"Well, let's take the offensive and make mincemeat of them. That's what he means."

"I see," I said, thinking this over for a minute. "That's a good idea."

"He thought you'd go for that. We won't be able to get you your job back, but at least you'll get some brownie marks for good thinking."

"Does Senator Hollinger know about this plan? " I asked.

"He's been told. He'll play along."

"Relations between him and me are somewhat strained," I announced.

"Don't worry about him, Friedrich. The President knows how to handle him. All the strings will be pulled at the White House. By the way, are you going to the reception at the French Embassy tonight? "

"No. What reception? "

Normally I tried to avoid the Washington diplomatic cocktail circuit, except if I had strong business reasons.

"Oh, it's just an ordinary reception in honor of some visiting fireman. But I think it might be a smart move to be seen in high places at this time. Can't do any harm. You never know who might be there. Wouldn't be a bad idea to corner the Minority Leader of the Senate, and have a word or two with him."

"All right, Bill, I'll go."

I did not meet the Minority Leader of the Senate. The reception was of momentous importance to me for an entirely different reason.

I arrived late. This didn't matter, since it was one of those huge affairs. There must have been more than two hundred people in the room. No one paid much attention to me after I had passed through the reception line. I saw a few familiar faces, and one or two people recognized me, but this was not my world. I knew the German ambassador and his wife, but they had never cultivated me, and I saw no reason to run after them. A number of other ambassadors — such as the Yugoslav and the Greek — I had had professional dealings with during the last three years or so had come, and we exchanged courtesies. Of course Bill Bush was there, busy as a bee. I was trying to think up some suitable Wilhelm Busch quote with which to embarrass him. Did he have a family? I had no idea. Suppose he was recently married, I would try this on him:

Vater werden ist nicht schwer,
Vater sein dagegen sehr.

Becoming a father is not difficult,
Being one, however, very.

As I was pondering this, I heard a heavily accented voice.

"Mr. Bierbaum? "

I turned around and looked at a face that seemed vaguely familiar.

"My name is Lermontov, Boris Lermontov," the face said.

Of course! The Russian ambassador, famous all over Washington for being a great wit and a great flirt. He was the best-dressed man in Washington (he had all his clothes made in Italy). He was very much part of the new Russian diplomacy: the grimmer the Chinese, the gayer the Russians. The Chinese had been very grim lately. So far my record as a non-fraternizer of Bolsheviks had remained virginally clean, and I saw no reason to be particularly friendly now. But it wasn't the liveliest party, and there was no reason for me to be unduly rude, either.

"How do you do, Excellency," I said. "I don't think I've ever had the pleasure of meeting you before."

"A source of many regrets on my part, I assure you."

Lermontov wore a goatee à la Lenin, but that was all that was Leninesque about him. He had a twinkle in the eye, moved fast in a birdlike manner, and behaved more like a French movie star than a Russian diplomat.

"It's very opportune that I should meet you today," he went on, coming very close to me and lowering his voice, "since, according

191

to what I hear, you're the man of the hour. Yes, it is a stroke of very good fortune that we should meet today. *Garçon!* " He beckoned one of a dozen white-coated waiters who were carrying trays of glasses, bubbling with champagne. "Was it not one of your great poets who said that a true German could not abide Frenchmen, but liked drinking their wines? "

"I see you know your Goethe," I smiled.

"I served in Berlin for six years, and got a little tired of quoting Marx in German. Those long involved sentences! Goethe is much more fun. In any case, it is fortuitous — now *that's* a nice word, isn't it? — that we should meet today, since I've been wanting to speak to you. Why don't we go to that corner over there, " he pointed to a little Louis XV alcove, "and sit down for a few minutes? I hate talking about *important* things standing up. Besides," he continued in the manner of a man about to pronounce a particularly delectable *bon mot*, "those elbows that people keep sticking into you *have ears!* " I laughed dutifully. We walked across to the alcove and sat down.

"Well, my friend," he began, rubbing his nose as though it was itching, "I have a little *bonbon* for you, which I will give you out of the goodness of my heart. I know what you're asking yourself: why should the Russian Ambassador give *me* a *bonbon*, me, Friedrich Bierbaum who doesn't even like Communists? Now, confess, my friend, that's the question you're asking yourself. Right? "

"Since you mention it, Excellency," I replied, smiling.

"I have my reasons. *Le coeur a ses raisons.* Diplomats, too, have their reasons. They're not too difficult to guess, as a matter of fact. They have to do with the rather *colorful* relations we have with our friends, the Chinese. Anyhow, whatever they are, and whatever you think of us, what I'm about to tell you is true. There's only one little hitch. If you make use of the information I'm about to impart to you, our 'friends' will poison your soup, as certainly as these bubbles " he held up his champagne glass, "go from the bottom up rather than from the top down."

I frowned.

"Poison my soup? "

"Oh, there are many ways in which the Chinese can do that," he said, with a nonchalant gesture of the right hand. "They may not do anything so crude as to bump you off right away, but they're a very ingenious lot. They have much native intelligence and long traditions. And we've also taught them a good deal, you see. We share a common heritage that originated in the formidable brain of your fellow German Karl Marx, or do you reject him since he did not come up to the high standards of the Nürnberg Laws? "

"*Please,* " I said, not concealing my annoyance at his tactlessness.

"I'm sorry, sir, I forgot that you are a reformed character," he continued. "As I was saying, the Chinese won't like it if you make use of this information. Therefore, if you want to survive you will have to keep it under your hat. You can't go blurting to the Americans: Tex Winter and his girl friend, Karin Hamsun, are in the pay of Peking! "

My heart stopped beating. *I swear* my heart stopped beating.

"Mr. Bierbaum," he said solicitously, watching my face in its agony. "Mr. Bierbaum, are you all right? "

"Yes, yes," I said. "Just give me a second to collect myself." I swallowed hard, and took a sip of champagne. Suddenly everything fell into place. Sun at eight o'clock in the morning. Americans tools of imperialism and materialism. Right from Chairman Mao. And Karin?

"Did you say *girlfriend?* "

"You did not know," the ambassador asked lightly, "they were — how shall I put it decently — *in love?* Oh, I see. A devoted couple, I understand. They pursue different routes in their common endeavor, but it's all for the same old cause. I'm sorry that this little tidbit has shaken you so much. Perhaps it was my clumsy way of talking that did it. My wife says I have as much talent for diplomacy as she has for bricklaying." And he began roaring with laughter. "As a matter of fact, she wouldn't be a bad bricklayer at all. Would you like to meet her? "

"That's very kind of you, Excellency," I said. "But I really think you will have to excuse me."

193

"Just as you wish," he said, bowing, like an actor departing from the stage, his performance over.

I have arrived at the climax of my story. My purpose was to document, for the sake of the historical record, how it came about that CRUPP fell into the hands of a Maoist agent. Have I succeeded? Or are you, dear reader, saying what my Latin teacher at the Hanover *Gymnasium* used to say to me when he caught me bluffing my way through Virgil, *Si tacuisses, philosophus mansisses*? If you had only kept silent, you would have remained a philosopher.

So it was, of all people, the Russian ambassador who opened my eyes to the true nature of Tex Winter. I had found his attitude towards the leisure project objectionable and obstructionist from the beginning. Of course, he never made any bones about his view that the solution to it was *political*. But who would have dreamt that his political solution was a Communist revolution, Chinese style? I am deeply ashamed to confess that it certainly was not I.

He must have thought America rotten to the core before he ever came to CRUPP. Most likely it was this which had turned him into a futurist. If you're a Communist, it's easy to be a futurist: you simply believe that the coming revolution will bring happiness to everyone but "the ruling classes." All the work he had done for CRUPP must have been grist to his mill: the studies of law enforcement and the administration of justice, of Foreign Aid, and — oh, what irony! — his paper on Disaster Simulation.

I wonder whether I will ever find out at what stage precisely he decided that he was the ideal man to become an indigenously American Maoist leader. His strategy was obvious enough. After all, what better platform for an eventual seizure of power than a Washington think tank? It is axiomatic by now that what counts in the contemporary world is not how much steel a nation produces, or what strength its currency may have, but whether it commands enough brainpower to deal with the ever-increasing sophistication of the technological problems facing it. Tex Winter must have realized at some early stage that his combination of gifts — the brilliant mathematical mind plus nasal western accent — was a political gold mine.

As for Karin, that enchanting nymph with her tousled *Bubikopf*, who smells of Swedish lawns in the spring, I am paralyzed by remorse. How come Paula knew instinctively that there wasn't an honest bone in her body? How come she sensed that she was at least in part responsible for my downfall? What an old fool I am!

The morning after my conversation with the Russian Ambassador, I phoned the FBI and asked them to check her out. Within an hour I had the answer. She and Tex had "joined up" on October 5th, 1979. What had triggered that union? I looked at my diary. There it was: Jerry Gorham went on television on October 3rd. The fifth must have been the day I cross-examined my staff.

The pounding of the heart, the dark spasm in the lower abdomen, which had seized me when first Senator Hollinger and then the Russian ambassador struck me their respective blows, returned, much intensified. Betrayal, humiliation, treason, on every front! Aren't these the situations when men my age (or even far younger) have heart attacks? Well, however piercing the pain, I wasn't going to have one. Instead, I swallowed hard and dialed Karin's number. She was at home, probably sitting in her futuristic living room, her eyes on the large oil painting depicting fifty copulatory positions which, as she had told me at our first digiting session an eternity ago, helped her with her "control brakes." Perhaps she had just had a shower in her space capsule and was wrapped in a towel.

"Oh, it's you, Friedrich," she said, her voice sounding slightly subdued. "How are you? "

"Not too bad, Karin," I said, trying to sound normal. "Considering. I want to ask you something. Did Tex tell you about his conversation with me? "

"As a matter of fact, he did," she said. "You two seem to have had quite a quicktran. I don't believe in quarreling."

"When did you and Tex start digiting? "

There was a slight pause.

"Why do you want to know? "

195

"I just want to find out whether it was he who made you tell all those lies."

"Listen, Friedrich," she replied without a moment's delay, "I used to like digiting with you. In fact, I still like it. But that doesn't mean I don't like digiting with others as well. There's plenty of room for parallel feeds. Tex is a great guy. And he's so devoted to his mission. I really believe him when he says he's going to change the world."

"Oh Karin, Karin, Karin," I said, uttering a deep sigh, "if you had lived as long as I have, and seen the things I have seen, you would stay away from people who think they can change the world."

"Well, I'm not going to," she replied sharply, "I have no use for people who don't believe in anything."

There was no use pursuing *that* line of thought.

"Why did you continue with me," I resumed, "if he's so wonderful? "

"Because when I told him I was digiting with you, he said 'go right ahead, don't let *me* stand in your way'."

Was that true, I wondered, or was that another lie — or, more likely, a half-truth?

"Is that all he said? " I asked. "Or did he go on saying that you should digit with me so much, so often, and in such a manner, that you would soon turn me into a wreck? That you would wear me out completely? All he would then have to do, when the moment came, would be to give me a little push, and I would collapse, and he would step into my shoes? Isn't that what he said, Karin? "

"I'm not accountable to you, Friedrich. This is not a master-slave system," Karin answered, quite amiably. "As you know, I have my own control tests. If I said no to your question, you wouldn't believe me anyway. Why should you, for that matter? We don't interface intellectually on any level. I suggest we should leave it at that. May I go now, Friedrich? "

"You may, Karin. You may. Good-bye."

196

So that was it. Tex hoped that Karin would turn me into something resembling old Jannings in the *Blue Angel*, a sex-obsessed, dithering old idiot. Well, he failed. He may be President of CRUPP, but *in that* he failed. Everything suddenly fell into place.

I remembered the change of attitude in Karin in the week after the Jerry Gorham explosion, her flatteries, her intention to "perfect my cyclic shift," the protestations of devotion and admiration, the declaration that she would "zero-eliminate" any other number I might wish to digit with, and, above all, her demands on me to achieve superhuman performances in bed. However, it was a source of the greatest comfort to me that when Karin and I "got together" in the first place — on her gorgeous round bed suspended from the ceiling — she had no ulterior object. It was only much later — six months later, to be precise — that she fell under the spell of her fellow mathematician, Tex Winter, that silent, strong cowboy with the PhD. His attitude towards me must have struck her as perfectly intelligible in terms of personal ambition: there was no need for a political explanation, and I'm sure the Russian Ambassador was all wrong when he said that the two of them were serving the same cause. Karin has no cause at all. She has no comprehension of politics. She may have some vague and fuzzy sentiments in favor of world improvers, but all she knows is computers, mathematics, and sex.

O dass sie ewig grünen bliebe,
Die schöne Zeit der jungen Liebe.

Oh may it thrive for ever green,
The spring of love that once has been.

Chapter 29

I shall never know whether it was to our advantage, in the long run, that the members of the Committee on Finance of the United States Senate, before whom the CRUPP hearings were held, seemed to be more involved in the proposed amendments to the Sugar Act of 1948 than they were in the rights and wrongs of our relations with the White House. Only Senator Cranbrook of South Carolina and Senator Tonbridge of Oregon showed any real interest, perhaps because they had been among the victims of the attack on the Shoreham Hotel, and were, therefore, on the wrong side of the issue. Tom Shrewsbury, the Chief Counsel, was distinctly hostile to us, too, certainly at first, because his wife — so he said — was still suffering from the after-effects of the tear gas. (He himself had been spared.)

The rest of the Committee had their minds on the sugar production of the states of Hawaii and Puerto Rico, and such matters, and visibly suffered from difficulties encountered in keeping apart the testimonies of — say — Richard Toshima and Richard Rosenberg, the lawyer representing the Columbian Sugar Producers Association. Even Senators Cranbrook and Tonbridge occasionally lapsed and asked our people questions about excise taxes and reciprocal trade agreements. The version of the hearings which eventually appeared in the *Congressional Record* was carefully expurgated. Why our case appeared before the Finance Committee, rather than the Committee on Government Operations or on Rates and Administration, I shall never know. Hardly any question was asked about the financial relationship between CRUPP and the White House, which might have been the original *raison d'être* for this arrangement. In any case, the excerpts I shall quote below come from my memory rather than from the official transcript.

Our tactics had been carefully prepared with the help of Senator Hollinger, normally a member of the Committee, but disqualified from participating because he was, after all, Chairman of the CRUPP Board. He himself was in daily contact with the President. The idea was to allow our critics to "go to town on us" for the first two or three days, then to choose a moment where we would be sure to get maximum publicity to make a statement revealing CRUPP's discovery of the real causes of the leisure riots, and finally, when the Committee was in a more pliable mood, to unleash the Reverend Soren Andersen with his ideas on how to deal with the riots in future.

As you will see, we managed to stick to this plan pretty faithfully. The only thing we had not expected, as I have mentioned before, was the confusion between the leisure riots and the demands for higher tariffs to keep down the import of sugar from the Bahamas, Madagascar, and various Latin American republics.

I hope I shall be forgiven for presenting only very brief selections of the highlights. The hearings began on March 30th, and lasted eight days. Every member of the CRUPP staff was cross-examined at length, plus Mac.

Let me begin with a short excerpt from Mac's testimony.

Senator Hawkhurst - Utah: It is our understanding that the CRUPP people induced you to submit to some special psychological treatment from which you suffered severe mental and physical damage. Is that correct?

Mr. MacIntosh: The damage was not severe, Senator.

Senator Hawkhurst: From what we understand, it was severe enough. You realize, of course, that Mr. Bierbaum used to be special assistant to the late *Reich* Marshal Göring, the second man in Hitler's Germany. Were you not reminded of the kind of experiments men like Bierbaum conducted in German concentration camps?

Mr. MacIntosh: No, Senator. Not for a minute. None of those recovered completely within a month, as I did.

Senator Benenden - Idaho: Mr. Chairman, I think the witness should stick to the point. We were discussing the sugar beet production in Peru.

199

Another illuminating moment occurred during the appearance of
Karin Hamsun.

Senator Cranbrook - South Carolina: Miss Hamsun, was it ever
possible to utter any free criticism of Mr. Bierbaum, or did he
run the place, as one would expect, in a strictly authoritarian
manner?

Miss Hamsun: Those of us who kept out of his way had very
few sum-check subtractors. But others, who worked directly
within his gigacycle, often suffered a great deal of negative
picoseconds, and sometimes even reached a macro-decollator.
Personally, I found his vector mode display highly defective,
especially during the last few dump-checks.

Senator Tenderden - Virginia: I don't know, Mr. Chairman,
whether this is the place for personal statements of this nature.
Are you merely speaking for yourself, or for the sugar interests
of your state *in toto*?

Miss Hamsun: I was speaking entirely for myself, Senator.

During Tex Winter's testimony, I had the greatest difficulty
sitting still. If only I had been able to get up and say to the
assembled Senate Committee: "Don't trust this hypocrite!
Don't listen to his high-minded sanctimoniousness! This man
is a Maoist! A paid agent of Communist China! He wants to
take over America! He is the new Quisling, an American
Hitler! "

Mr. Shrewsbury - Chief Counsel: Now that you have succeeded
Mr. Bierbaum as President of CRUPP, is it your intention to
cultivate the White House connection the same way he did?

Dr. Winter: I will not engage in personal deals over lunch with
any of the President's assistants, if that is what you mean, sir.
My relations will be open and aboveboard.

Senator Hawkhurst: It's very good to hear this, Dr. Winter.
One of the difficulties in these hearings has been that so many
statements have been — how shall I put it? — slightly less
than candid. For example, I have trouble believing the assurances
of the gentleman representing the Sugar Syndicate of Mauritius —
I'm afraid I've forgotten the name — who claimed that a lowering

of imports into the United States would inevitably lead to a Communist takeover of his country.

The Chairman: Senator, we were discussing the affairs of the CRUPP Institute. Would you continue, please, Mr. Shrewsbury.

Mr. Shrewsbury: Well, Dr. Winter, do you think that it is proper for a private research institute like CRUPP to have such close ties with the Administration?

Dr. Winter: Surely that depends entirely on the social purpose behind such a relationship. If it is calculated to bring about maximum publicity for CRUPP, if not cash, then my answer is no, sir. If, on the other hand, the purpose is to throw new light on the ever-worsening social and political climate in this country, then my answer is a categorical yes.

That was the general tone of the hearings before I made my statement. Hilde, Toshima, Cedric presented their testimonies calmly and competently, and in each instance attempts were made to make them say things casting the severest aspersions on my integrity. They behaved admirably. I shall never be able to thank them enough for their loyalty and devotion.

On the fourth day of the hearings, Senator Hollinger suggested to me that the time had come for me to ask the Chair's permission to make a statement. At breakfast, Paula gave me some advice which perhaps I should have followed.

"They'll never pay attention to you," she said, stirring her coffee, "unless you make a big production out of it. Obviously, their minds are on other things."

"Please, Paula, let *me* decide how to conduct my affairs," I replied proudly.

"Don't be stubborn, Friedrich," she went on. "When they call your name, get up, go before the television cameras, and say defiantly, in the words of Martin Luther at the *Diet of Worms*, '*Hier stehe ich! Ich kann nicht anders. Gott helfe mir! Amen!*'"

"That would be *insane*, Paula."

"All right, do it your way."

As the following transcript reveals, perhaps I should have done it Paula's way. I had the greatest difficulty catching the Chairman's eye, and when at last I did, his first response was to rebuff me.

The Chairman: We are not yet ready to hear your testimony, Mr. Bierbaum. We will call upon you when the time comes.

Mr. Bierbaum: I would like to have the Committee's attention for an important statement on the nature of the recent disturbances.

Senator Tenderden: Mr. Chairman, may I suggest that we hear this witness. He may be able to throw light on the troubles in Northeastern Brazil. After all, virtually all the sugar imported into the United States from Brazil under the existing quota system comes from that part of the country.

The Chairman: May I remind the distinguished Senator from Virginia that the witness's name is Friedrich Bierbaum, the former president of the CRUPP think tank?

Senator Tenderden: Did you say CRUPP? I didn't know they were doing research on sugar imports. But they're good people, and perhaps we should listen to them.

The Chairman (after a private conference with members of the Committee): All right, Mr. Bierbaum, if you make it short. But first, Senator Cranbrook wishes to address a question to you.

Senator Cranbrook: Do you think that it is no coincidence President Roberts chose you, and your think tank, to work on the leisure riots? After all, his authoritarian propensities are well-known, and you are an old Nazi. You are, in fact, birds of a feather. Besides, isn't it true that there is something inherently fascist about an institution like yours, responsible to no one but itself, exercising such an overwhelming influence on the Executive?

Mr. Bierbaum: No more fascist than any research department or university that is consulted by the Government, Senator.

Senator Cranbrook: Come, come now, Mr. Bierbaum. This Committee has yet to hear of a university having the President in its pocket. So you don't think it's surprising that the President chose someone like you, who sees a Communist behind every door, to investigate the riots? Haven't you always thought they were convenient scapegoats?

The Chairman: That will do, Senator Cranbrook. The witness wishes to make a statement, and we want to get back to our hearings on the Sugar Bill. Let us get it over with. What is it you wish to say, Mr. Bierbaum?

Mr. Bierbaum: I will be brief, Mr. Chairman. We at CRUPP are the only people who have established, beyond a shadow of a doubt, what the true cause of the leisure riots is. The rioters are not Communists, not drug addicts, not kids, not homosexuals, not members of the Women's Liberation Movement. They are upholders of the American system of free enterprise *par excellence:* ordinary, usually law-abiding, middle-class executives who have been prematurely laid off their jobs, or whose work week has been reduced to the bare minimum. They riot because they're bored, because they don't know what to do with their time without work, without jobs. Thank you, Mr. Chairman

I had hoped that this statement would hit the Committee like a bombshell. As I had predicted, the press the next day *did* give it ample space on the front pages, and the media generally grasped its significance, even if my account of CRUPP's competence, and my own role in the proceedings, was treated — let's put it mildly — with the utmost skepticism. But after a few minutes of desultory cross-examination, the Committee returned to its consideration of the Sugar Act, on which it spent the following twenty-four hours.

When the Committee resumed its examination of our affairs, it was in a distinctly different mood. It treated Soren Andersen with a respect it had conspicuously withheld from the rest of us, particularly from me. Senator Hollinger's calculations proved to be correct: Soren's testimony provided the climax of the hearings. It may well have been the purpose of our Board Chairman to have me personally discredited, while sustaining CRUPP's role in the total picture. If that was so, he succeeded admirably, even though the press — as I shall report later — was far less kind to Soren than the Committee had been.

203

Senator Cranbrook: I understand, Reverend Andersen, you are a distinguished theologian. Does it not seem strange to you that you should be working in an institute that deals with very practical down-to-earth problems like urban planning, ecological concerns, technological questions, that sort of thing?

Rev. Andersen: There are moral and religious dimensions to all these things, Senator.

Senator Tonbridge: A man like you must have found it intolerably hard to work in an organization whose head has displayed over so many years the most blatantly naked opportunism?

Rev. Andersen: By no means, Senator. I've always found his management of CRUPP responsible and intelligent. From the beginning, the fundamental question posed by the leisure rioters has been the most profound question any person can ask, namely what am I to do with my life on earth? They seem to be very sure of their answer, which is to WORK. But of course that's nonsense.

Senator Tonbridge: To many, life without work is empty.

Rev. Andersen: Of course. Because one does not know what to do with one's time. As a Christian, I believe the purpose of life is not work, but *play*, serious play. I interpret play as ranging all the way from the celebration of God to ping-pong. Play is any human activity with a meaning beyond itself in which one engages for its own sake, and not for the sake of its consequences. A delight in the pursuit of knowledge and beauty is play. Love is play. Art is play. Religion is play. Much of politics, Senator, is play. The love of secrets is play. Competition is play. The only activities that are *not* play are those that satisfy the basic appetites of life. Survival is not play, gentlemen.

Senator Tenderden: Let us come to the point, Mr. Andersen. Are we to understand that you wish us to tell the leisure rioters that they're wrong to want to work, that they should learn to play?

Rev. Andersen: It's very difficult at the moment to tell them anything, Senator, since they don't want to listen. But when the right moment comes, yes, I *would* tell them that they shouldn't be so hung up on the word '*work*,' that much of the work they *did* do when they had jobs was boring and meaningless, that we now have a marvelous opportunity in America to spend our lives doing more important things than wasting our time in factories and offices performing useless and demeaning functions. After all, for the first time in human history the problem of scarcity is close to solution. This has been the bane of our existence up to now, and it still is for most of mankind. More and more people *can* have a good life, if they know how to do it, and in my book the good life is one that is spent in serious play.

Mr. Chairman: Thank you very much, Mr. Andersen.

It will have been noted that the Senate Committee did not once stray from the point during Soren Andersen's testimony. It did not confuse his definition of serious play with a cost benefit analysis of sugar imports from Guatemala. This may have been due to the traditional respect owing to a man of the cloth. But I believe it was more likely an intuitive recognition of the fact that Soren had touched the nerve center of the work-leisure problem. Unlike other members of my staff, Soren had not come up with any concrete recommendations as to ways and means to deal with the leisure riots: all he wanted to do was to put forward his ideas in circumstances where he was bound to get maximum publicity, in the hope that others would translate them into practice.

This hope was fulfilled with lightning speed. The day after his testimony, Senator Tenderden made a speech in the Committee.

"I was much impressed," he said, "by the cogency of the Reverend Andersen's remarks. However, it's too bad that the gentleman has so little practical sense. He does not seem to realize that we all need work, just as we need air to breathe. But I think he's quite right: the world would be a better place if we could all devote ourselves to the pursuit of the arts and philosophy, and all that. But we won't do it, unless we *call* it work. Therefore, I herewith move that we establish a sub-committee to study how play can be translated into work."

A majority of the Committee backed him, and the first session of the sub-committee was called for the following Monday.

* * *

The mass media mangled Soren Andersen's arguments atrociously.

"PLAYFUL CRUPP MINISTER ATTEMPTS WHITEWASH,"
read a headline in the *New York Daily News.* Matters were
not helped very much when the National Association of Work-
Seeking Executives and Professionals began broadcasting from
a pirate radio station on a ship just outside Norfolk, Virginia.
So there *was* a national organization, after all. They quoted
my Senate statement every hour on the hour, and inter-
spersed the endlessly repeated playing of the top ten with
moderate and reasoned pleas for jobs. While urging its members
to continue with "peaceful leisure rioting," they considered
it their prime responsibility to convince the public that their
demands were fair and attainable. They urged the unions to
discontinue their closed shop practices, and to open their ranks
to former members of management on humanitarian grounds.
They also declared their intention to begin lobbying systematically for their cause in Washington.

Three days after the hearings were over — on April 11th — the
Russian Ambassador called me at home.

"I just wanted to say *Guten Abend, Herr Bierbaum,* that's all,"
he said, making it quite clear that there was something else
he had to say. "I hope you are not bleeding too much? "

"Thank you, Excellency, it is kind of you to ask. No, I'm
all right."

"Well," he went on, "if one believes, as you do, in the blessings
of a capitalist free press, I suppose one has to be prepared for
this. In Moscow we do things differently."

"So I understand, Excellency," I replied.

"Please don't think that we are angels, though. We're just a
little different from our American friends, that's all."

"I know." What *zum Teufel* was he after?

"I thought you behaved admirably, Bierbaum, considering the
circumstances. I trust your telephone is not tapped? "

"Of course not," I laughed.

"Good. I'm trained to be careful about these things. The Americans have learned a lot from us. Anyway, I have great admiration for you. If we invited you to come to Moscow to teach us how to get rid of *our* Protestant work ethic, would you come? "

"You are very kind, sir, but I don't really think I would, frankly. I don't know enough about you people, really."

"No need to be so polite, Bierbaum. But let me tell you why I really phoned you. I hope I'm not incommoding you? "

"Not at all." I felt in my bones that what he was about to tell me was of vital importance.

"I think it would be wise if you left the United States quickly. It doesn't matter very much where you go, Europe, Mexico, Canada, anywhere, but I think you would be safer if you left this territory fast. Within three weeks, I would say."

"May I ask why? " A spasm of fear seized the lower part of my abdomen.

"I have reason to believe that your successor would *prefer* you to go abroad. Am I making myself clear? That your presence so close to his would be considered a little *inconvenient*. That he might resort to some means of his own to create a little distance between himself and you. He knows very well that you have important friends, and that you are not the devil the press is making you out to be. He doesn't want you to establish a government-in-exile next door to him. I might feel the same way if I were him. Wouldn't you? "

The thought had never occurred to me.

"Oh, I don't know," I said weakly.

"You see, the new man, I understand, knows very well how loyal your staff is to you. If we learned anything from the Senate hearings, we learned *that*. It would be intolerable to him to have them drop in on you every evening for a drink, to tell you all about the mischievous activities he intends to engage in. I have a great deal of sympathy for him, as a matter of fact. No, my friend, you have to leave. By May 1st, I would say."

"Why should I have to leave the United States? "

"It's a psychological thing, my friend. Canada, for example, is only an hour away from Washington, but you might as well be on the moon. No, if you go to Canada, your successor will feel absolutely safe. After all, who's ever *heard* of Canada? "

All this struck me as utterly plausible, and I was amazed that I had not thought of this myself.

"I'm very grateful to you for telling me this, Excellency. But why are you taking the trouble? "

He laughed.

"Did I not tell you the other day that diplomats always have their reasons? *Les diplomates ont leurs raisons que les autres ne connaissent pas*, to improve on Pascal. There's another thing I want to tell you."

"Yes? "

"In your exile you will find time moving a little slowly. Perhaps you will want to write an account of all the things that have happened to you recently."

"Perhaps," I said. "I really don't know."

"Well, if you do write something, could you send me a copy, please? But, whatever you do, you must resist the temptation to *publish* anything. Our yellow friends wouldn't let you get away with it. Of that I have no doubt whatsoever. Please be *very* careful. But it's more than likely that I'd find it useful to have a copy. I might be able to push things along a little. Am I making myself clear? "

"I guess so, Excellency. At the moment I can't think so far ahead, though. Please forgive me."

"Of course, of course, my dear Bierbaum."

"But I'm very grateful to you, Excellency. I will think about what you have said."

"Do so. Do so, " he responded.

* * *

Paula and I left Washington for Montreal on May 3rd, precisely a year and two months after Bill Bush's initial phone call telling me — it seemed an eternity ago — about those earliest phases of the leisure riots. Paula bore up magnificently the loss of our sumptuous house in Bethesda, with the swimming pool and the Buddha.

"What will I ever do? " she asked dismayed, but quickly pulled herself up like the daughter of the parade ground General von Lichtenfelde-Königstein. "I will find a way to keep busy where-ever I am."

"Bravo."

Hilde arranged a party for us in Room 332 of the Mayflower. It was a subdued affair, semi-surreptitious. Of course, Tex and Karin had not been invited. We were all very brave.

Thus I said farewell to my loyal troops, like Napoleon after the Battle of Waterloo.

* * *

The island in the St. Lawrence I see when I look out of my window in Montreal's *Habitat* is called St. Helen's Island. Napoleon wrote his memoirs in St. Helena, and here I am, writing the final sentence of *my* memoirs.

One hundred and sixty years after Napoleon's death, people are still arguing about his place in world history.

What will they say next year about mine?

END OF ORIGINAL MANUSCRIPT

Postscript

As it turned out, it was not St. Helena. It was Elba.

Today is August 5th, 1980. Here we are, Paula and I, high
up in the Swiss Alps, in the *Waldhaus Sils Maria*, just two
lakes away from St. Moritz, only a few miles north of the
Italian border. I used to spend my summer holidays here
with my parents, more than half a century ago. It's the
same old, sumptuously comfortable hotel, inhabited by
the cosmopolitan rich from all corners of the earth, just
right for us, for me anyway: Paula might have preferred
the slightly more modest *Hotel Margna*, on the other side
of the *Chasté* peninsula, where Nietzsche used to go for
long, somber walks, thinking deep thoughts. Anyway, here
we are, in just the right atmosphere to look back at everything that happened, from the top of the world. I remember
as a boy I used to have prolonged nosebleeds here, because
of the *Höhenluft*, the thin air, high up in the mountains.

How extraordinarily well everything turned out in the end!
I still have the greatest difficulties believing it. To think
that I finished the manuscript only one month ago today!
As I had promised, I immediately sent a copy to the Russian
Ambassador in Washington. I personally went to Ottawa, to
deliver the parcel to the Russian Embassy, to be sent by diplomatic mail to Washington. I hoped that Boris Lermontov
would soon have an opportunity to disclose parts of it — or
even perhaps all of it — to the State Department, or the CIA,
whom no doubt he frequently provides with information
about Chinese activities in the United States. There could,
of course, be no question of publication in my lifetime.

210

My fortunes changed dramatically two days afterwards. In fact, circumstances took such a radical turn for the better that on July 20th — the day President Roberts was nominated for a second term in the White House — I happily yielded to the demands of one of America's most distinguished publishers (one of two hundred and seventy-eight who made a bid for it) to publish my memoirs by October 10th, in good time for the election. I accepted his offer not only because he was prepared to pay me more money than all the others, but also because of his reputation for integrity and quality. It may well be that he received a little "encouragement" from Bill Bush — probably nothing crude like money, but rather some slightly more dignified incentive, like the promise of first refusal of President Roberts' memoirs, when the time came — since it's obviously very much in the President's interest to put before the voters in good time a full record of the way his initial "hunch" about the causes of the leisure riots was subsequently borne out by scientific research. I promptly invested a microscopic fraction of the proceeds in this well-earned and well-deserved two week holiday in Switzerland. (I have always been amused that in German the same word — *verdienen* — covers both earning and deserving.)

The extraordinary thing is that my publisher wants to publish the manuscript in its original form, without a word changed, including — for reasons best known to himself — all the unsavory personal passages which I would have thought of no conceivable interest to the public at large. At first, Paula thought this was "too childish for words" — *eine entsetzliche Kinderei*, to quote her literally — but once I explained to her

a) that the publisher was offering a sum equivalent to the Gross National Product of Prussia in 1813; and

b) that there was a very real danger the Russian Ambassador might release the copy of the original (he was not to be trusted, as I soon discovered), and I would have the *Teufel* of a time explaining any changes; and

c) that she emerged as the true heroine of the story,

she finally consented, with a contemptuous smile.

The CRUPP Board gave its blessing without any reservations
whatsoever, convinced that this "authentic inside look at the
inner workings of the nation's most important think tank"
was an invaluable contribution to a better understanding
of the way vital governmental decisions are made. In fact,
they were delighted, and only reluctantly agreed to my
keeping the whole of the proceeds.

Here is how it happened..

On July 7th, a tall, well-dressed gentleman called on me
around four o'clock in the afternoon. Paula was out shop-
ping, making her weekly trip to Sepp's, which has fifty-
seven different kinds of German sausages and is the only
pre-World War II German butcher shop that has survived
in Montreal. He said his name was Larsen. He wanted to
consult me about getting up a think tank modeled on
CRUPP in Ottawa. Could he have the benefit of my advice?
After all, was I not the Herman Kahn of the late seventies?

He came at just the right moment. Having concluded my
manuscript, I was beginning to be bored. I told him I was
most interested and would be delighted to cooperate.

He thanked me profusely, took out a little spray gun and
put me to sleep with some stuff that smelled like Karin's
perfume — Swedish lawns in the month of May. It was
delicious. As I dozed off, I remember saying to myself:
"The Maoists have got me after all! How come the
Mounties let this man get through? "

He left a note for Paula, faking my handwriting to perfection,
saying that unfortunately I had been summoned to Washington
at a moment's notice, and would phone her tomorrow.

I woke up in Senator Hollinger's office. I had been unconscious
right through the long car trip to Washington.

"My dear Bierbaum, how *are* you? " he said.

He seemed genuinely delighted to see me. I rubbed my eyes. My throat was dry. I was starving.

"You must forgive this playful little ruse of ours. But we were afraid that, after all that's happened, if we just asked you to come, you'd refuse."

"Would it be possible for your secretary to get me a cup of coffee, and perhaps a piece of toast? " I asked, grasping for my old aplomb as if it were air.

"But *of course*, my dear friend. I should have thought of this myself."

He rang for his secretary.

"May I come straight to the point? " he went on, while I tried hard to collect myself. "We've had a spot of bad luck at CRUPP. Tex Winter was arrested last week. It seems he was in the service of a foreign power."

I was sufficiently in possession of my faculties to feign surprise.

"Really? "

"It is not entirely clear," the senator went on, "which foreign power, but I have reason to believe it is the Soviet Union."

"Are you serious? " I was hardly able to contain myself.

"Oh yes," he continued, his expression as suave and slick as ever. "The circumstances of his exposure are not as yet entirely clear. But I understand what first raised the suspicions of the authorities was Tex Winter's newest research project, which he claimed was a logical extension of his previous work, under your guidance, on legal and judicial matters. He has now branched out into constitutional reform, and has just started a program exploring the possibilities of amending the Constitution to have the position of the President of the United States changed into that of Chairman of the Federal Secretariat, and altering the electoral system into one based on computerized referenda on specific issues, the technical details to be worked out by a task force headed by Miss Karin Hamsun."

"Charming," I said.

"Indeed. That's a very good word for it, Bierbaum. As for her, she appears to have been somewhat careless in her personal relationships. Indiscreet is perhaps a better word than careless. She should have known better than to spend weekends with the Russian Ambassador in Las Vegas, and to be seen there — not only by CIA agents, but also by reporters of the *Los Angeles Times* — gambling through the night at the Desert Inn, and then sharing one of the bridal suites with him (they have some fourteen, I understand) during the day."

For a second or two I was seized by pangs of jealousy of the wily and cunning Boris Lermontov. What an old master! I wonder whether he'd had time to read the copy of my manuscript, and compared notes between his cyclic shift and mine. Oh God!

I pulled myself together.

"Was there anything else in Tex Winter's work," I continued in the manner of a curious journalist at a press conference, "which suggested that he might not be entirely reliable, Senator? "

"Well, looking back at it now, Bierbaum, I must admit his entire research program was somewhat unorthodox. I mean, for example, what is one to make of a project examining the possibilities of socializing the *New York Stock Exchange*, and making the *New York Times* the investigative branch of government? No, no, all this seemed to me from the very first as somewhat eccentric, but, as you know, it has always been my policy to leave the choice of subject areas very much to the staff. I believe in leaving responsible people alone. Think tanks can only prosper in an atmosphere of completely free enquiry. My concern has always been to protect CRUPP's reputation, and to maintain the connection with the White House. You can imagine that under these circumstances, I've found it rather difficult to discharge these responsibilities."

"I quite understand, Senator," I said.

"I knew you would."

I took a close look at him. He seemed to have aged considerably in the two months I had not seen him. His Cary Grant face was gray and lined. He now looked like the late Gary Cooper.

"And so you have decided," I said, "to invite me back to my old function! "

"I'm afraid it's not quite as simple as that," he said slowly. "I don't think we could get away with it, considering the circumstances of your departure."

"Oh? "

"You must remember that in two weeks there will be a convention nominating President Roberts for another term. We didn't think it would be wise at this point to give his opponents any weapons gratuitously. No, we had something else in mind. In fact, we have already taken steps. We have asked someone else to assume the presidency of CRUPP, and to have you second-in-command. But we could not get an acceptance unless you are in agreement."

"Someone else? " I asked, frowning heavily.

"Yes," he said, obviously not wanting to tell me who.

The secretary came in with the coffee and toast, while I pondered this.

"And you couldn't tell me this on the telephone? " I asked.

"I was afraid you would misunderstand and slam the receiver down, Bierbaum," he replied, a little timidly. "Also, I must confess, I rather enjoy the cloak and dagger touch occasionally.

"I see."

"The President and I think this new head an ideal choice," he went on. "I don't know whether you've kept up with the news, but we've had terrible leisure riots in the last two months. That association of theirs has turned very militant. It has managed to bring the cultural life of America practically to a standstill. Theaters are closed, concerts canceled. Every museum, every art gallery is picketed. Not to mention all adult education activities in the country. Your — er — successor has developed a plan to deal with the riots. We think it may well be the correct answer. We want it worked out in time for the nominating convention. It's the most marvelous opportunity CRUPP has ever had to make a vital contribution to the national life of the United States."

"When do you think I can see him, if it *is* a 'him'? "

"As a matter of fact, the new president is waiting in the room next door."

He stood up and flung open the door. I was wondering whom I would find. An unknown person? Soren Andersen? Hilde? But there sat Mac!

"Hello, Mr. Bierbaum," he said, smiling a little uneasily. "It's good to see you again."

"I don't know what to say," I said, truthfully.

"I think I will leave you two alone together," Senator Hollinger said. "I will see you later."

"Now tell me precisely what you have in mind, Mac," I said, after the Senator had gone. We both sat down on two deep leather armchairs in the corner.

"Do you remember, Mr. Bierbaum, that I had mentioned I was working on a plan of my own? "

"Yes, I do," I replied. "I'm sorry I didn't have time to listen to it."

"Well, it's very simple. In fact, it's beyond me that CRUPP hasn't thought of it before. It's really too obvious for words."

"What is it, Mac? "

"You see, judging from my own experience, Americans *have got* to work. It's not money or status that's important, it's *work*. The world is all wrong about America: it thinks Americans are crazy about money. That's not true. Americans are crazy about work. I think they have that in common with you Germans."

"That may be possible," I said, wondering what he was up to.

"Also, Americans appreciate only what they are paid money for, or...." He paused significantly.

"Or? "

"Or what they pay money *for. So, instead of paying them to work, let them pay for work.* The most wanted jobs, of course, will cost the most. The more senior the employee, the more his job will cost him, and so on. All we have to do is work out a kind of reverse salary scale, that's all. There's nothing to it. People like myself who need to work or they'll become dangerous will simply buy themselves the jobs they need. The rest, well, they'll stay at home. They're perfectly safe, devoting themselves to serious play. Since they'll stay off the job market, there'll be plenty of work to go around. It's so simple," he repeated, "I don't see why nobody else thought of it."

"You're a genius, Mac," I said, jumping up. Then I suddenly hesitated. "How much will my job as your assistant cost me? "

"I'll let you do it free, to start. A kind of free trial period," he laughed. "If you find you like the work and decide to stay, the reverse salary will go up. It's all going to take a lot of computer work to figure it all out, but CRUPP's good at that."

"Oh, excellent," I said.

Suddenly he turned serious.

"Has Senator Hollinger told you about the new board? "

"No, what board? "

"Well, you see, Mr. Bierbaum," I noticed that Mac was acutely embarrassed telling me this, "a lot of unpleasant questions have been asked about your ...how shall I put it? ... *background.*"

217

"Come on, Mac," I said, cheerfully. "I know all about that. What did old Senator Hollinger cook up? Out with it! "

"Well, he's appointed a new Board, what he calls 'a broadly based one.' I'm to be President. You're to be Vice-President. And the rest of the Board is to prevent CRUPP from ever again being accused of Nazism. And in view of your...*background*...they've appointed the following people to become members of it. Dr. Norman Cohen, head of the American Jewish Congress; Professor Abraham Cohen, president of Brandeis; Mr. Robert Cohen, Assistant Secretary of Defense; Dr. Eric Cohen, Nobel Prize winner for medicine, 1977; Professor Philip Cohen, president of B'nai B'rith, and Mrs. Chaim Cohen, president of Hadassah."

I put on a stiff upper lip.

"Very nice," I said bravely. "They sound like a very eminent group of people. I'm afraid I don't know any of them, but I'm sure we'll get along very well."

"Of course," said Mac, "I *know* you will! "

"By the way, how is Karin? " I asked. "Is she still with Tex? "

"Oh, haven't you heard? She was appointed head of the Department for Computer Sciences at Brandeis. She left Tex and I hear she's now taken up with the President, Dr. Abraham Cohen. I thought you *knew*."

"No, Mac, I hadn't heard," I said.

"I'm perfectly relaxed about *her*, " he volunteered. "I'm *cured*, you see."

* * *

Paula flew down to Washington the next afternoon. We were staying at the Georgetown Inn. I was exhausted and went to bed early. She was too excited to join me. She kept repeating how happy she was for Mac.

"Remember what you used to say when watching the American Commander-in-Chief in liberated Berlin? 'A little child shall lead

them! The meek shall inherit the earth! ' " Her voice dropped.
"It's nice to be home again, eh, Friedrich? "

I uttered a contented grunt.

"But let me tell you one thing, my boy. Don't start anything
with another Swedish morsel, or I'll pack my suitcase. *Verstanden?* "

"I promise nothing," I said drowsily, watching her through half-
closed eyes as she ran her finger along the windowsill.

"This place needs dusting," she said, conclusively.

bummy - 113 - familiar

Bill Bush
doesn't speak US
idiom - 28

I read it approp - in 9's 16 min
I go to good lecture

p. 16 - Think tank w.
human touch -
the proprile of staff "the last
I like touches like
Skinner"

costumes ego purses -

Louisville
St. Louis
Courier
Ohio State

Goethe world
love
p. 38

p. 67 - I laughed out
loud -
dinnerware course - ?

Gay secy of defense
p. 15 - reu
soveu c's
report